Zoe Lea lives in the Lake District, UK, with her husband, two children, dogs and peregrine falcons. As well as writing, she helps manage an animal tracking company used for raptors and other wildlife. She's previously worked as a teacher, photographer and in the television industry, but writing has always been her passion.

Also by Zoe Lea

The Secretary

CLOSER THAN SHE THINKS

ZOE LEA

PIATKUS

PIATKUS

First published in Great Britain in 2024 by Piatkus

1 3 5 7 9 10 8 6 4 2

A CIP catalogue record for this book is available from the British Library.

ISBN 978-0-349-42269-5

Printed and bound in Great Britian by Clays Ltd, Elcograf S.p.A.

Papers used by Piatkus are from well-managed forests
and other responsible sources.

Piatkus
An imprint of
Little, Brown Book Group
Carmelite House
50 Victoria Embankment
London EC4Y 0DZ

An Hachette UK Company
www.hachette.co.uk

www.littlebrown.co.uk

To Aidan and Talia

PROLOGUE

Is he dead?

Did I ask that out loud or was it in my head? My mouth is numb with shock. I can't tell if it's moving or still. I can't even put my fingers to my lips to check. I'm frozen. I can only stare at him lying on the floor.

Is he dead? Is he dead? Is he dead?

A detached part of my mind starts replaying what's just happened as I watch his blood pool on the tiles, funnelling into the grouting. Another part marvels at my ability to do this. I feel like I'm separating from reality.

Did I just see that? Did I just see him die?

His body on the floor is the anchor keeping me tethered to the room.

He was shouting. I can't remember the words he used, but 'gormless bitch' were among them, as was 'stupid'.

And then he was dying. Dying right in front of me. And I did nothing. I just watched. My feet stuck, my hands in tight

1

balls as the blood slipped from his head and created a new, more interesting pattern on the floor.

My heart thumps in time with the question in my head.

Is he dead? Is he dead? Is he dead?

I can feel its terrified beat in the tips of my hair, on the underside of my fingernails. My whole body rattles with its jerky, horrified banging.

'Is he dead?'

Hearing the question outside of my own mind makes me jump. I forgot I wasn't alone.

'It was an accident. Anyone will see it was an accident.'

'What are we going to do now?'

Panic washes through me.

I've spent my life waiting for things to happen, watching from the sidelines, and now I'm finally centre stage, I don't know what to do.

'Just be quiet for a moment.' I lean on the table, my breath coming in short gasps. 'Let me think.'

'You going to call them? The police?'

'I don't think we can do anything else. Can we?'

There's a moment before I go to my phone. A moment where we look at each other. Everything will change as soon as I make the call, and a million unsaid words rush between us, a million silent conversations.

I try to enter the passcode. It takes three attempts, my fingers slippery and clumsy. I hesitate on the last try.

This is it.

After this phone call, nothing will be the same. My life will change irrevocably, but then hasn't it already?

I thought I'd only just started this journey; I didn't for one moment think this was my destination.

ONE

Six weeks earlier

'Lou? It's Rick.'

I press my phone to my ear; the January wind is biting, and his voice is faint.

'Rick. Is everything . . .?'

His hesitation answers my question, and my stomach drops.

''Fraid not. She didn't want me to call you, but I thought it best.'

'What now? What's happened?'

He takes a long intake of breath, and when he speaks, his voice has a flat, placating monotone to it. It makes my insides clench and my throat go tight.

'She's fine. Well, you know your mother. She's as fine as she can be. Batted me away when I tried to help. She was brushing the drive at the side of the house. Trying to sweep up leaves, I think. I saw her go down. I helped her, got her back inside,

3

and she's OK and I don't want to worry you. She told me not to call, but I thought . . .'

'No, no, thank you for calling.' I reach my car and throw in my laptop and books. 'Where is she now?'

'Watching that game show she likes with a cup of tea. It's her arm. She wouldn't let me take a proper look at it, but she was holding it. At the elbow. Looked sore.'

I thank him again. Apologise again. Thank him some more.

I've spoken to my mother's neighbour, Rick, more in the last six months than I have in all the four years he's been living in the bungalow at the back of her house. Starting the engine, I hear his flat voice in my head again – *She's fine* – and feel something squeeze at the base of my stomach. My mother is not fine.

Checking the clock on the dashboard, I groan. The lesson overran. Again. It was with Gary, or Handy Gary, as I like to call him. The manager of the off-licence on the high street who talks endlessly about his Spanish girlfriend who he met online, while he sits a little too close and invades my personal space a little too often. This time he wanted to learn the words for 'caress' and 'canoodle'. I found it hard not to roll my eyes as I spent the best part of an hour trying to teach him Spanish phrases he could say over Zoom. All the while he was asking me what I found romantic and I was trying to make sure he didn't put his hand on my thigh.

I have fifteen minutes to get to the community centre for my weekly pensioners' lesson. I'm going to be late. But after speaking to Rick, it looks like I might not make it at all. Now is not a good time for my mother to be having another fall.

She's fine. Rick's voice in my head again. *As fine as she can be.* What does that mean exactly?

4

That she's fine to wait until five, when my lessons for the day are over and I can make the twenty-minute journey to her house? Or fine as in, you'd better get here quick because she probably needs a check-up at A&E as her arm might be broken?

I pick up my phone and go to recent calls. No, I can't call him back, can I? Poor bloke. It's kind enough of him to see to my mother, to pick her up and patch her up and call me. I can't ring back and ask for a detailed explanation of what she's done and if, in his opinion, I need to be there. This is her third fall in as many weeks, and each time Rick has come to the rescue.

Going past his name, I select the next one under recent calls. MOTHER. It rings out. I look heavenward as I listen, mentally seeing her getting up out of her chair and walking to the phone on the side table. Even though I've told her a thousand times to keep it with her, to put it in her pocket, she never does. It lives in its cradle as if it's still attached with a cord.

Brushing the drive. What was she doing brushing the drive on a January morning? The frost will be thick there. That end of the house never gets the sun, and it's bitterly cold. I end the call and look at the next number: PAUL, my husband. I hesitate. He's at work. In the taxi rank, trying to drum up business, and I can hear the conversation in my head before it happens.

You're going where? She was doing what? She'll be fine. If it was bad, Rick would've taken her to hospital. You know Rick, what a fusspot he is. He's probably exaggerating, and you can't just drop everything for her again.

But I will. I have to.

I put the car in gear and murmur aloud to myself as I drive, mentally going through what I have to cancel and change. As a Spanish teacher, my pupils are a mix. The majority are kids and young adults studying for some kind of exam. Then I have people who want to learn the language for holidays, or business, or, like Handy Gary, an online relationship. I have my weekly class with the local pensioners and a few students I teach online, but as I don't have a PGCE, I'm not qualified to teach at the high school or college, so I take what I can get.

Once I'm out of the village and on the dual carriageway, I start making calls on hands-free. I ring Harriet, the manager of the pensioners' club, apologising. Then I call Lucy, my two o'clock, studying for her A level, and try to rearrange a double lesson next week, but it doesn't work out. I have an online lesson at half three but will hopefully be back by then, and I need to tell Paul, who will not be happy with any of this.

The last time Mum fell, I spent the best part of two hundred pounds buying her some new shoes that promised better balance. Two hundred pounds and they've improved nothing. Paul also missed a darts tournament because I forgot to pass on some vital message as I was busy arranging an appointment with her GP. I swore to him I'd find a solution to this, that I'd work something out. Stop letting her deteriorating health dictate our lives, but here I am again.

By the time I get to my mother's, my mind is a scribble. I see a broom on the ground outside, a pile of leaves to the side of it.

'For heaven's sake.' I go to park, but have to stop to let a white van pull out of the shared driveway. Must be someone working over at Rick's, or one of his customers. I step on the accelerator before they've fully passed me. The car jerks forward and the van stops sharply. I flush and raise my hand. Bloody hell, that was almost a bump. Almost a car repair we can't afford and another argument between me and Paul. I look away, my heart pounding. I'm not making eye contact with the driver. I just want to get inside and see to my mother.

The van drives around me at a snail's pace. I can feel the driver's eyes on me, like they're making a point, and although I know it was my fault, I swear at them under my breath as I finally park and switch off the engine, my heart still going at a million miles an hour.

'Mum?' I walk through the hallway and into the lounge, and the heat hits me as soon as I open the door. It's similar to when you go abroad and get off an air-conditioned plane. That wall of heat that slams into you? My mother likes to re-create it in her lounge.

'Mum? Rick called. He ...' I stop when I see her. Her jaw hangs softly open, her eyes closed. A slight snore.

Switching off the gas fire and the television, I go to open a window and then come back to have a look at her. There's blood on her sleeve, her cheek has a scratch, and her nose is cut slightly along the top. I gently lift her arm and look at the elbow, the one Rick said she'd been holding. A dark blush of blood is forming under the skin, pooling into a bruise. He was right, it does look sore.

'Oh Mum,' I breathe. 'What are we going to do with you?'

TWO

The house is an oddity. My mother insists the Gothic architecture is beautiful, but I think it looks sinister. As a kid, I used to tell friends at school it was haunted, and they believed me.

If you didn't know better, you could be forgiven for thinking it was an illusion. Your mind playing tricks on you as you come out of the small village of Dilenby, heading towards Manchester. A large old house with a pitched roof, arched windows and stone pillars in front of the porch, like something out of a bad horror film, nestled in among the red-brick estates, off-licences, chip shops and industrial parks.

As the story goes, my grandparents inherited it from a distant uncle who made his money in something to do with coal. When my grandmother died, she left it to my parents, and by the time I was born, it was a given that either my brother or I would get the house. There was never any question of it leaving the family. It would go to one of us, and then on to our kids, and so on and so on.

Which is why I've never really thought of it as my house. As soon as I became a mother myself, from the moment Felix, my son, took his first breath, the place has always been his.

It was built in the 1800s, an old farmhouse with four bedrooms, two reception rooms, a kitchen and dining room, and it must once have been quite grand. An estate agent would describe it as having 'period charm' and 'immense character', but in reality, the charm has long since gone and its character is now a bit like my mother's: cranky, fraying around the edges and in need of some serious modernisation. It was once part of some lord's estate until most of the other buildings and land surrounding it were sold off to developers.

Over the years, people have tried to buy it. The land is now worth more than anyone could've imagined, but the house is a family legacy. Memories fill every crack. It's where our ghosts live, and my mother refuses to leave them. It's why she won't hear of sheltered accommodation or even home help. As she puts it, 'I was born here and I'll die here and I don't want a bunch of strangers watching me do it.'

As she sleeps, I look out of the large picture window at the back, at the garden that leads towards the bungalow, Rick's house. My dad used to tell us that the bungalow was the gamekeeper's hut or the servants' quarters, and we were living in the rich people's house. It was a great game, pretending we were loaded, even though the carpets were threadbare and we couldn't afford to heat half the rooms. My dad worked at a telephone company, something to do with sales, and Mum had a part-time job in the local bakery, so money was tight, but we always had the house.

A place that stopped my friends making fun of my one pair of school shoes, my dad's beat-up car and my clothes off the market. They looked at the house and assumed we had money and it was just that my parents didn't enjoy spending it

I went along with it, pretending to be the rich version of myself that they saw, and now I always get an overriding feeling of fear whenever I remember my childhood. Like someone is going to uncover the truth about me. I think it's why I used to hate that bungalow. I used to resent how joined to us it was, how we were permanently overlooked, the shared driveway being a constant reminder that we weren't alone, that someone knew the truth, but now I am so, so grateful for it.

Even with my near miss that morning, I'm thankful for the way the houses are connected. It means that Rick sees my mother when she falls, when she forgets her keys, when she tries to sweep the driveway on a frosty January morning.

Rick is in his mid sixties, with mobility issues himself. He lives alone and is always warm and smiling, insisting it's no bother every time he comes to the rescue, but it is. It is a bother. His normally bright voice is now flat whenever he calls. We share a love of true crime; the first time he came to my mother's rescue, we got chatting over the latest Netflix documentary and have been swapping books and TV recommendations since, but as Mum's falls have become more regular, he's not as chatty. Doesn't want to talk as much as he did about serial killers and alibis. It's starting to get him down.

My mother is eighty-three, stubborn and getting more so every day, and however nice Rick is, he didn't volunteer for any of this.

'Hello, love, when did you get here?'

Her hand goes to her elbow. Confusion momentarily clouds her face, until she remembers, and then a flush comes to her cheeks.

'Rick tells me you've been trying to do the salsa outside with a broomstick.' I'm sitting on the wing-backed chair opposite her. Even though I've turned down the fire, the air is still stifling, and I pull at the neckline of my jumper. 'What was it this time?' I ask. 'King making a visit, is he? The driveway needed to be cleaned up for his fancy car?'

She bats away my words.

'I told him not to call!' She tries to slam her fist on the armrest and winces. 'Interfering old—'

'Rick's not interfering. If anything, he's extremely helpful. I don't know where we'd be without him.'

'He's an old worrywart.' She pulls her cardigan around her, trying to hide her arm. 'Always overreacting. I just had a little slip. I was fine. I was getting up when he came hobbling over, all dramatic. *Vivienne, Vivienne...*' She does an impression of Rick's high voice and I find myself smiling. And then I stop, close my eyes.

'Mum,' I look at her, 'you were on the driveway. In this weather. Without your stick.' I look over at her walking cane, abandoned by the door, and go to get it. Put it by her chair. 'If Rick hadn't come over all dramatic, you'd still be there now.'

'Would not.'

'Mum ...'

'Oh, don't bloody start. It was those shoes, stupid things you got me. They want throwing out. They haven't got any grip.'

It's always something. Shoes. A bump on the floor. A misplaced object she tripped over. It's never her, never her age. Never her losing her balance or being stupid thinking she's younger than she is. I take a deep breath.

'Let me see.'

'It's fine.'

'Let me see.'

'I've told you, I'm—'

'Either you show me your arm now or I call the doctor and you show him. Your choice.'

She tuts and holds out her arm like a naughty toddler. She takes a quick breath as I test the elbow, moving her arm back and forth, pressing slightly on the skin, which is now dark and menacing.

'That's a nasty bruise,' I say, 'but it doesn't look like it's broken. How does it feel?'

'What a daft question. How do you think it bloody feels?'

'Sore.' I raise my eyebrows. 'Stay there, I'll go get an ice pack. Anywhere else hurt? How's your—'

'Fine, fine. All fine. Don't fuss. That's your problem, you fuss too much. You're like Rick.'

I go into the kitchen and make for the freezer. The ice pack is on the top shelf, not long since used. It was only two weeks ago when Rick called me to tell me she'd fallen in the kitchen. Loose tiles on an uneven floor. He'd been driving past when she'd flagged him down. She'd been trying to make some kind of bandage out of bedding for her knee and asked if he could cut through the cotton.

'Looked swollen,' he told me. 'And Lou, I think the bed sheet . . .'

'The bed sheet?'

'The one I cut up for her bandage. I think . . . I think it was vintage,' he said finally. 'Looked like Laura Ashley. I tried to save it, but it was no use. She'd already been at it with the scissors.'

He's an interior designer and was distraught over the ripped vintage fabric, and as I look across at his bungalow, his artistic style is apparent. Before he moved in four years ago, the bungalow had been home to a retired couple. It had a low-maintenance front garden with a rockery and was covered in yellow pebble-dash. He's renovated it into a Zen-like hideaway. I look at the bay window, the rendered walls and symmetrical paving amid carefully swept gravel and potted plants that surround a bench.

I wonder how it must feel to have money to spend on stuff like that. All the people involved when the work was going on. All the customers he has visiting him there now. Cars are always making their way past my mother's on their way to his.

I look up at the sagging suspended ceiling above me and the mouldering window frames. He must hate staring back at this house. Must hate that his customers have to drive past the chipped paintwork, ratty garden and walls that needed a coat of paint years ago.

My phone vibrates in my pocket. Pulling it out, I see it's a message from Handy Gary.

You left your cardigan with me.

I put my hand on my arm. Shit. He's right.

I'll be in the Duck and Bucket at nine and could bring it then. Will I see you there?

I shudder. No, Gary. You will not see me there. The last thing I want to do is encourage him by meeting him at the pub.

I quickly send a message back saying I'll get my cardigan at our lesson next week, and see I've missed a message. It's from Felix.

Not in tonight. Will eat later. Out with Sophie.

Sophie again. His new girlfriend from work. Why is he

always out with Sophie and never in with her? It's like he doesn't want us to meet her.

I go to reply when a message comes in from Paul.

Don't forget to pick up my parcel from the garage.

Need it urgently for tonight.

I stare at the screen. More second-hand darts accessories, little screws or flight protectors or whatever the hell he spends hours on eBay searching for. I think about texting them both back:

Mum's had another fall. If Rick hadn't found her,

she'd still be lying on the driveway. I think she's

What do I think?

That she's frail. Yes. That she's prone to accidents, obviously. But there's something else. Something about the way her eyes cloud over sometimes, about the way she's started forgetting what she is saying right in the middle of saying it.

The way she's become less opinionated, less vocal. The way she just nods sometimes, like she's remembering something, trying to pull at something from far-off. And the other things, like the tins of salmon I'm trying to ignore, stacked up in the cupboard, and the way she brushes me off when I ask her what they're for.

I think she's—

I squeeze the ice pack, then send a quick message to Felix asking when he'll next be home, and one to Paul about picking up his parcel, and then put away my phone.

I look around the kitchen, the brown wallpaper with little pictures of onions on it, the brown doors, the broken and chipped floor tiles under my feet, the leaded windows. Everything is vintage in this house. Including me.

We have touched nothing since the accident. Since my

brother and father died and our world imploded. They left us as shrapnel and now she's leaving me too. I can feel her slipping away, and I feel as old as the faded onion wallpaper. Exhausted and scared and, I realise with a shock, alone. So very alone.

THREE

'You're right to worry,' Paul tells me that evening. 'Worry that if you don't do something, you'll lose all your clients. Harriet won't be happy about you cancelling the pensioners' club, your only regular gig, and it's not like we don't need the money, Lou, we do.'

I make pasta with a cheap sauce from the Co-op for dinner. It isn't what Paul wanted; he wanted to eat at the Duck and Bucket, get one of their meal deals after training with his new second-hand darts. Darts that promise to make him into a 'champion player'. He told me he's entitled to a special discount now, as he's part of the official team. But when I asked him how much of a discount, he got vague, so pasta and sauce it is.

He takes a mouthful and nods at his own words. 'You can't go on like this. Dropping everything whenever she calls.'

'Paul, she had a fall, I couldn't just—'

'Rick said she was fine, you told me so yourself. You could have phoned her and—'

'You know she never answers the phone. I had to go over there. To check she was OK.'

'Of course you did. I get that. Of course you need to check on her, but you could've done it *after* your lessons. She'd have been fine waiting a few hours and you wouldn't have lost the job and be out of pocket. That's all I'm saying.'

The back of my neck aches, my shoulders feel like they're up around my ears. I close my eyes, a headache building. Why did I even mention the fall to Paul?

'I can get back the money I lost today,' I say. 'I'll work late next week.'

I pick at my meal. Paul's getting ready to meet the other members of the darts team at the pub. A group of mostly middle-aged men, all getting excited over throwing sharp stabby objects at a board, and for the life of me I can't understand why he does it. I don't know how he talks to them all, plays the game (though 'game' seems a bit of a stretch) and stays awake at the same time.

'Maybe it's time—' He begins, and I cut him off quick.

'Paul, please don't start with that again. It's been a long day.'

'She's not going to get better,' he holds up his hands, 'that's all I want you to understand. She's not suddenly going to get younger, be light on her feet again.' He stands and pats his stomach, as if to feel where the food has gone. 'And if we put her in a home, we can rent out the house until Felix is ready to move in.' He lets out a burp and apologises before carrying on. 'Tony was saying an Airbnb is the way to go. House that size, just outside of Manchester, it's a brilliant location. Imagine the—'

'Paul . . .' My voice holds a warning, but he takes no notice.

'He reckons it would bring in enough to cover the cost of

the care home and more. I could speak to him tonight. He said just to give him the word.'

I take the dishes to the sink. This is not a new conversation.

'He's doing us a favour,' Paul goes on. 'You know that. He should really be trying to persuade us to put it on his books, rent it out through him, but as a mate, he says we should try it ourselves first. He's offered to come over, have a look, give me some free advice.'

'You know what we could do?' I turn to him. 'What we should be doing? Moving her in here, with us. Or us going to her, living with her in that house, we could—'

I'm stopped by Paul laughing, his high, hollow laugh that shuts me down.

'We've been through this, Lou, it's a non-starter. You ser-iously think me and your mother in a house together would work? That she would even consider it? Where would she go here?' He points to the dining room. 'In there? With you at her beck and call? And do you think for one minute she'd let us move into that precious house? That she'd allow us into your brother's bedroom, your father's—'

'OK.' I hold up my hands, admitting defeat. Anything to stop him carrying on. 'You don't need to be mean. It was just an idea.'

'A bad idea,' he says, his voice softer. 'The good idea is moving her somewhere she'll be happy. Looked after. By professionals. Where they have the time and resources to take care of her.'

I turn back to the dishes.

'And then the rent from her house pays for that care and a bit besides . . .'

I focus on the bubbles, on swishing the water and watching the foam build. I do what I always do when Paul talks like this, I shut out his words and let my mind wander to Spain. I imagine the other me, the me in a parallel universe who finished her degree and moved away like she'd always planned. Who didn't have to stay at home and be there for her mother.

She walks the polished streets of Malaga in sandals and floaty dresses; she eats tapas at the bar by the cathedral and drinks sweet Spanish sherry from oak casks. She has a brother and both parents back in England and she calls them daily, hears about their lives over digital connections.

It's seven o'clock: what would the other me be doing now? Far too early to have eaten yet. Perhaps she's getting ready for the evening. Going into the centre to meet friends at one of the crowded bars, sitting on a high stool and watching the tourists pass as she sips a cocktail. Perhaps she is—

'Lou!'

I blink rapidly. Paul is dragging me back into our dining room with its yellow overhead lighting and the chill in the air.

'You were daydreaming again.' He clicks his fingers in front of my face. 'Did you hear what I said?'

'Sorry, it's been a long day.'

'The house.' He grabs his jacket. 'I'll arrange for Tony to have a look, just tell us what kind of money we can expect if—'

'No, Paul.' I turn, my hands dripping wet suds on the kitchen floor. 'Not yet. You can't, she's not ready.'

'She is.' He comes forward and gets hold of my hands, presses a tea towel into them. 'Love, your mum needs more than you. She needs proper care. You can't put your life on hold every time she has a little trip.' He pauses, staring at me. 'You say she's not ready, but maybe you're the one who's not ready. Have you thought about that?'

He kisses the top of my head.

'I'll kip in the spare room again tonight; I'll be home late.'

I give a brief nod and watch him go. The house settles around me, the silence suddenly loud.

It's not supposed to be like this. I'm not meant to be doing this alone. I had a brother. I had Mark. He was the practical one. He was the one who would know how to handle this situation, what to do.

When the accident happened, I had counselling briefly and I remember the woman telling me I wouldn't always feel like this. That although it was a cliché, time was a healer. But she lied. Time ticks slowly by, and every second is like a prodding needle. Time doesn't heal, it hurts, and I have no idea what to do about it.

I look up and see my reflection in the kitchen window, my frizzy brown hair escaping its ponytail, my shoulders high, my blue woollen jumper that's seen better days, and I wrap my arms around myself briefly before going to my phone.

Felix hasn't replied, but I have a new message from Gary. He's put a sad-face reaction to my message saying I wouldn't be going to the pub.

I'll keep it until we next meet . . .

I cringe. Three dots at the end as if it's a date or something. I give it the thumbs-up emoji, the least encouraging thing I can think of, and imagine him at the Duck and Bucket. Probably propping up the bar and trying to chat up some poor woman. What would happen if I went in? Had a glass of wine? Watched Paul play darts with his teammates and pretended I was interested? Let Gary come over for a chat? Fake-laughed at his jokes and . . .

Gary's face is suddenly large in my mind.

The way he grins with his tongue between his teeth, all

spittle and gums, his eyes half closed and always too close. The smell of his breath and his clammy hand when it brushes against mine. I recoil, flinching back. I will never be that desperate. Even if Paul is there, albeit by the dartboard, I'm never spending time with Gary when I don't need to.

I go to the back door. I'm certain Paul has locked it. He always does, but I need to check just in case. As if Gary might suddenly think of returning my cardigan in person. It's a long shot, but I wouldn't put it past him.

I lean against the door for a moment, hating the blackness out there. The way the shadows hide things. I stare past my reflection into the night beyond and a shiver creeps along the back of my neck. At the uncertainty of who might be out there, looking in. At the uncertainty of everything at the moment. It takes a lot not to go to the fridge, open a bottle of wine and pour myself a large glass.

But it's a school night. I have a busy day ahead of me, and no matter how much it feels like it, getting drunk is not the answer. Going into the lounge, I turn the television on loud, pick up my phone and start a long scroll of social media, looking over all the people who seem to be living a better life than I am.

FOUR

The next day, I skip breakfast and take an early drive to check on my mother, making it back in time for my first lesson. She's fine, bruised and as stubborn as always and shooing me away, telling me again what a fusspot I am.

It's another bitter day, the wind biting and the cold seeping into my bones. I walk through the village, and it feels as depressed as I am. All the Christmas decorations are waiting to be taken down. No longer needed and just hanging about on the buildings and lamp posts until someone from the council comes and gets them. It always amazes me how one week it's all twinkly lights and people smiling, and the next everywhere is dull and people keep their heads down like they're just getting through.

I pass the estate agent where Tony, Paul's friend, works. I almost go in, almost ask to speak to Tony and tell him to ignore Paul, but I hurry past instead. I didn't say anything about it to my mother. I thought about it, the words almost leaving my lips, but I couldn't do it. She'd get herself worked up, into a state, and the thought is absurd. Renting out the house? Airbnb? Who would want to holiday somewhere that needs fully redecorating, with window frames that are slightly rotting and patches of damp with the smell of mould in the unused rooms?

I pick up my pace, walking quickly to the Crooked Kettle, where Helen is waiting for me.

'Didn't think you'd make it,' she says as I dump my bags on the floor and fall into the chair opposite her. 'I was just about to text and offer to come to your mother's, meet you there. Turn these coffees into takeouts.'

'God no.' I take off my jacket. 'That's the last thing I want. I need to get out. Breathe some clean air that doesn't stink of Germolene. Talk to someone who doesn't have dentures.'

'How do you know I don't have dentures?' She gives me a goofy grin, and I'm reminded of everything I love about her. My oldest and dearest friend, who still has the ability to make me laugh even when it's the last thing on my mind.

We met in the baby group twenty-two years ago. I was still reeling from the accident and from becoming a mother, and Helen was reeling from falling in love with a Brit and having his children when she should only have been in the UK for a couple of years. Our bond was one of mutual shock, and we've been close ever since.

'How is she?'

'She's good. Well, good as in she told me to stop fussing and leave her alone.' I take a sip of the coffee, warm and delicious. 'But, y'know.' I place my phone on the table between us. 'I live in fear of that going off and it being Rick again. Or Paul, who seems to resent every minute I'm at my mother's and just wants to put her in a home. He's threatening to call Tony, from Chatting Estates, get him to go over there and see how much we'd get for renting out the house.'

'No!' Helen's eyes widen. 'What does Viv think about that?'

'She doesn't know,' I let out a huff of air, 'and she won't ever know. Paul doesn't have it in him to arrange it, and even if he did, she won't talk to him, so he won't be able to sort a time for Tony to visit.' I shrug my shoulders. 'And that will be that.'

Helen takes a mouthful of coffee. 'Y'know, it isn't such a bad idea.'

'Oh, not you as well.'

She holds up her hands. 'I'm not agreeing with Paul, I just think that—'

'You think she needs to go in a home? Somewhere they'll sit her in a chair and forget about her all day, on the other side of Manchester where I'll never see her?'

'I love Viv,' Helen says carefully, 'you know I do, but Lou,' she reaches across and puts her hand on mine, 'you're worn out. Look at you. Won't you consider getting carers in again?'

I glance down at my shirt and realise I haven't ironed it properly. And there's a slight stain on my jeans from last night's meal. I pick at the dried pasta sauce with my thumbnail.

'You look thin,' she tells me. 'Too thin. Not thin as in, "whoa, let me know what diet you're on", thin as in, "whoa, you need some rest and a huge meal". Why not give the carers another go?'

'I don't know if I could go through all that again.' I give a slow shake of my head. 'All the chopping and changing and ringing up the care company to say that she didn't like this person or that person and could we try someone else.' I look up. 'She just hates having strangers in her house. People she's only just met fussing and ...' I look away and remember my mother being outraged when one of them went in her wardrobe without asking to get her a cardigan. 'And being personal with her so quickly,' I finish. 'It's the cost of it all as well.' I wipe my hands over my face. 'I just can't think where we'd find the money.'

'But when was the last time you did something for you? Had some time off?'

I laugh. 'Time off? Who has time off from their mother?'

'Me, for starters.' Helen gives me a slight smile. 'Much as I love my mother, I'm glad she's thousands of miles away back home in Utah and I only see her on this,' she holds up her phone, 'when and how I like.' She leans in. 'You need help. Can't Paul or Felix go and ...'

She stops when I start laughing. The very idea that Paul would go to my mother's and offer to help is hilarious. As for Felix, he commutes to Manchester, where he works as a graphic designer, and when he isn't at his office, he's with Sophie, his elusive girl-friend, or out with his mates. I don't want to involve him in all of this, tie him down and stop him from living his life.

I shake my head. 'It's just me,' I say.

Helen pats my hand and I steer the conversation to her, ask her about work, her twin boys, anything so I don't have to see her sympathetic face at the state of my life.

Later that day, I make my way to the local Co-op. When I was a kid, Dilenby village had all the necessities, butcher, fishmon-ger and a Saturday market, but then it was as if word got about that it was the place to be, and the high street changed from practical to useless. The market went from fruit and veg to some farmers' thing that only seems to sell different versions of jam and cake. Wine bars, artisan bakeries and small boutiques opened up. What had been the butcher and the fishmonger were sold off to make way for a new Italian restaurant. Dilenby became fashionable and house prices soared.

I go over to the yellow sticker section and see what's there. What I can buy at a discount and make a meal from. It's slim pickings: there's a bag of peppers, a bit of bacon and a few pork pies. I put the peppers and bacon in my basket, thinking I'll add a tin of tomatoes for a pasta sauce. Pasta again. It feels like I might turn into a piece of fusilli, but what else can I do? I went to fill up my car the other day and nearly had a panic attack at the price of fuel. We can't seem to get out of our overdraft, and the loan we took out to pay for Christmas is coming to the end of its interest-free period, which I'm trying to pretend isn't happening.

My phone buzzes and I jump. It's Helen.

Forgot to ask – golf club, next Saturday night? Live band! Get Paul to take the night off. You need a night out!!!

I smile.

Can't, I type back. No money and no . . .

I stop. I was about to put no desire to go, but this is Helen's idea of a good time. She's being nice in asking Paul and me along, so I delete the last part and leave it as No money. She'll understand that. They do this kind of thing every weekend, even though they're both working full-time and must be so tired. She claims to like it, says she enjoys getting dressed up and putting on make-up, but she sees Simon every day. Has seen him every day since they got married over twenty years ago. And the cost! It must cost them a fortune just to go out and sit together somewhere different. She calls them 'date nights' and the whole thing baffles me.

Have a good time!

I stare at my message as it sends. No doubt she'll tell me all about it the next time we meet, full of golf club gossip. Paul never asks me to go out with him. Not to the pubs he goes to or the darts tournaments. I imagine, for a moment, if he did ask me. If we actually went out together. Getting dressed up, forcing my feet into heels, make-up drying out my skin, wearing something tight and uncomfortable, sitting across from him and talking about . . . what?

I give a laugh at the thought of us sitting in silence, staring at our phones, just waiting until we can get back home to our normal routine of sweatpants and television.

I put the phone back in my handbag and pick up a tin of tomatoes, already hating the meal I'm going to cook. I drop it in my basket, knowing that Paul will probably get a curry anyway. He'll find out its pasta and make excuses why he won't be home, and then most likely get a takeout and eat it at the office, where I can't see him do it.

My phone rings, and I smile. Helen isn't taking no for an answer.

'I can't,' I say before she has the chance to speak. 'I have no money and there's no way Paul would take me to a dance. He hates dancing. If I went, it would have to be just you and me. I might try to wangle that.'

There's a moment of silence.

'Is this Louise? Louise Whitstable?'

It's not Helen.

'Sorry? Yes, this is Lou. Who is this?'

I pull the phone away from my face. Unrecognised number. Damn. My cheeks go hot at the thought of what I've just said.

'Sorry, I thought you were my friend,' I say quickly. 'If you're ringing about Spanish lessons, I am taking on new students but I do have quite a full schedule. Were you—'

'I'm not calling about Spanish lessons.' His voice is soft. I can hear the smile behind the words. 'I'm ringing about Viv. Vivienne is your mother?'

I close my eyes. The squeeze at the base of my stomach is back in an instant.

'She is. What's happened? Can you—'

'Everything's fine, she's fine, it's just . . .' Another pause, and I hear him take in a sharp breath. 'My name's Oscar. I'm over at Rick's, I'm working for him, and there's this guy doing the rounds, claiming he's from some kind of charity. He was here and I told him to clear off, and then he went to your mother's, and I know it's none of my business, but he's been in there for half an hour now and I know how these guys operate. I was just . . . well, she could be signing her life away, so I called Rick and he gave me your number. I just thought you should know.'

FIVE

I pull up in my mother's drive, the car jerking as I slam on the brakes. I left the food in the basket, didn't even put it back on the shelf, just abandoned it in the aisle and ran out. I rang the student I was meant to be meeting and cancelled, and the rest of the twenty-minute journey was made in a state of panic as my mind presented various nightmarish scenarios.

She's given this man all her bank details.

She's left him alone in the lounge and he's working out what he can steal. He's mugged her, hitting her over the head while he fills his pockets with what he can find.

'Mum . . .?'

I can hear voices in the lounge, a low one and my mother's. I straighten my shoulders and open the door to see her sitting opposite a heavy-set man with reddish hair in need of a cut. They are both drinking tea and there's a set of A4 papers on the side table and one on my mother's lap. I can see something printed on it, a photograph, and some words, all in red.

'Lou!' Mum beams at me. 'Come meet Josh, he's here raising funds.'

'Nice to meet you.' Josh smiles at me. He's late twenties and dressed in a shirt and tie with a jacket that has dirty imitation fur at the cuffs and collar. The kind of jacket that doesn't look good over a shirt and tie.

'Mum, what is all this?' I ask her, ignoring him. 'What's going on?'

'Josh is raising money for the people in Ukraine. Awful, just awful what's going on, and he's doing something about it.'

I look over at him; he smiles at me over his cup.

'We already give to several charities for Ukraine,' I tell him.

'Vivienne did tell me that,' he says, sitting forward in his seat, 'but as I explained, this is for the children over there. I'm collecting funds that will go straight to them.'

I lean forward and pick up the papers from my mother's lap. A horrific image of a child has been printed out, and underneath are some bank details.

'I'm not following.' I look up at him. 'Where's the name of the charity you're involved with? The official—'

'Oh, it's not official, as yet.' He gives me another smile. 'We're taking matters into our own hands and raising this way and then transferring the funds.'

'Transferring the funds?'

He nods. 'Once we get to a decent amount, we'll transfer the funds to the children's charity that deals with—'

'OK, I think I've heard enough. Time to go.'

'Lou!' My mother blinks up at me. 'Don't be so rude! Josh here is doing something wonderful; he's collecting money for—'

'Collecting money for charity *is* wonderful,' I agree, 'but calling on vulnerable adults and asking them to donate to a private bank account that isn't with a registered charity is a bit much.' I turn to him. 'Don't you agree, Josh? That preying on my mother, in her eighties, who doesn't really know you, or that you won't just keep the money, is a bit out of order?'

He raises his eyebrows and goes to stand.

'As I said, once we have a decent amount, we're transferring all the money—'

'A decent amount?' I feel rage build in my chest. 'Why not just get people to give straight to the charity? And which charity is it?' I lift the page. 'You say it's for the children, but which charity exactly are you donating to?'

He looks at me. Staring me out.

'You do know I could call the police? Tell them that you're—'

'It's not illegal to cold-call on houses.'

'But it is illegal to commit fraud.'

'Lou!' My mother stands up, leaning heavily on her cane. 'Josh isn't doing anything like that. He's—'

'Mum,' I take a deep breath, 'did you transfer any money?'

'I was just getting my bank card,' she tells me. 'I told Josh I wasn't sure how to make a bank transfer, and he was going to talk me through it.'

'I bet you were,' I say to Josh. 'Leave now, please.'

'I promise we're giving it all to the charity,' he says as I lead him to the door. 'Here, look.' He fumbles in his bag and brings out a key ring. A flimsy piece of ribbon attached to a silver chain and ring. 'To show our appreciation,' he says as he holds it up, 'we give one to everyone who makes a donation, and we also have some novelty items, a selection of small toys and—'

'What's a key ring got to do with anything?' I cut him off.

'My mother doesn't need a key ring or a bookmark or anything else you have in that bag that you use to rob people of their money, and if you come back, I'm ringing the police.'

He gets to the front door and pauses a moment, looking past me towards the hallway and the kitchen beyond.

'Lovely house,' he says, almost to himself, as he puts the cheap key ring back in his pocket. 'All the way out here, miles from anywhere,' his eyes meet mine, 'and your poor mother rattling around all on her own.'

'She's not on her own,' I say loudly. 'I'm here.'

'Not all the time though, eh?' He raises his voice, speaking to Mum, who is still in the lounge. 'Just saying you want to be careful, Vivienne, out here on your own. You might get all sorts trying to take advantage,' his eyes flick back to mine, 'at any time.'

I hold up my phone, and he raises his hands.

'Bye, Vivienne,' he calls, 'lovely to meet you. Maybe we'll meet again soon.'

I watch him leave with my stomach churning. My mother is still going on about how I'm being rude and that she's perfectly capable of giving whatever money she likes to whatever charity she likes.

'You can,' I tell her once the door is closed and locked, 'but not to any random bloke who knocks on the door. Mum, he didn't have any identification, nothing to say he was working for a charity. What were you thinking, letting him in like that?'

'You heard him. He was collecting first and then giving it to the charity.'

'He was collecting to put it in his pocket.'

We stare at each other for a moment. Her eyes are angry,

but then I see them cloud over as my words sink in. Confusion rests heavy on her brow, and she suddenly looks so small. Her hands go together at her chest, and I almost cry to see her so visibly upset but trying to hide it from me.

'What else?' I ask her gently. 'Did you give him anything else? Cash?'

She looks away, a bit sheepish.

'He seemed so nice. Genuine.'

'Oh Mum, how much?'

She shrugs, and then her face crumples a little. 'Just what I had in my purse. Twenty pounds or so. I was going to make a bank transfer for the rest.'

'The rest?'

'Josh said a couple of hundred would provide shelter for some children for . . .' She puts her hands to her face. 'But he was so polite, so nice. Said I had a lovely home, that he'd love a tour . . .'

I go over to her and put my arm around her.

'It's OK,' I say softly, 'it's fine. Twenty pounds isn't that much. I'm just glad I arrived before he made you do that bank transfer. Oh Mum.'

I stay with her a while and then go into the kitchen to put the kettle on. Thank goodness I came when I did, I think, and it hits me again. How vulnerable she is.

I hear an engine passing the house, and I look out of the window expecting to see Rick's Volvo, but instead it's a white van. The van I almost crashed into the other day. My stomach drops a little as I realise this must be the man who called me.

I open the back door and raise my hand to slow the vehicle. *Dilenby Gardening Services* is written on the side in blue, and I smile at the shadowy figure in the driving seat. Without him warning me, my mother could have signed over her entire savings. I need to thank him.

I fold my arms tightly and walk towards the van as it comes to a stop. The air is cool; there was a frost again last night and this side of the house gets no sunshine. I take my time, not wanting to fall, as the ground is hard and slippery under my feet. The driver's door opens, and as he gets out, the smile on my face freezes.

He isn't what I was expecting.

Because he called me from Rick's, and Rick is in his sixties, I assumed he was an older guy. The way he warned me, and the way he looked out for my mother, made me think he was at least middle-aged, but the man who climbs out of the van is anything but. He's young. Late twenties, and tall, has to be over six feet.

He takes his time getting out, and I watch, transfixed. He's wearing a cotton T-shirt, even though it's freezing out here, meaning I can see the outline of his broad shoulders, the set of his muscles underneath the material. And his forearms are tanned, in a kind of I-work-outdoors sexy way. In January. Who has sexy tanned forearms in January?

'Louise?' He smiles. If he was aware I was checking him out, his expression doesn't betray it. It's a friendly smile, an honest one, and shows off a set of amazing cheekbones. I swallow. 'It is Louise?'

No one calls me Louise any more. I nod, and finally find my voice.

'Thank you so much,' I say, holding out my hand. 'I got here just in time. She was about to give him her bank details.'

He steps forward and takes my hand. There's dirt under his fingernails. His skin is warm and rough. I look at my small hand in his and it's an effort to take it back.

34

'I'm just glad I called you,' he says. 'He came by asking for Rick, walked all the way up the drive. When I said Rick wasn't here, he asked me if I knew the old lady who lived next door. I did think about calling the police, but they could've taken an age, and in that time . . .' He trails off, glances at my mother's house. 'Rick was just going into a meeting, couldn't call you, but he said you wouldn't mind if I did.'

His gaze locks on mine. God, he's good-looking. His eyes are a strange colour, a light grey, and his black curls look impossibly thick, the kind of hair you only see on models, or in movies.

'Is she OK?' He smiles expectantly. For a second, I've forgotten what we were talking about. 'Viv?' he prompts. 'Hope she's not too shook up.'

'She's fine,' I tell him. 'A little embarrassed, but fine.'

'Good.' He turns to leave. 'Glad I could help. See you around.' He goes to get back in his van, and then stops. 'Oh, and be careful out here, it's icy. Not good when you're trying to brake, or trying to stop someone from driving into you.' He gives me a meaningful look, and as I flush, he laughs. But it's almost affectionate, like we've known each other for years and he's pulling my leg.

I watch him turn off onto the main road and drive away. *Who and what was that?*

I walk back into the kitchen and lean on the closed door, my face still hot from his teasing, and I realise that he must know my mother. He used her name. He must have chatted with her before. He's probably driven past the kitchen window a hundred times. I glance out to where he just was. We must have passed each other often, but this is the first time I've seen him.

SIX

'*Te gustaría un café?*'

   '*Te gustorio une caff?*'

I smile tightly. 'Try again,' I say and point to the words. 'Repeat after me, *gustaría.*'

   '*Gustorio.*'

'Almost.' I go back to the book where Gary has written the phrase and underline it. We've been doing this for almost five weeks and he's only marginally better. 'You need to practise. You're almost there, but without daily practice you won't get the pronunciation correct. Now, what was it you wanted me to translate? A letter from your girlfriend?' I look up and jump. He's close. Too close.

Gary does this. If I don't watch him, he inches forward, invading my personal space, getting as close as he can without actually touching me, and he's done it now. When I was distracted by the book, he leaned in so our faces are now ridiculously close. I move back a little and he smiles, enjoying watching me squirm.

'OK!' I lean over to my bag, looking inside for something I don't need just to get some space between us. 'Do you have the letter with you?' I look at him expectantly. It has been a long hour and there's still ten minutes left. I will not let this lesson overrun again.

'I'll send it to you,' he says. 'It's upstairs in my flat, but I'll photograph it and email you a copy, then you can translate it and bring it back next week. Is that OK?' He grins. 'I don't mind paying extra.'

I nod.

'And perhaps you could,' he raises his eyebrows, 'help me reply? I hope you don't mind, it's a very private letter, and I think she asks questions about ...' He gives a high-pitched giggle and trails off. I stare at him.

'Then perhaps,' I say slowly, 'if the letter is very private, be-tween the two of you, you should translate it yourself.'

He stares at me a moment longer than necessary and then nods. 'Perhaps that would be best, if you think so.'

'I think so,' I say, and give a tight smile. 'I'm sure you can do it.'

'If I get stuck,' he leans in, and I have to force myself to keep still and not recoil, 'if there are some words I don't know, I'll ask for help. My girlfriend, she's very poetic. Did I tell you about her dreams of writing a book?'

I nod as I scoop up my books and papers. Gary has told me many times about Josie. His chance meeting online with her, his late-night conversations where they communicate in fits and starts with what little English she knows and the Spanish I've managed to teach him. I know about this girl's likes and dislikes, her family, her dog, and all about her upcoming visit he's in the throes of planning. She'll stay in his flat, where he'll speak bad Spanish to her and goodness knows what else. Poor girl.

I go to the door that leads to the shop. I like to keep it open so that Trudy, the girl who works in the off-licence, can see and hear us, but Gary always manages to close it at some point. I open it now and meet Trudy's gaze; she raises an eyebrow and I give her a look that makes her grin and shake her head. A silent conversation that says everything. How she works with this man daily, I will never know.

As I walk through the shop, he calls my name. I turn. He's holding up my cardigan, the one I left behind the previous week.

'Forgetting this so you have a reason to see me again?' He laughs. 'Leaving it here so you can ring me up? Make a date?'

I laugh back politely and hear Trudy mutter something that sounds like 'creep'. As I take the cardigan from him, I wonder how best to tell him that I forgot it because I was so desperate to get away.

'See you next week!' he calls out as I leave, gulping in the cold air as if I've been suffocated.

I text Helen as I make my way to my car parked outside his shop.

Handy Gary is the worst. I swear as soon as I get some more students, I'm cancelling him.

What this time? she replies. The usual leering?

Private translation, I write back, letter from his girlfriend. Don't ask!

She sends a being-sick emoji and I smile.

I should stop going. Or tell him to keep to his space. Just say, 'Gary, please don't sit so close,' but then what? He'd get offended, cancel, and I can't afford to lose another student. Just this morning, the energy bill arrived, and Paul read the riot act while I told him he needed to tighten his belt as well. It isn't just me. We both need to try to save money somehow.

Prices are soaring, and we don't have enough in the account to keep up. The taxi firm is struggling, has been ever since a new firm opened in the neighbouring village, and I'm not bringing in enough to cover the shortfall. I tried to explain that if he gave up his precious darts team and weekly outings to the pub, we could save a bit. But of course, as usual, it was all my fault because I wasn't earning enough. Whenever I mention him giving up darts, he comes back with me giving up Spanish.

'You'll have to get a proper job,' were his last words, 'full-time. I'm managing the place and working double shifts to save on drivers, doing everything I can. It's you that needs to pull your weight. They're looking for people in the Co-op. You could do that, stack shelves, serve customers. You don't need much experience for that kind of work, so they'd take you on. Minimum wage, it's more than you're getting now.'

I almost choked on my toast. My Spanish lessons aren't lucrative, but they're the only thing that's mine. They keep me alive. Rolling the vowels around, the words taking me back to a time when it was all I thought about, the life I was going to live out there. I can't *not* teach Spanish. I can't give up that small piece of myself. The only piece I have left. So if Gary wants to put his face close to mine while he repeats verbs, if he wants me to translate love letters from his girlfriend, so be it. I'll just have to advertise for more students and work longer hours.

I run a hand over my face. My eyes are hot, stinging with tiredness. How exactly am I going to work longer hours when I have to visit my mother every day? Nights? Take on translation work instead of sleeping? I lean my head back against the seat and close my eyes.

There's a sudden tap at the window and I let out a small scream of surprise.

He starts to laugh at my reaction, his face full of amusement, and I go hot as I wind down my window.

'Sorry!' He holds up his hands. 'I didn't mean to scare you. I just . . .' He shows me a bottle of water and looks back to Gary's shop. 'I thought it was you. I was going to leave you alone, but I saw you put your head back like that and I wanted to make sure you were OK. And then I end up scaring the life out of you.' He shakes his head, black curls moving softly. 'I'm such an idiot. And Viv, has she recovered after her visitor last week?'

Oscar.

I tried not to think about him. Mainly because every time I did, I went hot with embarrassment.

I swallow. *Get a grip.*

'She's great,' I say, and force myself to behave normally. 'She was just a little embarrassed, but she's fine. I feel I didn't thank you properly. That day, it was all rushed, but I'm so glad you called me. Told me what was going on.'

'Me too,' he says, and am I imagining it, or do his eyes linger on mine a little longer than they need to?

'I'll tell her you were asking after her,' I say. 'I'm just on my way there now.'

He smiles. 'Me too. Rick's having a pond put in.'

We stare at each other a moment. Is there . . . *something*? Is that . . . And then he taps the roof of the car and leaves.

'See you around,' he says.

I watch as he gets into his van. He's so agile, opening the door and swinging himself in in one fluid movement. Like he's a dancer. Like his thigh muscles are ... I give myself a mental shake.

'Stop that,' I murmur as I start the engine.

When I glance up, I see Gary at the shop window. Staring at me. His face serious.

'See you next week,' he mouths, and I nod. He stays there watching me as I pull out into the traffic. I shrink into my seat, as if trying to shake his stare off me.

At the lights, I see Oscar's van a couple of cars in front and realise I'm going to follow him. We're making the same journey, and it feels weirdly intimate. The cars in front turn left as we head straight on, and suddenly I'm right behind him. We slow in the traffic, and as I catch a glimpse of his face in the side mirror something whooshes up in my chest.

Can he see me? I wonder. Can he see me staring at his side mirror? Staring at him?

I take a sudden right. It's the wrong direction, but I can't do this for another twenty minutes. I pull in at the industrial estate, feeling embarrassed and annoyed at myself, and realise I'm by the sports shop, the one Paul wants to buy that dartboard from. He's been talking about it for weeks, but I keep telling him we can't afford it. I'm about to turn around when I see a car. Dilenby Taxis, orange lettering, little light on top. I'd know them anywhere. I frown and watch as Paul exits the shop.

I let out a sigh. So I have to get a full-time job, but *he* can spend money on a dartboard we don't need? But as I turn off the engine, ready to get out, I see he isn't carrying a dartboard. He must've just gone in to look at it again.

41

I smile, give a small laugh and my hand goes to the door. Then I stop as a woman comes out behind him, high blonde ponytail swinging as she walks. She is carrying a large bag. A large, heavy bag. Paul takes it from her, and I watch as he pulls out a dartboard. They both look at it a moment, then he laughs and kind of leans into her, one of his hands going to her shoulder.

I frown, but stay where I am. He puts the dartboard back in the bag and takes it over to a small red Mini. I watch as he puts it on the passenger seat, then says something before getting into his own car. The blonde woman drives off, and Paul follows her.

The car park is suddenly empty again, and I'm not sure what I've just seen and why it's making me feel so uncomfortable.

'Who the hell was that?' I ask aloud. I grab my phone and start to text.

Just missed you. I'm at the sports shop where that
fancy dartboard is and saw you
Saw you what?

I delete what I've written.

It sounds like I'm accusing him of something. What *am* I accusing him of? Helping some woman buy a dartboard? She's probably on his team.

Am I being stupidly sexist? Thinking that all darts players fit one stereotype?

I flush, embarrassed by how easy it is for me to jump to conclusions. I'll ask him about it later, find out who she is and why he's helping her buy a dartboard instead of working at the taxi office.

My phone buzzes in my hand. A message from Paul.

Working late tonight, sorry! Got waylaid today so don't bother making me anything for dinner. Will grab something while I'm out.

SEVEN

Dilenby Library is one of my favourite places. Aside from Spain, obviously. I'd rather be in Malaga any day of the week, but the next best place is the library. It's small and has two floors, a small non-fiction section on the ground floor, and then upstairs to the fiction department, which has a few tables and some padded chairs.

It's old, the same layout and feel to it as when I was a kid, and going in there brings back memories, good ones, ones that I like to revisit and remember. Memories of Mum and me spending ages browsing, me taking armfuls of picture books, Mum with her romances. Although I progressed from picture books to travel books to true crime, Mum still likes her romances and I'm there almost on a weekly basis collecting and returning books she's ordered.

I breathe deeply as I walk in. The smell of old books is calming, I always think. If Spain hadn't seduced me when I was a teenager after idly picking up a travel book, I could've been a librarian. Worked with books in some capacity. Breathed in their scent all day and got lost in their worlds.

'Hello, you.' Ruth, the librarian, smiles at me warmly. She's known me since I was a child, knows everything about me, and I find that both comforting and hard. She's one of the few people I see on a regular basis who knew Mark and still talks about him.

'Got them here,' she says, and goes to the shelf behind her. 'Didn't get through them all last time, hey? She must be slowing down. I don't think in all the time I've worked here your mother has ever done that.'

I frown as I look at the pile of books Mum has ordered. I pick up the first one, the cover illustration of a woman dressed in a nurse's uniform looking very familiar. I look at the next one, frowning.

'She had these the other week.' I glance at Ruth. 'I remember the expression on that nurse's face, the way she's biting her lip.'

Ruth nods. 'I'm guessing she wants to read them again. Or didn't get a chance. She could've just called and renewed them. Maybe it was a mistake. Oh, and these are for you. We were going to try to sell them, but I thought you might like them.'

I open the bag she hands me and see a pile of books, all black covers and bold lettering. True crime, thrillers, the kind of thing I love curling up with and forgetting myself in for a few hours. I offer to pay for them, but she refuses, as always, so I thank her, put Mum's books in the bag with mine and leave with a niggle at the back of my mind. Mum never reads books twice, especially this kind. She always says that she can guess the ending from the first page and that's the fun of it, but she couldn't read them all over again.

45

Perhaps Ruth is right, she didn't get chance to read them first time around.

I pretend that the dragging feeling in my stomach isn't because of the library books, but because of what I've got to do today, and maybe it is.

Paul is taking me to my mother's, and I feel a little sick at how it will play out. He's going to take a look at the gutters, which have got clogged up with leaves, causing water to pour down the side of the house. Mum wanted to call somebody, but once Paul heard about it, he thought it was a great opportunity for him to take some pictures for Tony. See what needs doing if we're to rent it, even though I've told him time and again that she won't leave. I'm dreading him bringing the whole thing up with her and upsetting her.

'Ready?' He's waiting outside the library in the taxi, the engine running. 'That's a pile, isn't it?'

'Some are for me.'

I don't tell him about the books. I don't say much at all as we make the journey. Paul turns up the radio and I look out of the window. I hate riding in the taxi with him; it reminds me of when we first met. Thinking back, I can't remember exactly when we became an item. Paul was just there. I knew him from school, he was a friend of Mark's, and after the accident, when I dropped out of uni and wouldn't leave the house, he started coming round.

It's funny in a way, because I think it was Mum who encouraged the whole thing, and now they don't like each other at all. She used to call up the stairs, 'Lou? Paul's here for you again, come down,' and because he was one of the few people I could talk to about Mark for hours, I would come out of my room.

I turn and study his profile as he drives. He's started dyeing his hair.

'Paul?' He glances at me. 'The other day, I was at the sports shop . . .' I falter. He's frowning in that way he does, his hands tight on the steering wheel.

'What?'

'That sports shop over on the industrial estate, and . . .'

He looks at me. 'And what?'

I shake my head. 'Nothing. I just thought I saw you, but . . .' I trail off, not sure where I'm going with this.

'If it's about that dartboard, you can stop worrying.' He shakes his head. 'I changed my mind about it. You were right. We need to tighten our belts, look after the pennies and all that. That's what today is about.'

I nod, and we make the rest of the journey in silence.

'Why's Paul here? What are you doing bringing him with you? Hasn't he got work?'

I didn't prepare her. I thought it best not to say anything, and now, as she stands in the kitchen, leaning on the counter, staring at Paul through the window, I don't know if I should have.

'He's just here to clean the gutters,' I say gently as I fill the kettle. 'We won't bother him, and he won't bother us. Come on, you and me will go back in the lounge, watch that show you like about selling stuff you find at car boot sales.'

I usher her back into the lounge, and we sit, the TV blaring and the fire full blast, my stomach in a knot. I can hear Paul's ladder scraping across the side of the house.

'Look who's come visiting,' my mother suddenly says, and I look at where she's pointing. A robin sits on the windowsill over on the far side of the room, peering in at us. 'They say

47

robins are a sign that someone who's passed is thinking of you.' She picks up her biscuit and starts crushing it in her hand.

'Oh Mum, have you been feeding him? You'll have a whole flock if you're not careful.'

'I don't want to be careful,' she says, and I watch as she makes her way over to the window, opens it and puts a trail of biscuit crumbs on the sill. She turns to me, and we share a smile. The robin starts pecking at the crumbs. My mother claps her hands, delighted, and I feel my throat get tight.

'I got your library books,' I say after a moment, and she smiles. I look over at them on the side table. I almost don't do it, but it's like a bruise that you can't stop prodding, and so I go to them. Picking up the first one, the one with the nurse, I take it over to her.

'Looks familiar,' I say, and she takes it off me, reaches for her glasses and stares at the cover. 'You read that the other week, didn't you? The nurse? I remember her.'

As she turns the book over, reads the blurb on the back, I'm clenched tight, waiting for her to say, 'Oh yes, I've had this one,' so I can relax, but she doesn't. She shakes her head instead and peers at me over the top of her glasses.

'Looking forward to this one,' she says, and puts it down. 'Thanks, love.'

I want to push it, to make her read the first page, but instead I walk out to Paul, wrapping my arms around myself. She's just forgotten, that's all it is. Once she reads a few chapters, she'll remember, and besides, it's only a library book. So she forgot a book she's read. That means nothing.

'Ladder's too small,' Paul says as I reach him. 'We need one with an extender.'

I nod. 'I did think this was beyond your remit. I'll call someone, get—'

He shakes his head. 'No need. I've got someone. And . . .' he smiles at me, 'they're not only going to clear the gutters, but they're going to paint those window frames,' he points to the kitchen windows, where the chipped paint is falling off, 'and give the front of the house a makeover as well.' He takes out his phone and starts going through photographs he's taken of the house. 'I sent these to Tony just now, and he said it needs sprucing up before we can even think of listing it. People won't look at it; they'll drive by and not make an appointment. You need what's called kerb appeal to get them in. Make it look good on photos.'

'Paul,' I shake my head, 'I've told you a million times, she won't move. We can't put her in a care home. She won't go.'

'She will,' he says in a low voice. 'She can't continue like this. Soon she'll take a fall that'll cause more damage than she can handle, or she'll lose the plot. What was it she did last week? Lock herself out again?'

I think back to the latest phone call from Rick, just days after the fall on the drive. Mum had gone out to the back garden and somehow locked herself out. I had to drive over while Rick took her inside his bungalow. I offered to give him a spare key, but he refused, saying he didn't want that kind of responsibility, not that I can blame him.

'She'll do something one of these days and we'll have no choice but to move her out for her own safety, and in the meantime, there's nothing wrong with being prepared.'

I open my mouth to ask who's going to pay for all this, how I'll explain it to Mum, but the words stick in my throat as I see a familiar white van making its way up the drive.

'Here he is,' Paul says. 'He was just leaving Rick's before. He's working for him, putting a pond in or something, and as he drove past, he offered to lend me his ladders. He does odd jobs for Rick, that kind of stuff. So I thought, he can do the same here. And he's given me a great price.'

My heart rate quickens as Oscar parks up and climbs out of his van.

'Hello again,' he says, smiling. 'Your husband has hired me as a kind of handyman. Do a few jobs. Hope that's OK?'

'Of course,' I manage, trying to return the smile.

Paul begins talking about times and jobs and pointing to the house, and I nod. Half listening. My mind reeling.

Two weeks ago, I'd never seen this man, and now suddenly he's everywhere. Like when you find out you're pregnant and suddenly babies are on every corner. As Paul talks about the window frames, Oscar turns to me and we lock eyes. The air kind of shifts. Something unseen happens between us. I flush and look away.

Is he feeling it too? This weird pull?

I excuse myself and go inside. Back to my mother's safe kitchen with the sad onion decor. My heart is knocking against my ribs and something akin to shame washes over me. But beneath the shame is an emotion I'd completely forgotten. A feeling that's like revisiting an old friend from my childhood. It's a giddy, compelling excitement that flips my stomach and sends a rush through my chest. It takes my breath away.

I go into the ridiculously hot lounge and busy myself with sorting my mother's books, tidying up her things on her table. Then I go to social media and start to scroll. Beg the app to distract me and make the feeling and everything it wants to say to me go away. I don't want it. I don't want to feel like this at all.

EIGHT

'Louise Shelley Whitstable,' Helen giggles that Friday night. 'I never thought I'd see the day.'

We are in my kitchen, a bottle of Sauvignon Blanc open on the table between us. Paul is working nights again and Felix is at Sophie's for the evening, so I rang Helen and insisted she come over. Since meeting Oscar, I've got into the habit of reliving our meeting. Daydreaming about it. Summoning up the giddy feeling and testing it, asking it questions, wondering why suddenly *now*, and *with him*. I was driving myself insane with it. But as I look at Helen, a wide grin on her face, I'm not sure this was a better idea.

'Will he be there tomorrow?' she asks. 'If I were to drive past, will I see him? Up the ladder pulling out the leaves?'

I close my eyes. The worst part of all this is that I didn't say anything about how I'd behaved when I was around him. How he'd made me feel. How he'd reminded me of what it was to be *seen*.

But it seemed that none of that explanation is necessary when talking to your best mate. Because all I did was relay the tale of the man at my mother's, claiming to be from some charity, and how Oscar had phoned me, and then how Paul had hired Oscar to fix things around my mother's house, and Helen called me out on it. Immediately.

I open my eyes to see her still staring at me. The teasing smile still plastered on her face.

'Stop being childish.' I go to refill our glasses. 'It's not like that. For one thing he's half my age, and for two, I'm married. Did you forget about Paul? My husband?'

'Bloody hell, Lou, I didn't say you were about to jump into bed with him. I just said you like him. You fancy him, and being honest, I think it's marvellous news. It's the first time I've seen you with a light in your eyes in months.' She shakes her head. 'No, make that years. You look alive. You look awake. You look good.'

I take a careful sip of my drink.

'Oh God,' I groan, and she bursts out laughing.

'It was the way you went bright red when you said his name and wouldn't look at me.' She leans forward. 'Is he gorgeous?'

I think back to how he smiled at me, and my stomach does that involuntary dip. Helen starts to laugh again, and after a moment, I laugh with her.

'Is it a midlife crisis?' I ask her. 'Because you know me, and I never do this. Never. Have never done this. I don't know what's wrong with me, but it was like, as soon as I saw him ... And the way he looks at me. It's like he's thinking ...' I shake my head and put my hand to my face. 'I'll never be able to go to my mother's again while he's there. I'll have to start visiting her at night, early morning ...'

'Here.' She tops up my glass. 'You're overthinking this whole thing. I'll tell you what it is, a crush. A simple crush. Bloody hell, Lou, you're allowed to fancy someone. You're allowed to flirt. That's not being unfaithful, that's being alive.' She takes a swig of her wine and shakes her head. 'I fancy loads of people apart from Simon. I never do anything about it, would never, ever do anything about it. You know why? Because once you speak to them, once you actually talk to them and realise that the idea you have of them in your head is so drastically different from the real person, then poof!' She waves her hand. 'The crush and all that delicious drama is gone. All the steamy looks and wild imaginings gone. So enjoy it while you can. As soon as you have a proper conversation with him, you'll find out he's just as dull as the rest of them.'

I nod. That's all it is, an innocent crush that will evaporate as quickly as it came. A stupid set of feelings. Nothing more. I look at Helen. She's a terrible flirt, always saying how good-looking people are, always batting her eyes, leaning in close, smiling and laughing, but she never acts on it, just flirts a little, shares a joke and moves on, and she has the best marriage I know. So why am I so serious all the time? I shake my head and take another sip of wine. It's freezing cold and crisp, delicious.

'Good, isn't it?' She notices my reaction and lifts her glass in agreement. 'Simon got a crate of it from some supplier at the golf club. Expensive stuff. He got it especially for us. For you. Said to send you his love.'

I smile. 'Lovely Simon.'

We both take another sip. Helen drains her glass and goes to open another bottle, telling me more about the wine Simon picked out.

Paul is always polite to Helen, always has been, but he's

never taken time to get to know her. He thinks she's too brash, too American, even though she's lived in Dilenby for over twenty years and done more for the local community than he ever has. But as far as he's concerned, she is my friend, not our friend. It's the same with Simon. To Paul, they're my friends, and he steers clear.

He was like that when I met him. He had a group of lads he went out with who I barely met. They were all like Paul, all with wives who went out with their girlfriends while their husbands were with their mates.

'So, this Oscar,' Helen says after a moment, and I roll my eyes. 'I'm guessing he must be married too?'

I'm quiet a moment and then shake my head. 'I don't think so.'

'No ring?'

'I didn't look. It's just . . . he's young, can't see him with—'

'How young?'

I shrug. 'Late twenties? Early thirties?'

'Not that young then.'

'Fifteen years younger than me, at least.'

'Girlfriend, then,' Helen goes on, ignoring me. 'He's probably got loads of girlfriends. You know, I can't remember the last time you did this, talked about another man. In fact I can't remember you *ever* doing this. Even when I first met you, a new mum, not long married to Paul, and you never talked about him like—'

I grab the bottle.

'Sorry.' She holds up her hands as I fill my glass. 'Sorry, I got carried away. I just mean, we never talk men, never, and it's nice. Enjoy it. Flirt a little. Have a crush. Gossip about it with me. It won't kill you.'

I think for a moment, replaying the way I behave when I'm around Oscar, stumbling over my words, going bright red, hot flushes and my heart picking up speed.

I give a quick shudder. 'No, it's not nice,' I tell her, taking a gulp of wine. 'It's pathetic. Humiliating. I'm in real danger of making a fool of myself, like one of those fawning old women. It's all in my head and I need to stop it. Need to get a grip.'

She looks at me a moment and then goes for her phone.

'What?' I ask as she starts tapping at the screen. 'What are you doing?'

'Research,' she says, and I feel a sinking in my stomach.

'What are you up to?' I go over and sit next to her, and see that she has Facebook open on her phone. I groan. 'Helen!'

'Oscar Delany,' she says, 'Dilenby Gardening Services.' I watch the screen as she scrolls down. 'Five-star reviews,' she murmurs, 'lots of recommendations,' and then she starts to laugh.

I look over and see she's stopped on a photograph, a picture of Oscar in a sleeveless T-shirt looking right at the camera. It must have been taken in summer, because his skin is deeply tanned, there's a sheen to his shoulders and his hair is a little shorter.

'OK,' she says, laughing again, 'now I get it. Now I know what's so embarrassing. I think I'd make a fool of myself as well. Might get him to come and do some gardening over at my place, see how much of a fool I become. How much does he charge?'

I give her a friendly shove and change the conversation swiftly to her twins. I ask if either of them has a girlfriend and tell her about Felix and Sophie.

I bring up Felix's Instagram account and navigate to a

picture of the two of them to show her. It's one of my favourites, when they went to some posh charity do and Felix spent a small fortune on his outfit. His tall frame is clad in a light grey fitted suit, his blonde hair freshly cut in that short-back-and-sides style that is so popular, and a wide smile across his face shows his dimples. I run my thumb over his face. Those dimples were the first thing the midwife told me about him. His arm is draped around a stunning-looking girl wearing a silky green dress, her long black hair in curls around her, her make-up immaculate and a matching wide smile on her face. They look like something out of a celebrity magazine, like they should be famous, and I swell with pride.

'Whoa,' Helen says as she takes the phone off me, 'she's a bit special, and look at Felix! How handsome!'

'That's the suit that cost the earth,' I tell her. 'Hand-stitched, apparently.'

She shows me photographs of her boys and tells me what they're up to, and we finish the wine talking about how quickly time passes and remembering when they were all toddlers and how we thought those days would never end.

'Relax,' she says as she's leaving. 'I was only joking about all that Oscar stuff.' She takes a deep breath. She's drunk, and I put my arm around her as Simon pulls up outside the house. 'I know,' she begins, and leans in close for a hug, 'it's not right between you and Paul, but I know you'd never . . .' She shakes her head. 'I was just poking fun, just having a giggle. But you know you can tell me anything. *Anything.*'

I smile, hug her back and watch as she gets in the car, giving Simon a wave.

Later that night, I lie in bed and her words replay in my head. She knows *what* isn't right between me and Paul? I reach my arm out, feeling the empty space beside me. When was the last time we slept in the same bed? Did anything in the same bed?

He was only meant to be sleeping in the spare room while he was taking on double shifts at work, but the problem is, he's always working. I try to think back to when it wasn't like this between us, to when we were different, like Helen and Simon, and it must be the wine, because my mind is a blur.

I remember being busy with Felix, always busy with Felix and work, juggling his childcare and my Spanish tutoring. Trying to make ends meet. Running around making sure he went to all the after-school activities, the weekends of football and rugby, and Paul is there in all those memories, but I struggle to find anywhere he's being something other than just there. When it was just the two of us.

I rub my hand over my face, giving in to the fact that I won't be getting any sleep for a while, and reach for my phone.

As it jumps into action, I pause before going to the mind-numbing game I usually play when I can't sleep, and instead navigate to Facebook.

Dilenby Gardening Services.

I begin scrolling through the photographs. I know I shouldn't. I'm fanning the fire here, encouraging that whoosh and flip of my stomach, my daydream about how he looked at me, but I'm a bottle of wine in and I don't care. I go through the pictures of finished gardens to photographs of him. Photographs of his smile, his teeth so uniform, and his lips. His dark hair, his eyes. *What is it with his eyes?* The way they seem to know everything, like he can see straight into my soul. I zoom in and trace my fingers across his face and wonder what the hell I'm playing at.

The phone rings and I drop it on the cover.

'Shit.' I pick it up and my heart hammers as I see who is ringing. 'Mum?' I sit up, suddenly fully awake. 'Mum, what's wrong? What is it?'

'There's someone here,' she says, her voice a fierce whisper. 'Someone's outside the house. Watching me.'

NINE

'What? Someone's what?'

'Outside,' she says a little louder. I can hear the fear in her voice. 'I didn't want to ring, didn't want to bother you at this time, but I'm scared, Lou. He was out there when I went to bed, staring up at the house, and I just went to the loo and he's still there. Stood outside. Staring up at the window. Watching me.'

My heart speeds, an image in my mind of what my mother has just told me, a man staring up at her house from the pavement, his eyes on her bedroom, waiting for . . .

'I'm on my way,' I say quickly. 'Phone the police.' I jump out of bed. 'Phone them now and tell them what you just told me. I'll be there as soon as I can. And stay in your bedroom. Don't go to the door, don't open the window, just call the police and stay there.'

I grab my jeans and a jumper, my mind racing, and then go back to my phone.

'Pick up,' I hiss as it rings out, 'pick up, pick up,' but there's no answer. He must be on a job. I grab a hair elastic and pull my hair back. As I go down the stairs two at a time, I call the main office and Sheila answers.

'Dilenby Taxis. Where are you going to?'

'Sheila? It's Lou.'

'Hi, Lou! How are—'

'I'm trying to get hold of Paul, but there's no answer. I need a taxi.' My words rush out quickly. 'I need to get to my mother's.'

'Let me try,' Sheila says. There's silence apart from the faint tapping of a keyboard.

I take a deep breath. She'll be on the main radio now, trying whatever system they have in place, and I curse myself. Why of all nights did I have to drink the best part of a bottle of wine tonight? I switch on the kettle as I wait. A coffee for the journey will be good.

'Lou?'

'Yes?'

'I can't locate Paul. Must be on an airport run or longer. Sometimes they switch off the radio if it's a long journey so as not to be distracted, and Paul isn't on the rota like the normal drivers. But I've got Joe on his way round to your house now. Is everything all right?'

I shake my head. 'Someone's outside Mum's house. We had an incident with this bloke trying to scam her out of money the other week. I'm worried he might be back.'

'Bloody hell. Has she called the police?'

'I've told her to do that, but I need to be there. To go round and—' I hear a horn blare outside. 'Joe's here,' I tell her. 'Can you keep trying Paul? I'll ring his mobile, but if you—'

'Of course, I'll put a shout out. And you've got Joe with you, he'll sort out anyone who's there. Ring me when you get there, let me know your mum's OK.'

I run out and jump into the taxi, my heart pounding. The roads are clear, and as I tell Joe what's happened, he speeds up and we make the journey to my mother's quickly. I consider calling Rick, asking him to walk over, but then I remember his lack of mobility and the fact that he's in his sixties, and disregard the idea. I'd only be putting him in danger as well.

I berate myself for not calling the police when that man was at her house. When he was trying to get her bank details and sizing up what he could come back for. Guilt claws at my insides as I imagine him breaking in, shoving my mother aside as he ransacks the place.

I see blue lights reflecting off the windows of parked cars before we turn into my mother's street. A police car is outside the house, and I make a sound, a low moan. Joe mutters something about it being all right, but I shake my head. Whatever's happened is my fault. I should never have let that man leave. I should've called the police then. She's too vulnerable. Too helpless.

I get out of the taxi and run into the house, expecting the worst: my mother hurt, the house in disarray, things stolen, a window smashed, a door broken down, everything that my mind was able to catastrophise on the journey. What I find is an officer sitting in the lounge with my mother, drinking tea.

'Mum! Are you all right? Is everything . . .'

'It's all fine,' the officer tells me with a smile. 'Everything is fine.'

I look from him to my mother, confused, and she gives me a small smile.

'All good out there. No one and nothing in the garden.' I turn to see another police officer. 'I've checked everywhere outside. Nothing seems to have been disturbed.'

'I'm so sorry.' My mother glances from the police to Joe and then to me. 'I was certain there was someone there. I thought I saw them, thought I . . .'

'Don't you apologise.' The first officer leans towards her and smiles. 'We'd much rather find this than someone trying to break in.'

My mother nods and I go to her. She's shaking.

'I thought I saw someone,' she says quietly. 'I was so sure. So certain. I could see him in the shadows.' She frowns, and then looks down. She's so small, sitting there. So frail in her nightclothes, her white hair sticking up, her small frame visible under her cotton dressing gown. Shoulder bones sharp and her hands fiddling with the teacup she's holding. She looks lost, afraid and lost, and my arms go around her, unexpected tears biting at my eyes.

'You're the daughter?' the second officer asks, and I nod. He makes a slight movement of his head towards the door. 'Could I . . .?'

I give Mum another squeeze, and as I leave, I hear Joe telling her what a fright she's given us.

'There's nothing to report,' the officer tells me as we go into the hall. 'We've checked the perimeter, up to the bungalow back there, and found nothing.'

'Thank you for checking,' I say. 'It's just we had a man here the other week. Claiming he was collecting for charity and trying to get my mum to hand over her bank details. I thought he might have come back.'

'Did you get his name?'

I shake my head, and then stop. 'Josh, I think. I didn't get his last name, I just got rid of him. I should've . . .'

He nods. 'They're vulnerable at this age. My dad's the same. I found him with a Labrador the other day. Someone had asked if he wanted to take on a dog, and he just agreed. He can't walk down the street and yet there he was with this big dog that someone wanted to get rid of. It's at our house now.' He raises his eyebrows, and I smile. 'I won't give you an incident number,' he goes on, 'but you might want to think about installing an alarm system of some kind. They have cameras and you can access them from your mobile phone, so if you think anyone is outside, you'll be able to see them. Even one on the doorbell is useful.'

'Oh,' I look down at my phone, 'I didn't even . . .' but as I'm saying the words, I realise how obvious it is. Of course we should have an alarm fitted. Cameras. I've seen them, scrolled past adverts for them while I was shopping online. Why did I never think of that?

'Well,' he says after a moment, 'we'll be off.'

'Thank you,' I tell him as they both start to leave, 'thank you so much.'

I'm just telling Joe to go, that I'll spend the night at my mother's, when Rick appears.

'Everything all right?' He's panting slightly, his hand on his bad hip, and I wince at the thought of him racing over here. 'I saw the police car,' he says, 'and an officer came over to the bungalow. I thought . . .'

'It's all fine, it's—'

'Me causing a fuss again,' my mother calls over from her chair. 'I'm so sorry, Rick, my eyes have been playing tricks on me. I thought I saw someone lurking in the garden, but turns out it was nothing.'

Rick looks at me, and I can see his mind working. My mother, probably dreaming and still in her dream state, imagining all sorts and calling the police.

'It was me,' I say quickly, to stop the presumption that's going on in his head. 'I told her to call them. I thought it was ...' I trail off, exhausted suddenly. 'Sorry,' I tell him, 'we really didn't mean to disturb you.'

We watch the police car pull away, and the fact that we seem to be disturbing him *a lot* lately sits heavy in the air between us.

'It's OK,' he says after a moment. 'I'm just glad it wasn't anything serious.'

'Tea?' I offer, and he shakes his head.

'I'll try for another couple of hours' sleep. It's a long shot now that I'm awake, but I'm in the office tomorrow. Arranging a floor delivery for a house. Trying to source oak flooring these days is proving to be a nightmare, and it's going to be a long day.'

He looks over to my mother and then back to me.

'Is she ...?'

I nod. 'She's fine. I'm sorry. I'll ...' I can't finish the sentence, because what can I say? What can I do so he's not bothered by us again?

I watch him go, leaning on his cane as he limps down the shared driveway. A pang of guilt hits me hard, and I make a mental note to take him something by way of a proper apology. A bottle of wine, or a few of those crime novels we both love. Make sure we've not upset him too much with Mum's antics.

Joe leaves, and suddenly the house is silent. It's gone three in the morning, dark, quiet and cold. I settle my mother back in bed and shiver as I go to the kitchen.

The night is dark outside, a thick coat of blackness hiding everything. As it stands, anyone could walk down that shared driveway and around the back of the house if they wanted to. The only area of the garden that's fenced off is the oak trees where we scattered my father and brother's ashes, and what good is that? No one is likely to want to break into the memorial we have there, but this house? Even though it contains nothing of any real value, if you look at it from the street, you wouldn't think that. And if you knew the only person inside was a little old lady . . .

My phone rings, the shrill noise slicing through the air and making me jump.

'Paul?'

'I just heard from Sheila. Bloody hell, Lou, is everything all right?'

I glance at the clock; he must be finished for the night.

'Where have you been? I called and called, and Sheila couldn't get hold of you either.'

'I took a job on, long drive. A couple who needed to get to Cheltenham missed the last train and paid over four hundred for me to drive them down there. Couldn't refuse and turned off the radio as I was out of action. My phone must have been on silent.'

I close my eyes. They're hot and stinging.

'So it was a false alarm,' he says after I've told him about the events of the night. 'Your mum imagining things again.' I say nothing. I know what he's thinking.

'We need a security system fitted,' I tell him. 'The police officer advised it and Mum's agreed. You can get them with cameras. I'm ordering one tomorrow. Once it's fitted, I can—'

'Stare at cameras overlooking the street outside your

mother's? Put one in her lounge and stare at her watching telly? Like you did with Felix with his baby monitor? Obsessing over every sound, every movement?'

'Paul, the police officer said—'

'The police officer was too polite to say what everyone's thinking, Lou. Your mother is old. She's imagining things. Seeing things. Her mind isn't what it used to be. It's pretty obvious she's got the start of—'

'Not now.' I cut him off. 'Bloody hell, Paul, not now.'

I end the call and sit at the kitchen table. I'm not ready to go into the damp-smelling spare room, which has been shut up for an age, and make a bed with dusty sheets. I fill the kettle, and as I'm waiting for it to boil, I pick up my phone, thinking I'll do some research on the alarm I need to order.

There's a bang from outside, and I jump. I go to the back door, thinking it might be Rick, or the police officers come back.

'Hello?' I shout into the black garden. 'Anyone there?'

There's no reply, but a shiver creeps along the back of my neck. The same shiver I got the other night when staring out into the dark. I have the feeling I'm being watched.

TEN

I imagine Monday mornings are a frantic time in most houses. The alarm going off at what feels like an ungodly hour, the thought of work after two days of rest. It can be a time to dread, a roll of the eyes. I remember when it used to feel like that in our house. When Felix was at that age where he was starting to sleep in, just becoming a teenager, and it was hard work to get him out of bed. Paul was working something close to normal office hours and there would be the smell of coffee in the air, and I would be making Felix's packed lunch while getting ready for my students. We'd all be rushing about and shouting to each other across the house. The radio or breakfast television would be on, and it would be all *quick, quick, hurry up and chop-chop* and then you were out of the door, the day galloping ahead, and you had to run to catch up to it.

I sip my tea and listen to the quiet around me, the only sound the rhythmic thumping of my heart pounding in my head. Since Friday night, I've not really slept. My shoulders are tight, and I rub my hand on the back of my neck, trying to ease out the muscles.

'I'm overthinking it,' was what I told Paul when I got home. 'It was nothing, a false alarm. She was dreaming and thought she saw someone. No big deal.'

Paul didn't say anything, he didn't repeat what he'd said on the phone, and in a way, that was worse. He just put his hand on my shoulder, heavy and comforting, and didn't say the word that was in the air like a great big bloody elephant in the room as I made myself a drink and talked about taking a nap, but that word hummed around in my head like a trapped fly all night.

I googled it.

Against my better judgement, I found myself consulting the internet for symptoms like my mother is showing and found that it's a term used for the *inability to make decisions, think clearly or remember* ... and then I couldn't read any more because I felt sick.

I go to my phone now and look at the notification that's arrived. The alarm and security cameras I've ordered are due to be delivered between eleven and three. Oscar will be at my mother's from nine until twelve. Today is his first day there. I need to make sure he knows what he's doing and ask him to fit the alarm and cameras as well.

Before the butterflies dance in my stomach at the thought of seeing him, of having to talk to him, I remind myself that I have more important issues to focus on. Helen's words ring in my ears. *As soon as you have a proper conversation with him, you'll find out he's just as dull as the rest of them.* I will. Of course I will. She's right.

I think back to the stark words on the medical website that

explained about not being able to do everyday things, repeating words and stories, memory loss and confusion. I think of the library books, the police, and shake my head to get rid of them.

'She's not that bad,' I say out loud as I grab my car keys. 'So she forgot she'd read a few books and imagined she saw someone. She's nowhere near as bad as what I read on that website.' But my words don't do anything to move the heavy rock sitting in my stomach or slow my racing heart, a constant reminder that something isn't right.

My lessons pass in a blur, the way they always do. Years ago, when I started teaching, Paul made it clear that he never wanted any students at the house. Back then, Felix was little, and I could understand his insistence that none of it be brought home. His own working schedule has always been chaotic; as the manager he can work all kinds of hours, and we never knew when he'd have to work nights. He didn't want to be woken up by someone badly pronouncing how to order a coffee in Spanish.

When Felix was at university and Paul was working something close to office hours, I thought about doing my lessons here, asking the students to come to me, but it was then that I realised I loved the travelling about. I enjoy meeting my students in their homes, finding out about the world they occupy. I enjoy getting out of my own space.

The lessons always start as soon as I arrive. I try not to speak any English, and I absolutely love it. I love being the Spanish woman I never got to be full-time; I love it when a student gets the pronunciation correct or suddenly understands a word. I love being immersed in the language, the sounds, the syntax and definition of it.

That morning I have two lessons back-to-back with a mother and daughter. They're travelling along the Spanish south coast for the summer and want to know the basics. I spend a happy two hours teaching them individually and then together, and at the end, as I stand up to leave, the mother hands me a small box.

'What's this?' I ask, and she smiles as I open it. It's a hair clasp, jewelled and decorated in the colours of the Spanish flag. I feel my throat go a little tight.

'We wanted to get you a little something before our adventure begins,' she says, 'and we thought you could wear this the next time you're there. Wherever it is you go to in Spain.'

I thank her, wish them a wonderful journey and leave. When I get to my mother's, I open the box again and look at the clasp. It's beautiful. The other me, the me in Spain, would wear things like this instead of the plain elastics I make do with. She would put her hair up in this not for a special occasion, but just to go about her day.

I hadn't the words to tell the two of them that I never go to Spain. I was out there for six months when I was at university. I had a job, a placement for my second year, at a travel agent in the centre of Malaga. I had a flat in the square above a café that I shared with two other girls on my course, who both loved Spain and the language as much as I did. I stroke my fingers along the jewels and allow myself a small moment to think of them. Of what they're doing now. We lost touch when I came home abruptly and it was clear I was never going back. When the accident happened and that life was ripped from me.

I put the lid on the box and shove it in the glove compartment, out of sight, out of the way. Boxed up and shut away:

it's what I do with most things that are too painful to think about.

'You're a bit late, aren't you? Oscar's been here an age. I want to nip to the lavvy, but I thought I'd better be around in case he needed me for anything.'

Mum's eyes are wide as she blinks at me, and I give a laugh. 'What? You can go to the toilet. What do you think he's going to do? Ask you to shimmy up there and help him?'

She's got her hands pressed tightly together, and I inhale sharply as I take a good look at her and how scared she appears. She called me four times yesterday, five on Saturday, even though I visited her like I always do.

'I'm just checking in,' she said, like she was afraid of what might be happening. Like she needed a quick reassuring chat to bring her back to normality. I ended up staying Saturday and Sunday evening with her. When I helped her up to bed, she asked me to check the locks on all the doors and windows. She needed to hear me tell her she was safe.

'It's OK,' I say now. 'And I'm sorry I'm late. You can nip to the toilet. I'll go and see how he's getting on. Make sure everything is all right.'

I help her up out of her chair, and as she makes her way to the stair lift, I brace myself and head towards the back door. I can see the bottom of the ladder through the kitchen window, can hear a radio playing, and I take a deep breath. I'll ask him if he wants a coffee, chat to him like a normal human being, and by the time I come in to switch on the kettle, all this silliness will be gone because I'll have realised that he's just as ordinary and boring as the rest of us. Nothing special.

71

'Hello?' I step outside. It feels like it might snow. The sky has a dull, heavy appearance, the light is peculiar and there's that anticipation in the air, like the world is holding its breath. I look up. He's there. Right at the top of the ladder, leaning over. He looks down at me, and *boom*. My stomach flips, my heart speeds. Adrenaline whooshes through every fibre. Helen's advice about him being normal flies out of my head as I watch him climb down. This man is anything but normal.

'Hey,' he smiles, causing me to take in a sharp breath, 'I did knock, let your mother know I'm here, but there was no answer, so I just . . .' He lifts his hand to the ladder, and I swallow. I'd forgotten how tall he is. 'Everything OK?'

I nod, force my eyes to the ladder, to the leaves he's collected from the gutter. Concentrate on the dull metal and try to sound like I'm not on a roller-coaster, which is exactly how I feel.

'Friday night,' I begin. 'Nothing serious, but she had a bit of a scare.'

'Oh no, did she . . .?'

'No, nothing like that, she didn't fall or anything.' I brace myself and meet his eyes. 'She was imagining things; thought she saw someone watching her.'

'Watching her?'

'Stood out here.' I wave to the front of the house, to the street beyond. The feeling I had the other night falls over me like a shadow as a familiar shiver runs the length of my neck. 'We thought it might be that man who came before. The one claiming to be from the charity.'

Oscar goes to speak, and I shake my head. 'It wasn't. No one was here. We ended up calling the police, but no one was around. She just scared herself. Got herself into a state.'

His brow creases, and he looks to the street and then back to me.

'That man, he shook her up good and proper, didn't he?'

'She was just dreaming,' I tell him, and wrap my arms around myself against the cold, 'imagining things. It's her age, she gets confused and . . .'

I hear my words, the way I'm making excuses for her, and he gives me a look of understanding. The one I'm getting used to seeing when I talk about my mother, the one that usually makes me want to scream in the face of the person doing it, but with him, with him looking at me in that way, I find my throat closing in. My nose smarting. His sudden sympathy and understanding making me tearful. I look away, the rush of emotion blindsiding me.

'Anyway, I'd better . . .' I turn to go, before tears spring and it gets even more uncomfortable between us.

'So, the Spanish lessons,' he says, and I turn back. 'Your husband – Paul, is it? He said we could start with some lessons as soon as I've done the gutters. To speak to you about a time. I was wondering, is this afternoon OK, or is that too soon?'

'What?'

'The lessons . . . Paul said you teach Spanish.'

'I do.'

'And he said that you'd teach me, and in return I'd knock some money off for . . .' He waves to the house, and when his eyes lock back on mine, they narrow. 'He didn't tell you?'

I shake my head, my resolve to not get flustered gone.

He gives a small laugh, looks at his hands and slowly takes off his gloves. 'I'm planning to go to South America for six months or so, travel there, and I think speaking Spanish will make all the difference. So when your husband told me what you did, told me what you needed doing here, it seemed the obvious thing.' He pauses, and I feel my cheeks start to burn. 'If that's OK with you, of course?'

He stops speaking, and we stare at each other. Paul has made this arrangement without even talking to me about it. Without even letting me know. That's what he meant by getting a 'great price'. I feel a surge of anger towards him, for hiring me out as if me and my lessons are something he can barter with. And to not even ask me!

'Because it's no problem if not,' Oscar continues. 'I can do online classes if you're too busy.'

'No, it's fine, it's fine,' I say quickly, thinking of the price of the work here and how much the lessons will bring the cost down. Especially if I'm going to add fitting cameras and alarms to his list. 'I have a space next Monday. It'll have to be in the evening, but I can teach you then. If you're free?'

'Great. Next Monday evening.'

'About seven? I'll feed my mother and then . . .'

'Seven.' He nods, grins at me. 'It's a date.'

My heart is beating hard in a panic as I realise what I've just agreed to. I mumble something about putting the kettle on, and once I'm in the kitchen, I lean against the door, breathing heavily. I was meant to be spending less time with Oscar, not more, and now we have a date.

ELEVEN

It's been six days since I found out I'm going to teach Oscar, and I'm sitting at the dining room table staring at my laptop. I'm out of my depth. I'm so far out of my comfort zone, it isn't even funny.

Every time I even think of planning for our first lesson, my palms get sweaty and a nervous, anxious swirling starts in my stomach. It's pathetic, but I have no control. My body betrays me as soon as I bring up his face in my mind, and the thought of having to concentrate and focus while sitting next to him for a *whole hour* is too much. It's all too much.

In the past week, despite the bitter cold, he's cleared the guttering, worked out a plan for sanding and repainting the window frames and started to fit the security cameras. But he's doing more than fixing the house. He's making my mother feel safe. He's fixing her.

She talks about him like he's an old friend. She tells me snippets of the conversations they've had – his upcoming trip to South America, how he said she makes the best cups of tea, how he likes chocolate digestives – and I realise she's been spending far too much time alone. With only me popping in a couple of times a day, she's become isolated, and I've Oscar to thank for that realisation. I've Oscar to thank for making her feel secure in her own home again, into making her chattier again.

I purposely gave myself a full week before we had to start our lessons. A full week of waiting for Helen's advice to kick in, of waiting for Oscar to say something idiotic. And I'm still waiting.

I tell myself I'm behaving stupidly, but then he'll look at me longer than necessary, or smile at me for no reason, or say something a little suggestive, and any logical thoughts go out the window. Is he feeling the same pull? Is he, and I don't think this lightly, but is he actually *flirting* with me? That thought sends me spiralling.

I take a deep breath and look at my notes. Conversational Spanish. That's all I need to teach him. We're going to start with the basics, simple vocab and pronunciation. I look over my exercises for this kind of lesson and the words start to swim on the page. Between trying not to think about Oscar and worrying over my mum, along with the extra evening visits that have now become part of our routine, I'm exhausted.

'Hi, Mum.' Felix appears, placing a cup of coffee beside me. 'Thought you could do with this. Working on a Sunday.'

'Thanks, love.' I give him a smile. It's past two, and he's only just up. He looks tired, his face pale and puffy.

'Big night last night?'

'Got in about four,' he says, and gives a wide yawn. 'Might try a nap before heading to Sophie's later.'

I take a moment. I've been here before and know I'm on shaky ground. I need to be careful what I say, but I can't stop myself.

'It's serious with Sophie, then? You seem to be over at hers a lot.'

He shifts in his seat, and I wait, hoping I've not overstepped the mark. Sophie is the daughter of Felix's boss. He's spent so much time with them these past few months and I want to be a part of it, this new life he's forging, but I need to ask for that carefully.

The last time he brought a girlfriend home, it did not go well. It was someone he'd been seeing in his last year of university; she came to spend a weekend with us and it wasn't a good time. The rival taxi company had just opened up and Paul was under a lot of stress. It was the beginning of him working double shifts, working nights on a regular basis. He spent the entire weekend either at the taxi rank or talking about the taxi rank. It all came to a head on the Saturday afternoon, just before he left for work. We were watching the news and there was a feature about climate change. And Lucy, that was her name, made a comment about how more cars on the road were the problem. As soon as she said it, she knew she'd been a little tactless. You could see by the way she looked from Felix to me, but Paul took it personally.

He didn't rant exactly, or have a go, but he talked about why he thought global warming was a conspiracy theory or something to that effect. Felix started poking fun, talked about tin-foil hats in an effort to lighten the mood, but Paul had lost all his humour. He left for work and the atmosphere felt charged in his wake. I heard Felix murmur something to Lucy about him, and then they both went out for the evening.

Paul was fine the next day, more like his old self, trying to have a bit of banter with Felix over breakfast, but the damage had been done. Lucy, it seemed, was very sensitive, and even though Paul tried to make an effort with her before they left, Felix didn't bring her back again. In fact, he hasn't brought a girl back since.

And now Sophie, so pivotal in his career, with her flat in the city and those new friends he has. Well, it's a world away from Paul and me and our small semi in Dilenby. And even though I tell myself I'm wrong, I can't help thinking Felix is dreading the day he'll have to introduce us.

'Sophie has her own place,' he says eventually. 'She shares this flat in the centre of town, so it's just easier to stop there. And as we work together, it being a family business and all, it's just . . .'

'Of course.' I keep my voice light. 'And once you've got a car, it'll be so much better. You can spend more time here, get back and forth a little easier.'

'Yeah, about that . . .'

I look up at him.

'The money I've been saving. For the car. Well, the thing is, if I move, I won't really need a car. I mean, no one who lives in the city drives, the cost of parking being what it is, and it's just easier to get the trams. And this girl that Sophie shares the flat with, she's moving out. And it's really difficult to find places at a decent price, especially in the centre. I have mates at work who're paying a fortune to live in some really grotty places. So it makes sense. I mean, for me, to, well . . .'

'You're moving out?'

'It would just be . . . I mean, it just seems sensible, Mum.'

I stare at him.

78

When he was at university, I got used to the cycle of the school year. Every four or six weeks, he would be home. Half-term, Christmas break, summer holidays. He was gone, but not really. I knew when he was coming back and filling the house with his mess and noise again, knew when I was going to be cooking and cleaning and grumbling jokingly about him. The conversations I had with Paul used to be filled with Felix and what he was up to. It's bad enough now, with him hardly being at home, but if he moves out completely?

He reaches over. 'It's not like I'm moving miles away. It's Manchester! Up the road. I can be back here in under an hour.'

I laugh, embarrassed at the way his news has hit me.

'Of course you should move in with her,' I say finally. 'It makes perfect sense, it's just ... my baby boy, moving out!' I look about the house and feel its silence behind our conversation. The air is suddenly heavy with the ominous empty days, weeks and months that lie ahead. Felix is moving out. Leaving home. Not for university, but for good. I give out an embarrassed laugh and he puts his arms around me.

'Don't get all daft on me now,' he warns, and I push him away, laugh again and take a sip of the coffee he brought me.

'So, anyway, there's something else,' he goes on, and I feel my insides clench. 'Gran's house.'

'Gran's house?'

'Thing is, Mum, seeing you working like this,' he touches the laptop, 'and Dad with the taxi firm and everything ...' He looks up at me. 'And when you told me about what happened the other night. When she thought there was someone watching her. I think of her rattling around in that house on her own, frightened of her own shadow. Terrified of every little thing, and I'm worried that ...'

'You're worried?'

'Worried that you're not doing anything about it because of me. That you aren't selling, or renting, because you think I—'

'Shh.' I shake my head. 'Felix, there's no chance we're selling. That house will always be in the family. Once your gran . . .'

I stop then.

I've said the words a million times before, talked about how he'll inherit the house when the time comes, but the time is now, and the words feel different leaving my mouth.

'That house is worth so much money,' he says, 'and Dad told me about the taxi firm. How it's on the brink of going under. And you're working all the time. So I was thinking, if you want to sell it. If you need the money, and you're not selling because—'

'Stop.' My voice is louder than I intended it to be. 'That house, your gran's house, is *hers*. It's not for anyone else to decide about. We're not selling it. Ever. Your grandad and uncle's ashes are there. I keep having this conversation with your father, and I'm telling you what I tell him, that house is your gran's. Not mine. Not yours, not for us to do anything with until . . .'

I stop, not wanting to finish the sentence, and Felix looks away, shifts in his chair, every inch of him oozing with the energy of misunderstanding. He never met Mark, or my dad. Has only heard the stories about them, seen the photographs. To him, they are shadowy figures, not real people.

'My brother and father are there,' I tell him carefully, 'and one day, when you're older, you'll thank me for this. You'll have that house, and maybe you won't have children to pass it down to, maybe it will end with you, but it will end when I'm not here and can't watch. So no, Felix, your gran is staying there until—'

'OK.' He holds up his hands. 'Sorry I mentioned it. I just wanted you to know that if . . .' he points to the damp patch in the corner of the room, the wallpaper dark, 'if you wanted to redecorate, or get yourself a new car, you don't have to think about me. And Gran, she's . . .' he shakes his head, 'scared. When I spoke to her the other day, she didn't sound herself. She sounded frightened. She told me about what she thought she saw, someone staring up at her, she's—'

'She's just a bit spooked still. It'll be different when the cameras are fitted. She'll be better then.'

He looks at me a moment, and then comes forward and puts his arms around me. I let him hold me, breathing in the familiar scent of my boy.

He plants a small kiss on top of my head. 'Things don't have to stay the same,' he says before leaving. 'That's all I meant.'

I go back to my laptop and hear him turn on his music, start up the shower. I try to concentrate on the exercises I need to plan for Monday, but I can't focus. My mind is full of Felix leaving home. Him trying to give me advice about his gran's house. His inheritance. My throat goes tight with it all. When did he get to be this age? When did he get to be so thoughtful?

Change and everything it brings. The thoughts tumble over each other like a fast-flowing river, and my heart pounds, because I know that once it starts, once things begin to fall into the water and have to move along with it, I might go under and not make it back to the surface.

TWELVE

'Say that again?'

I glance at the couple walking their dog to the side of us and turn back to Helen. We're in the park in the centre of the village. I asked if we could have our lunchtime coffee outside because of what I needed to talk to her about. I didn't want to do it in the local coffee shop with eyes and ears everywhere, and I groan at my behaviour. I was afraid of people overhearing what exactly? That I have a new student? That my son is moving out?

'I'm being melodramatic.' I take a sip of coffee; it's too hot and burns my mouth slightly. 'But this whole thing feels melodramatic. I'm teaching him. Tonight. Verbs and nouns and ...' I shake my head.

'So not only did Paul arrange for this Adonis to do odd jobs at your mother's house,' Helen says, amusement in her voice, 'he's now arranged for you to teach him Spanish?'

'In return for a discount,' I say, and point to a bench, 'so that we'll get some money off the jobs he's doing.'

We sit down. Helen is smiling knowingly. The kind of smile you'd give a small child who's confessed to eating too many sweets.

'So you'll be up close with him,' she says in a low voice, 'just you and him in a tight spot.' She starts to giggle. 'Whispering Spanish at each other once a week . . .'

'Twice,' I interrupt, batting her on the shoulder. 'Mondays and Thursdays. Tonight's our first lesson. And it's not in a tight spot where we'll be whispering, it's in my mother's kitchen.'

She throws her head back and lets out a laugh. 'So what are you afraid of? That once you're alone with him in that sexy kitchen, you won't be able to control yourself?'

I take another sip of coffee and roll my eyes.

Since Felix's bombshell, my mind has skittered over shadowy versions of the future. Where I'd usually retreat into my daydreams of Spain, I find I'm returning to my daydreams of Oscar instead. It's unnerving. A threatening loss of control that I can't handle, and trying to articulate why this is so worrying is beyond me.

'That advice you gave me?' I turn to Helen. 'The stuff about once I speak to him he'll turn into an idiot and lose all attraction? Still waiting for that to happen.'

She looks at me more seriously. 'Lou, this has really got to you, hasn't it?'

'And now there's Felix,' I blurt out. 'He announced he's leaving home. Told me at the weekend. He's moving in with Sophie, who I've never even met.'

'Leaving home?'

'I know he already left home when he went to uni, but that was different. I knew he was coming back. Like you with the twins, you know they're home for the long summer and

Christmas. Oh God, *Christmas.*' I turn to her as it hits me. 'Is that it? Did I just have my last Christmas with him and didn't even realise?'

Helen's arm goes around me and she pulls me in close. 'Come on, let's walk.'

She stands up, stamping her feet against the late-January cold that's set in since we've been sitting.

'I'm dreading the twins moving out,' she says with a shudder. 'I'll go to pieces.' She looks at me. 'And I'll probably do much worse than develop a crush on an unsuitable man, so watch out.'

I give a small laugh, and she joins in.

'That's more like it,' she says as we start to walk again along the path and she quizzes me about Felix.

'Don't worry too much about your lessons with Oscar,' she says as we reach the end of the lane. 'I'm sure that in a few weeks he'll be just another student and everything will be back to normal. You're hardly going to seduce him over your mother's kitchen table with her in the next room, are you? It's just everything that's going on with your mum, and now Felix announcing he's leaving and you being an empty-nester. Oscar's your way of dealing with it all. He's your distraction at you reaching that age. Midlife crisis age.'

We hug goodbye and she leaves for her afternoon of meetings. *Empty-nester. Midlife crisis.* It's so clichéd it's funny. But as I get in my car, it doesn't feel funny. It feels sad and pathetic and something else.

'You're just scared,' I whisper to myself as I wait for the heaters to clear the windscreen properly. 'You're scared of getting old. Of being forgotten. Of this being it.' My heart starts to pound. 'And it's stupid,' I say, 'it's all stupid, because you're fine. No one is going anywhere. Everything is great. Oscar is just a crush. Nothing. Oscar is nothing.' But I hear the lie in my voice and the panicky, anxious swirling in my stomach picks up pace.

And that's when I see her. The swinging high ponytail, the jump between her steps. I remember her meeting Paul at the sports shop with the dartboard. The way they embraced before Paul drove off.

I watch as she makes her way past the park and into the village. She's wearing knee-high boots over skinny jeans and a puffed-up black jacket that's clenched in at the waist. The ones you see in ski resorts that look warm and fashionable. She's about the same age as me – a little younger, not by much – but has the type of figure you only see on celebrities. I glance down at my shapeless navy jacket that I bought in the sales, my usual uniform of jeans and jumper underneath. I try to imagine her playing darts with Paul. One of the lads, one of the team, and nope. I just can't imagine it. So what was she doing with that dartboard? What was she doing with Paul?

I sit for a minute before pulling out my phone and typing a message. We haven't talked properly about Felix leaving. In fact, we haven't talked properly in an age. Maybe that's all I need, time alone to talk it all out with my husband, and all these silly thoughts and my swirly stomach will calm down.

I look at my message.

Got the lesson with Oscar this eve, but home for about eight. Shall I pick us up a bottle of wine?

I pause for a moment, debating, then go for it.

We could take it to bed?

I hit send before I can change my mind, my cheeks going warm at my words, and an uncomfortable, itchy feeling descends. I'm embarrassed about sending Paul a suggestion like that.

I shift in my seat. When was the last time we went to bed together? The last time we had sex? And then I catch my breath as three dots appear. He's typing his reply.

It's Monday.

I stare at the words, my face burning, and then I remember. It's darts practice on Mondays. He goes straight after work to this bloke's house, who has a dartboard. They all take cans of beer and have mini matches and assess each other's techniques.

I look up at where the blonde woman was, think about that dartboard she bought. Wonder if the training is now at her house.

Of course! I text back. Monday night darts practice. I could run you a bath for when you're home?

I stare at my words. What am I, some seventies housewife? I can't remember the last time I offered to run Paul a bath, but maybe this is where I've been going wrong.

Don't worry, he replies. I have to head back into work after, won't be back until the usual time. Don't wait up.

I stare at my phone, and then another message comes through from him.

xxx

The uncomfortable exchange has left a sour aftertaste. I send a series of xxx back, and as I scroll through our conversation, I feel something clench. My heart is still beating fast, the itchy feeling still on me, and I'm hot. I feel like I want to start the car and drive to Devon and be someone else for a change.

'Daft cow,' I tell myself, and I put the phone away and push my thoughts to what I'm doing that afternoon instead. I have a lesson with a college student. I have to prepare my mother's meal and finish the laundry, and there's a bit of shopping I need to do. I'll clean her bathroom and then . . . A fizz of something shoots through my chest. It's so dramatic, so visceral, I put my hand to my chest. It clears out the itchy feeling but increases my heartbeat as if I'm running a marathon.

'Oscar is nothing,' I whisper as I put the car in gear, but the fizz doesn't hear my words. It bubbles and froths like champagne. 'You're just scared,' I repeat to myself, and I am.

I take my phone out again. Put the car back in neutral and return to the stilted conversation with Paul. I send him an emoji of a kiss, a yellow face puckering up underneath the three *xxx* I just sent, and the fizz stops at my pathetic attempt at whatever it is I'm trying to do. When was the last time I sent him an emoji of any kind? Let alone a kissing one?

The small notification underneath shows me that he has seen my message, and I wait for a response.

I stare at the stupid emoji and will him to send me one back.

'C'mon,' I whisper, as the itchy feeling of pity and fear rises, but nothing comes.

THIRTEEN

The room is hot. It's coming in from the lounge, seeping through the walls and into the kitchen. I've got out my laptop and my lesson plan is ready. I've done this a thousand times before, yet my heart is thrumming. It's ridiculous. *I'm* ridiculous. I keep repeating the words 'Oscar is nothing' to myself and going over what Helen said, but I'm still a bag of nerves.

'How long?'

'Just an hour or so. You won't know we're here, Mum.'

She narrows her eyes. 'I'll be watching my programmes.' She waves at my laptop on the kitchen table. 'What if I hear you? I'll have to come in and tell you to keep it down.'

The television is on full volume. The idea that she'd hear Oscar and me talking in the kitchen over the noise is laughable. If anything, we'll struggle to hear each other.

'Tell you what,' I say as I put a plate of custard creams on the tray along with her tea, 'once we get going, I'll pop my head around the door, and if we're too loud, you can tell me.'

'But what if I want to come in here? Get myself a cup of tea? I'll be disturbing you. Getting in the way in my own—'

'You could never get in the way,' I smile at her, 'and I'll bring you all the tea you need.'

'What is it you're doing again?'

'Teaching Oscar,' I tell her as I take the tray of tea and biscuits into the lounge. 'Get your stick and come and sit down in here. He's learning Spanish, remember?'

I put the tray down beside her chair, and as I turn to look at her, a jolt of panic passes over me. Her face is confused. She's looking at me like she's lost again.

'Oscar?' I hear the worry in her voice, and I take a beat.

I'm choosing my words, ready to remind her, when suddenly her face clears. '*That* Oscar.' She laughs at herself as she comes over to her chair, and I hear my own nervous laugh alongside hers. 'It's not that I mind,' she goes on, 'it's just that I like to get settled. You're normally not here. You come when I'm ready for bed. That's the routine we've got going now, isn't it?'

I nod as she sits down. I wish it wasn't the routine. I wish we were like before: me leaving after teatime and seeing her in the morning.

She stops suddenly. 'Nice though,' she says, and smiles, as if she's just realised. 'Nice that you're in there. So long as I can still hear my programmes. Will it be every night?'

'No, just Mondays and Thursdays.'

I hand her the remote as she puts her feet up on the footstool and smiles at me. I stroke her hair and smile back. It *is* nice seeing her at this time of day. When I'd normally be at home, alone. Cooking a meal for Paul and putting it under tin foil just to throw it away the next morning when he hasn't eaten it. Fixing something for Felix that he might . . . I stop.

He's leaving in two weeks. The other day he brought home a load of cardboard boxes, said he'd got a mate to help him take his stuff. I told him he could leave it all, that we'd keep his bedroom as it was in case he came back, but he laughed it off. Told me to make the room into an office, 'so you're not hunched over the dining room table any more'. He didn't see how upset I was at the idea.

'It's that girl,' Paul said when I told him, 'this Sophie. She's a different kind. The kind that doesn't think about money like we do. She probably put the idea into his daft head about not buying the car but using all his savings on clothes and night-clubs instead. Did you see that jacket he bought? Ridiculous. It'll be the same as that flash suit. Wears it once then it lives in his wardrobe in a plastic wrapper.' That was it. Our son was leaving home and we were discussing the cost of high street fashion.

I leave Mum in the lounge and wonder when we'll meet the elusive Sophie. It can't go on like this for much longer. Not if he's leaving home to live with her.

I go to the back door, ready to undo the bolt for when Oscar arrives. We arranged that he'd come in this way so as not to disturb my mother. It's not locked. The safety catch is on. Has it been like this all week? I use the front door so haven't noticed until now. I go to tell Mum, to have a go at her for leaving the door unlocked, but stop myself.

This is because of when she locked herself out the other day. She obviously put the catch on so the door wouldn't lock behind her, but forgot to take it off again. All the talk of people being outside watching her and she's forgetting to lock the door. I mentally curse myself. I should check these things. I've been putting her to bed and just assuming the back door is locked. A heavy feeling descends. A knowing that I can't depend on her to do anything any longer.

As I go to take the catch off, Oscar opens the door. He stops suddenly when he sees me right there in front of him, and breaks into a laugh.

I laugh with him, shocked, pressing my hand to my chest in surprise, and he takes hold of me. His hands on my upper arms.

'Sorry! Didn't mean to—'

'No, I was just . . . the door was . . .'

It's like his hands are electrified. I can feel them through my cardigan. The door is still open and the blast of cold air helps me. It cools the heat in my cheeks and gives me something to talk about.

'So cold out there!'

He closes the door, and we talk about the ice, the freezing rain that has put a hold on his painting, the icy winds that have prevented him from working at a speed he would've liked. He's been doing what he can, but the weather has stopped him from completing anything. And even though the frost makes everything look beautiful, underfoot it's deadly. Black ice hides on pathways and roads. I've thrown salt on the driveway and doorsteps and given my mother strict instructions that she's not to venture outside.

Everyone is wearing layers upon layers, hats under hoods, scarves over coats, but Oscar has his jacket open. As if it's midsummer. He tells me about the weather forecast for the next few days, then in one fluid movement he takes the jacket off. He's wearing a thick shirt, and he takes that off as well. In the process, I get a flash of his stomach. Pale flesh. A line of dark hair travelling down below his belly button that I'm unprepared for.

'I'm lucky,' he tells me, 'I don't feel the cold.' He throws the shirt over a chair, and I stare at him. I wasn't ready for any of this.

The energy he brings. His quick, animated movements. The way he fills the room.

'Good to go.' He grins at me.

The table seats four, but with Oscar being so tall, I have to move my chair so our knees don't touch, and it feels oddly miniature. A table for a doll's house. There's a dining room we could've used, but it's full of junk and I didn't want to have to clear it. But now, sitting so close to him, I wish I had. I wish we had space between us. He leans towards me, light dancing in his eyes, and pushes back a lock of black hair that's fallen over his forehead. I can smell the cold air on him, the taint of smoke from the chimneys of open fires; see a smudge of dirt on his upper cheek. I force my eyes away from it.

'So, we're going to get straight into it,' I say briskly. 'Tonight we'll go over some basic pronunciation and do a little role play. Order a cup of coffee, that kind of thing. How does that sound?'

'Role play?' He raises his eyebrows. 'I like a bit of role play.'

I lose my focus with that eyebrow raise.

'Er ...' I look at my laptop.

Did he just flirt? Is he flirting? That was definitely flirting.

I swallow, go to my lesson plan and ignore the voice in my head.

'Let's start.' I don't look up, I stare at the words as I say them, and the next hour goes by painfully slowly. I stick to my plan with a kind of rigour I've not had since I started teaching. I try not to look at him. Try not to think of anything other than the words and whether they sound right. It's exhausting. But I discover that Oscar is good. He has an aptitude for language, and he picks it up fast.

I usually get a feel for how a student is going to progress on the first lesson. I can tell if Spanish is going to be something that will become a part of their life as it did mine, or if it's going to be a struggle, and for Oscar, with his enthusiasm and ability to remember words, I know it'll be no problem. In the four months we have before he starts travelling, he'll be doing more than basic conversational stuff. He'll be good. By the time he's spent a few months out there, he'll probably come back fluent.

'That was brilliant,' he says as the lesson comes to an end, 'really great. I've been doing bits myself, got an app, but it's nothing like this.'

'Good,' I hear the relief in my voice, 'glad you enjoyed it. Next time, we'll build on what you've learned tonight and get a conversation going.' I pull out a sheet. 'Homework.'

He lets out a laugh, a deep sound that fills the room. 'Homework! I've not had that since school.'

I smile. 'It's only filling in the words you learned tonight. And you need to practise saying them, over and over.'

'Over and over,' he repeats, and I laugh too.

'Practise makes perfect,' I say, 'if you want to be good.'

He looks up at me, and as our eyes lock, I stop laughing.

'I want to be good,' he says. 'I want to be the best student you've ever had.'

We stare at each other a moment and then his face breaks into a grin. He disarms me so much; I can't tell whether he's joking or being serious. It's like we're playing a game and I don't know the rules.

'Over and over,' he repeats, holding up his homework before grabbing his jacket and leaving.

The room becomes my mother's kitchen again. The energy and unstable atmosphere gone. I'm drained. I feel my shoulders drop and relax a little. My jaw unclenches. I rub at the back of my neck, thinking about how teaching Oscar is going to be a bit like taking an exam. Focusing on what I'm being asked. Concentrating hard on every answer so I don't make a mistake, so I don't get anything wrong.

I go to the sink and start rinsing out our mugs, my hands slowly going over Oscar's, rubbing away all traces of him. I stop and decide to put them in the dishwasher instead. I'll get my mother's things and load it up, put on a wash before I get her ready for bed.

As I go to open the dishwasher, something outside the kitchen window stops me.

There was a glimmer.

In the black of the window, there was a faint reflection of something.

I turn to the kitchen behind me, wondering what the light could've reflected off, or if it was something outside. I lean closer but only see my own face staring back at me, and it passes over me again, the feeling of being watched.

The hairs prick up on the back of my neck. A tingle spreads over my skin and I take a step towards the door, thinking of it being unlocked for goodness knows how long. And out of nowhere, Josh's voice is suddenly right in my ear. *You want to be careful, out here on your own. You might get all sorts trying to take advantage, at any time.*

'Lou?' my mother calls, and I jump. A shocked laugh escapes me. 'Are you finished in there? I think I'm ready for bed.'

I put my hand to my head. It's hot. I'm flushed, and now I'm getting paranoid. Letting Mum's fears take hold of me. I let out another laugh at myself, at my dramatics, the heightened events of the night now affecting me in a different way.

I run my hands over the now locked door. Check it again. Check the windows.

'All finished,' I shout back to her. 'Everything's fine.'

But the shiver is still creeping along the back of my neck. The sensation of someone watching is not going away.

FOURTEEN

'Lou! *Mi amor!*' Gary kisses me on both cheeks, his hands on my shoulders.

I give a shocked laugh at the wetness on my skin, the proximity of his face. He's tried to kiss me hello once before, but I dodged him that time, backing away, telling him I had a cold coming on. Today I wasn't as prepared.

'Oh!' I long to wipe my cheeks.

'It's the Spanish way, isn't it?' he asks, still holding me. 'A kiss on each cheek?'

'Air kisses,' I say crossly and try to pull myself away. 'You don't actually kiss at all.'

He stares at me a moment and his grip tightens.

'And it's *mi amiga*,' I tell him. '*Amor* means love. You meant to say *my friend*, and that's *mi amiga*.'

He slowly opens his hands, releasing me, and I have to stop myself from moving quickly away from him and grimacing.

'*Mi amiga*,' he says lightly. 'I'm so sorry, I have so much to learn! I read that in Spain it's a kiss on each cheek, so I thought I was doing the right thing.' He says it behind a smile that feels cold, and I just know he's lying. I've been through all this with him before, told him the same things I am now.

I drove here in a daze, forgetting that my lesson was with Handy Gary, and I'm ill prepared. Normally I take time to psych myself up, ready for whatever he throws at me, but my head is so crammed with thoughts of Oscar, of Felix, of my mother, that I wasn't ready for his unwelcome behaviour.

He kissed me and wouldn't let go.

I hear Trudy mumble something under her breath as Gary leads me to the back room, and I quickly use the cuff of my jacket to wipe my face. I stop as we get to the door.

'That's not the usual table.' I look at the small table, two chairs close together. 'It's not big enough, we'll have to sit—'

'Sorry.' Gary walks into the room. 'The other table broke this morning, one of the legs just went. This is all I could get in a rush.' He moves one of the chairs. 'It's small but it will be enough for your laptop and my paper, won't it?'

He will be closer than ever, his leg touching mine, numerous excuses to be in my face, the smell of his breath, the smell of him.

I begin unbuttoning my coat as I look round the airless room, boxes of stock and piles of storage boxes surrounding the tiny table and chairs.

'D'you mind,' I say in a voice Trudy will be able to hear, 'if we hold the door open with something? It always gets so hot in here.'

Gary stares at me for a moment, looks outside at the frozen landscape. 'Hot?'

'We can just keep the door open a little, can't we?'

Trudy watches from the counter and then looks off to the boxes yet to be unpacked.

'What about some of those?' I ask, and she gets a four-pack of lager and places it on the floor as a makeshift door stop. We both turn to Gary. He gives a small shrug, and Trudy goes back to her counter.

'Thanks so much, it's just ...' I fan myself a little with my papers, and realisation crosses Gary's face.

'Of course, of course, no problem. I understand, a woman your age, all those hormones running through your body ...'

I have to stop myself from correcting him. Gary thinks I'm menopausal. I nod. Playing along.

'But the noise?' he says as I go to sit. 'The customers? I won't be able to concentrate, to focus. Shall I get a fan? I have one in my bedroom, I could—'

'Let's try without, shall we? Now, I thought we'd try the difference between the feminine and masculine nouns today.'

He stares at me blankly. Going over Spanish grammar is a step too far for Gary, but I wanted to blindside him a little. I open my laptop and find where we're up to. We've done likes and dislikes, all the basics, and essential vocab.

'Y'know, Gary,' I say, looking at him, 'I had planned to go over some more conversational phrases, the greetings and farewells we've been learning, but shall we take it a step further? Would you like to learn about the definite and indefinite articles?'

He blinks at me. I want him to be confused; I want him to be so out of his comfort zone that he doesn't have time to leer or look at me or sit too close. I scratch at my cheek, which still feels wet.

'You're different today, Lou,' he says as I put a worksheet in front of him. 'You seem ...' He shakes his head, waves to the door and Trudy beyond.

I want to tell him that this is what he needs to know if he wants to improve, but I stop myself. I need this job. I *really* need this job. I'm forgetting myself. Gary might be the biggest creep going, but he's one of my reliable and regular students and he has two lessons a week. That's not money I can just throw away. I need to keep him onside, not be so bossy and try to teach him Spanish grammar when he's not remotely ready for it.

'How about the days of the week again?' I smile, and he looks at me warily. 'We'll go through the days,' I say, 'and then recap the weeks and months.'

He puts one of his hands on my shoulder, and I fight my instinctive reaction to move away.

'That would be better.' He grins broadly, as if I've just admitted a secret, and gives a conspiratorial nod. 'I understand,' he whispers. 'Hormones. No problem.'

At the end of the hour, we arrange the time for his next lesson, and he stops me before I leave.

'Valentine's Day is getting closer,' he says. 'I want to write a special message to Josie. Reply to her letter. I thought,' he looks up at me, 'I might write a poem for her. Poetry is very romantic, isn't it? Do you like poetry, Lou?'

I shake my head a little. Gary will never cease to amaze me; the way in every lesson he seems to shoehorn in a question about what I find romantic.

'I've never really thought about it, to be honest,' I begin, and a smile spreads across his face, self-satisfied and smug.

'You'll love my poetry,' he says, and nods, 'but first I need your help. I tried, but I can't translate the letter Josie has sent to me. It's difficult going through her words. It's too much. I wanted to ask if you wouldn't mind. I'll pay. Just let me know how long it takes, and I'll pay extra. I just want to be able to write back to her, understand her words and write a lovely letter and poem back. Like the things that she writes to me about.'

I smile through clenched teeth. I thought I'd gotten away with translating this private letter between him and Josie, but it seems not. I think of the extra money and tell him I'll be glad to help, and that it'll be at my normal hourly rate.

'We're old-fashioned,' he says before he leaves to fetch the letter from his flat. 'Most people email, but we like to write to each other, to hold a piece of paper as we read the words. It means so much more when it's delivered that way, don't you think?'

I give a non-committal nod as he leaves the room, thinking how only Gary could make writing a letter sound off-putting.

As I'm packing up my things, I look around the room properly. It's the first time I've been alone in here. There are stacks and stacks of old magazines and newspapers. I wander over to them and see that they're not recent. They date from months back. I'm absently wondering why he's keeping them and if he's one of those hoarders, when he comes back into the room.

'Here,' he says, holding up a folded piece of paper, and then gives a low laugh. A laugh that reminds me it's essentially a love letter he wants me to translate. It makes me want to tell him I've changed my mind.

He picks up my folder and opens it. 'I'll put it safely inside,' he almost whispers, 'so you can translate it in private.'

I smile, hating the way he's trying to imply something, and hold out my hand, ready to take the folder from him.

'Oh,' he says, pulling out a piece of paper, 'Oscar Delany. You're teaching him now?'

He's looking at the lesson plan that I've prepared for Thursday night, Oscar's name at the top, with the date of the lesson underneath.

'Yes.' My hand is still outstretched, waiting for the folder. 'Do you know him?'

'He drinks in the Duck and Bucket sometimes, and he did some work for me a while back,' Gary says, and slowly puts the paper back into the folder. 'Some . . .' he waves to the shop, 'maintenance.'

There are no gardens near Gary's shop, so Oscar must have done something similar to what he's doing at my mother's. Odd jobs, gutter clearing, maintenance.

'Is he better than me?'

The question throws me.

'At Spanish,' Gary prompts. 'Is he a quick learner?'

I give an embarrassed laugh. 'I can't talk about other students,' I tell him as I take my folder back. 'It would be unprofessional.'

'He's a very good-looking man,' Gary says as he walks towards me. 'Trudy couldn't stop staring at him in his vest. He got all the ladies worked up when he fixed the shutters. He's the same at the pub. Likes to show off, a bit of a peacock. Don't you think, Lou?'

My face goes hot. Even with my head down, concentrating on my bag, I can feel Gary's eyes on me, scrutinising my reaction, and in response, the flush increases in my cheeks. I'm rattled, and I hate him for it. I give a non-committal shrug.

'Hadn't really noticed,' I say, and when I look up, Gary's eyes lock with mine and I feel the lie catch in my throat.

'You're blushing.'

I try my best to keep my expression and demeanour professional, to resist the urge to wipe my brow or pull at the neck of my jumper. I want to tell him that it's none of his business, but luckily, a loud crash from the shop stops me from saying anything.

Trudy swears.

'Again?' Gary shouts as he walks past me. 'You need glasses, your eyes testing. No one can be this clumsy.'

I walk out to see a bottle of wine smashed on the floor from where Trudy was stacking shelves. I say goodbye quickly and leave them to the clean-up while customers walk around the mess.

Once in my car, I take out my folder and look at the letter Gary wants me to translate. I've heard so much about Josie, his Spanish girlfriend. I'm interested to see who would find a man like him attractive. It's typed, rather than hand-written as I imagined, and I begin to read, translating in my head as I go. The words and phrases are clunky. It doesn't read like someone Spanish wrote it at all.

Gary, I miss you. I can't wait until us to be back with you. I wrote all this many words for you and . . .

A wave of nausea washes over me, along with pity. It's obvious that Gary has typed this himself, probably using Google Translate. The thought of having to work through it and then help him write a poem in return fills me with dread. And something else. Something close to revulsion.

A bang on my window makes me jump, and I turn to see Gary watching me, my finger frozen over the printout. I push it back into the folder as I wind down the window.

'I didn't say goodbye,' he says. 'I wanted to ask you something about our next lesson.'

'Next lesson?'

'The back room,' he glances at the shop, 'it's not right in there any longer. You're too hot and I'm too distracted.' He pauses a moment. 'Is there anywhere else we could go? Where is it you teach Oscar? Do you go to his flat? Sit in his lounge?'

'Oh.' Of all the things I expected him to ask, it wasn't this. I'm on the back foot. 'No, there's nowhere else, I'm afraid.'

'Next time you can come up to *my* flat. We'll get cosy on the sofa together and—'

'No!' The idea of going up to Gary's flat, without Trudy or customers close at hand, makes me snap. 'I mean, Oscar comes to my mother's house. I teach him there as he's doing some work there. The back room here is fine, it's no problem, and we need a table so it wouldn't be right in your flat.'

He smiles at my panic. 'No problem,' he says slowly, and then starts to nod his head thoughtfully, 'no problem at all. The next time you come, I'll have a fan ready. Two fans!'

I laugh, relieved to be going, and remind him of his home-work, then wind my window up and drive out of the shop car park.

Gary watches me go. The way he always does. I catch sight of him in the rear-view mirror and run my hand over my cheek, trying to shake off the memory of him being so close. The thought of the awful letter he wants me to translate is huge in my mind, and as I imagine what he'll want me to write in return, I feel sick. An image of him dictating sleazy erotic poetry makes me gag, and the idea of that happening on his sofa, in his flat, away from the safety of the shop, is terrifying.

FIFTEEN

Later that afternoon, I make my way over to Rick's. The air is still cold, the late-January day has got a bitter feel to it and the light is flat and dull. It's only three, but the darkness is creeping in. I wrap my arms around myself as I walk. I hate these months before spring, and January always seems to drag on for ever. I've met no one who relishes this bleak time, and if I did, I'd pick their brains until they could tell me something good about it. An icy wind makes me shiver.

I saw Paul yesterday before he went back into the office, and he said things were in awful shape there. The worst he's seen. He was pale, a kind of grey tinge to his complexion, and I asked if he was sleeping enough, getting enough rest. He told me he napped on the sofa in the office when he wasn't driving, and that he'd had to let some drivers go as the fares were so few and far between.

'It's the time of year,' I told him, as I stirred the stew I was making to take to my mother. 'Everyone is doing Dry January and driving themselves about. It'll pick back up again soon. It's the start of February in a few days. You need a night off. A full night's sleep. Napping on a sofa in the office is not proper rest,' I warned him.

He scoffed at the suggestion, and I mull over his words as I walk. He talked about selling up, closing the place down, and as I think about our huge overdraft, the loans and debt we have from putting Felix through university, from years of thinking things would pick up, a slither of panic squirms in my stomach. There is no way I can even think of cancelling Handy Gary.

Without the taxi business, Paul would do what? Get a job? Work normal hours? But what could he do? He's worked in the taxi rank since leaving college, taking his father's place as manager when he retired. It's all he's ever done. I doubt he's even employable. Could he actually work for someone else? The slither of panic builds as I remember his last words. Words he says every time the subject of money comes up.

'You'll need to get a regular job with a steady wage. Your money from teaching isn't reliable, it goes up and down too much. We need something we can bank on.'

I take a deep breath and look down at the pile of flyers I'm holding. I hastily printed them off earlier this morning: an image of the Spanish flag and a sales pitch that includes ten per cent off the first lesson. I posted the same thing on my Instagram account, now determined to do more on social media than just scroll. Start actually using it as a way to pick up students, instead of the sad mix of personal and the odd professional post that it currently is.

I take out my phone and check my account: @spanish-teacherLou. It's the first post I've done in over a month, and it has a couple of likes but no comments, and no messages asking for lessons. I think about doing another post later, maybe one of me at my desk, showing how I work, and cringe a little at the thought.

I reach the bungalow and Rick opens the door.

'Hello, you,' he says, 'nice to see you up this end.'

I hold up the bag filled with books I've brought him, and his eyes widen.

'Ooh, what have we here?'

'Ruth at the library,' I say, 'and I bought you a couple off the bestseller list to say thank you. Again. And sorry for the other night. I don't know what I'd do if you weren't such a good neighbour.'

'You didn't need to do this!' He pulls out a book and starts to read the blurb, something about a holiday that ends up in murder. He looks up and smiles at me. 'But I'm glad you did. Have you read this one?'

I shake my head.

'I'll read them and then hand them back in order of which is best,' he says as we go inside. 'Did you see that documentary the other night? The one about the woman who used her dog to swindle people?'

I tell him no, and smile as he relays the gist of it, glad we're back on safe ground, that he's not too upset about my mother's latest antics.

'You look like you could do with a strong coffee,' he says. 'If you have time?'

I nod. I hadn't planned to stay long enough for a drink. I was just going to drop off the books and make sure everything was all right with him, but Rick's house is a sanctuary. Beautiful light wooden floors with deep-pile rugs, pale green walls and two large picture windows showing the expansive lawn at the back of his house.

Sinking into the white sofa, I look at the modern art on display, the book he's been reading open on the chair opposite me, and think how lovely it all is.

Our house is nice enough, but not like this. I'm not someone who can put together a room. The things Rick has thought of in here, scented candles, bright cushions and throws, are things I've never even considered. I look around and wonder how this place feels more like my home than my own house.

'So,' he says as we wait for the kettle to boil, 'how are you? More importantly, how's Vivienne?'

'Better than the last time you saw her,' I begin, and then pause. 'We're getting some cameras fitted. An alarm for peace of mind.'

'Good idea,' he says. 'That way, if she hears something alarming, she can see exactly what's out there.'

I nod.

He leans in. 'I didn't like to say the other night,' he says, 'didn't want to upset her any more than she was already, but I do need to tell you something . . .'

I look up, see his face and freeze. His expression is serious, the easy smile gone, replaced by heavy concern. My stomach drops.

'Rick? What is it? Has she . . .?'

'I've thought hard about telling you this,' he goes on, 'but after last week, I'd never forgive myself if something happened to her. If she hurt herself and I hadn't said.'

'Hurt herself?'

He takes a deep inhale, his chest rising as he prepares himself.

'It was a while ago. I forget the day, but there was that cold snap and it got frosty early on.'

I think back. When was that? It's been so cold recently, the weather is making the days blur together.

'I was putting out the recycling,' he goes on, 'and I heard a noise. Sounded like moaning, a wailing sound. Someone crying. I thought it might be a trapped animal. It was coming from your mother's house, so I looked over in case a cat had got stuck or something . . .' He pauses, looks away. 'It was your mother.'

'My mother?' I frown. 'What . . . I mean, she never . . .'

'I think she was sleepwalking.' Rick's face is tight, his words stilted. 'She was in her nightdress, and when I spoke to her, she called me Andy.'

Time stops. Andy was my dad's name. I swallow, and it's difficult, like I've got something lodged in there.

'I'm so sorry,' Rick says, and he leans over, puts his hand on mine. 'I helped her back inside the house, waited until she'd locked the door. I was going to call you, but I thought if she was just sleepwalking . . . Well, it was late, and I didn't want to get you out here at all hours.'

I put my hand to my throat, swallow again and feel the constriction. Sleepwalking? Calling Rick by my father's name?

'Andy?' I whisper, and he nods.

'There's something else,' he says, and the tightness in my throat gives way to nausea.

'Oh God, what? What else?'

'She was holding a doll.'

'A doll?'

He nods. 'One of those cheap plastic ones.'

I stare at him. I can't imagine it, my mother wandering around holding a doll.

'Did you . . .?'

'I didn't ask her about it,' he says quickly. 'She was clutching it tightly, and I wondered if it meant anything.'

I shake my head, not really able to comprehend what he's telling me.

'I thought it was a one-off,' he goes on, 'that she was just sleepwalking, but after the other night, when she thought she heard someone . . . Perhaps she was . . .'

'You think she was sleepwalking again?' I look up at him, 'Imagining people were there?'

We stare at each other in silence, both thinking the same thing but not saying the words aloud.

'I'm sure there's nothing to worry about,' Rick says finally, and a sound escapes me that is a cross between a laugh of disbelief and a moan. 'Really, Lou,' he smiles, 'let's not be dramatic. She got confused, I helped her back into the house and she was fine. After a couple of minutes, she woke up properly, saw it was me, apologised and took herself off to bed.'

I stare at him as I think of what she was like the night she called me, her panicked, terrified voice on the phone and then her confusion and apologies as we realised that no one was there.

'Oh God.' I put my head in my hands and feel Rick pat my shoulder.

'Was I right to tell you?' he asks, and I look up.

'Of course.' I give him a small smile. 'And thank you for coming over and checking on her. I clearly need to buy you more books.'

He laughs, tells me not to be silly and starts talking about the documentary again. I nod along, make all the right noises, but I can't really focus on what he's saying. My mind is full of my mother and what medication she's on. Does she take something to help her sleep? Perhaps it's too strong. Or perhaps she's sleeping too much in the day. I do find her napping a lot in front of the television. Maybe I need to wake her up so she's really tired at night ...

'And those?'

I blink at Rick; he's stopped talking and is pointing to the flyers on the seat next to me.

'Oh.' I hold them up. 'It was just an idea. Oscar's doing some work on my mother's house, and in return I'm teaching him Spanish, and it got me thinking. You see people all the time, and perhaps they'd like lessons, and I need more clients, so if you wouldn't mind handing some of these out ...'

'Of course! I'll pass them around, put a few in the shop.'

'Thank you. You're an absolute star.'

'So you're looking to expand your business?'

'I need the money,' I say, and he smiles at my bluntness. 'Paul's taxi place isn't doing too well and I need to up my game.'

'Very enterprising,' he says. 'So I'm guessing Oscar wants to brush up on his Spanish for his trip to South America?'

'Yes, his trip.' I try to make my face and voice neutral, to give nothing away. 'With his girlfriend.' I look up. I'm surprised at myself. I didn't even know I was going to say that until the words left my mouth.

Rick blinks at me. 'His girlfriend?'

I can see her in my mind. Young. Fresh-faced. A lithe, muscular figure from all the yoga she does. Long hair and piercing eyes, brilliant style and—

'I didn't know Oscar had a girlfriend.'

'I just assumed ...' I leave the sentence hanging, hoping Rick won't realise I'm fishing for information.

'No. No girlfriend as far as I'm aware,' he tells me, and something in my chest lifts. Despite all my worries and anxiety over my mother, there is still this. There is still Oscar. And now I find I'm rushing to thoughts of him because he's such a welcome distraction, such a relief to slip into. My all-encompassing, absorbing thoughts of Oscar and the ability they have to push everything else out.

We talk a little about his trip, my Spanish teaching and a designer Rick knows who might be interested in lessons, and as I go to leave, he puts my flyers down next to a glossy brochure.

The house market is booming, it reads, *the prices are reaching highs . . .*

'Oh Rick,' I look up at him, 'please tell me you aren't moving?'

He smiles at me and says nothing.

'Please don't,' I say. 'We'd miss you so much. I mean, who else will I talk about nefarious dog-owners with?'

He lets out a laugh. 'So Viv didn't get one of these?'

'Oh, probably. And it's probably gone straight in the bin. She won't ever leave that house, you know that.'

'Of course, of course.' He shakes his head. 'I'm sorry I even mentioned it.'

I pick up the brochure and for a moment let myself imagine the course of events if she did want to sell. It's from some developers who want to build studio apartments; they don't mention an amount, but skirt around figures, high figures. I think of the money.

'Pretend you never saw it.' Rick gently takes the brochure from me, and I smile, let out a laugh. It's all a pipe dream. My mother is never selling, and no amount of money will change her mind.

As I leave, the thought that Rick might be considering moving sits heavy in my head. He's been such a help, such a godsend. I falter suddenly as the idea that he's thinking of moving because of my mother takes hold. I put my hand to my face and look back at his bungalow, his gorgeous bungalow so lovingly restored. He wouldn't leave that unless he was completely fed up with his needy neighbour and her late-night sleepwalking.

The realisation hits me like a smack just as my phone dings with a notification. A text from Paul.

Felix bringing Sophie for his farewell meal tomorrow night. I'm taking the night off work; can you cancel your lesson?

SIXTEEN

Felix has requested a roast. Roast chicken, to be exact. Apparently Sophie likes the thigh, but not the breast. She also likes honey roast parsnips and roast carrots, but not roast potatoes – that's the one thing she doesn't like roasted.

The evening is going to be a pain, as I have to buy the ingredients, see to my mother, then get back in time to cook the meal, and somehow in all of that be pleasant and calm enough to meet Sophie and give a good impression.

I sent Oscar a message last night.

So sorry, need to cancel our lesson tomorrow eve.

Can we rearrange?

He's finally replied, and in that time, I've checked my phone what feels like every five minutes.

Friday night?

Friday night. I've not had plans on a Friday night in months.

Great, I type, then change it to OK, and then to Friday is fine, see you then and press send before I dither myself into a state.

I'm about to put my phone away when I see three dots appear. He's sending a message back.

Pint afterwards in the Wilmot? We can talk through those cameras, there's a few things I need to go through.

The Wilmot.

The pub.

The pub with Oscar?

To talk about the cameras? What does he need to discuss that he can't talk to me about in my mother's kitchen?

My mind races through the scenarios until it finally dawns on me that I asked him to fit the cameras *after* we negotiated our deal. It isn't part of the skills swap we arranged. He probably wants to talk about money, and is being nice by offering to do it over a drink.

Still.

It's the pub, on a Friday night. With Oscar.

My stomach does a pathetic somersault as the word 'date' flirts around the outskirts of my mind like a taunting teenager.

I push it away and go to type a reply, and then falter, wondering how to put in a text that I'm sorry for giving him extra jobs without talking money first, for assuming he has the time, and how the pub isn't necessary. Annoyance at my indecision gets the better of me and I type Great and hit send quickly.

Three dots appear and I hold my breath.

A thumbs-up emoji pings onto the screen. I exhale in a kind of half-laugh, my heart pounding.

Get a grip, I tell myself, and throw my phone in my handbag.

But the exchange won't be ignored. His message inviting me to the pub is like a glowing neon sign inside my head as

I go about my day, along with the thought that it might not be right. That I might not be allowed. And it makes no sense, because of course I'm allowed. I'm an adult. I can go to the pub on a Friday night. But then it's not really just about going to the pub, is it?

I go through the motions of the day with that thought hounding me, as well as what Rick told me about my mother sleepwalking. I've decided not to broach it with her yet. Not to ask her about any of it: the confusion, the name, the doll. I tell myself it's because I want more information; I want to check her medication, see how she is in the coming days. See if it was maybe just a blip. But the truth of it is, I don't want to have the conversation with her. I can't even bring myself to talk to her about the cost of the work that Oscar's doing, let her know that we can't afford it, see if she can pay, and with every hour that passes, it seems to get a little harder. And so I talk to her about food, and what's on the news, and skirt around the questions I should really be asking her.

Back at home, I print out some more flyers with the intention of putting them around the village in the morning. I stare at them. If anyone does actually contact me to start lessons, when will I be able to do them? I'm exhausted as it is. Between my existing clients, my mother and now Oscar twice a week, the only other time I could teach is in the evenings or at weekends, and maybe that's the answer.

My weekends aren't full of social engagements and outings; most are spent cleaning, reading and binge-watching true-crime documentaries. Paul has talked about decorating Felix's room now that he's moving out, making it into an office or, he suggested with a laugh, a gym, but I don't want to be around for that. I'd rather work.

115

'What's that you're printing? Those cartridges cost a bloody fortune, you know.'

Paul comes over to the dining room table and picks up one of the flyers, frowning as he reads it.

'Ten per cent off?'

'Only for the first lesson. Thought I'd go into some shops in the village, see if they'll put them on the counter. I've got zero interest from my social media posts, so these might get more attention. I gave some to Rick the other day. He's handing out a few. Putting them in his shop, which is so nice of him.'

There's a loud cheer from the living room, where there's a darts match on television. Paul turns to go, and I stop him.

'Paul? Your darts team,' I say, not really sure of what is coming out of my mouth. 'Is there a . . . I think I saw one of your teammates in the park the other day. She had a ponytail, blonde . . .'

'Denise?' Paul raises his eyebrows, and I watch him. Try to see if there is anything in his look, anything that means something. His face suddenly breaks into a smile. 'I'm teaching her.'

I stare at him as if he's just announced he's going skydiving. He nods as if to confirm it.

'She's just joined the club but has no idea how to play at all. Her dad's got dementia, and though he doesn't talk any more, he still plays darts. So she wants to learn so she can play with him. Said I'd help her when I heard that. What with the state of your mum, it just seemed . . .'

Before I know what I'm doing, I go over and put my arms around him. He laughs, pats me on the shoulder.

'You have a heart after all,' I say.

He shrugs me off. 'It's no big deal. Just giving her a few tips here and there.'

I hold up my hand. 'You don't need to explain,' I tell him. 'I'm just glad that you're . . .' I stare at him, unable to find the words to tell him that it's nice to see him showing compassion. Sympathy. It reminds me of how he used to be. It's a whisper of the Paul who had all the patience in the world for me, who had grace and tenderness. 'It's a nice thing to do,' I finish, and smile at him.

There's another loud cheer.

'Oh, and tomorrow night,' I say quickly, 'Oscar, the guy who's working at my mother's, is taking me to the pub after his lesson. Going to talk through the cost of it all. Now he's fitted those cameras and alarm at the house, the price will be different. I won't be back until late. You could come along if you . . .'

Paul pauses by the door.

'Working,' he says. 'Friday night is one of our busiest, and we need all the money we can get, especially if all those daft cameras and alarms are going to cost the Earth.'

'They're not daft, they're . . .'

'Expensive,' he finishes, and we look at each other.

I open my mouth to tell him they were reasonably priced and that it shouldn't cost too much to fit them, but stop myself. I've no idea. No idea at all what figure Oscar will present me with. It could be another couple of hundred, and I bite my lip.

'You can always offer more lessons,' Paul says. 'Oscar seems keen. You could lay it on thick. Tell him he needs to know as much as possible, as no one speaks English in South America. That kind of thing.'

I look down at my flyers. 'These might . . .' I shrug. 'And Rick did say there's this designer he knows who might be interested.'

'Well then,' Paul says.

He goes back into the lounge and leaves me tidying away the printer and my flyers. The sense of dread I had earlier intensifies. At the end of February, the interest-free period on our latest loan runs out and then it shoots up. That's in five weeks' time, and if things haven't got better by then . . .

I tell myself they will. They have to, because the alternative doesn't bear thinking about.

SEVENTEEN

My cooking is a success.

Sophie is lovely, and watching her and Felix together is a strange thing. They laugh at each other when nothing is really funny. He sits close to her and always seems to be in contact with her, his hand on her arm, his head bending towards hers. His eyes linger on her, and she has his full attention at all times. Watching them together fills me with a feeling I can't describe. I've never seen him like this. His other girlfriends have been perfectly nice, but this is different.

I know it's serious because there's a sense of something in the base of my stomach. An aching, along with a feeling of being proud.

Once I pinpoint this, I find it odd. I'm proud of Felix for being with Sophie? For how he's behaving? But as the evening goes on, and the wine flows, I realise it's because I think my son might actually be in love.

By the end of the meal, I'm sentimental. I'm in very real

danger of becoming one of those mothers who hugs her son and tells his girlfriend how lucky she is.

I look at Paul over my wine glass, trying to remember when we were like that. The beginning of our relationship was blighted by death and loss. I clung to him like a lifeboat, and as I think back, I remember him being so kind with me. So affectionate in those early days, helping me navigate my grief as well as my growing love for him. I used to feel so guilty for being alive when my brother and father were not, and Paul helped me with that. He treated me gently and compassionately and showed me what it was to be loved after the horrors of life had made me feel so abandoned. I loved him fiercely back then.

I give him a wistful smile, remembering who we were, and then blink and turn back to my wine glass, which I've just drained. The temptation to fill it to the brim again and marvel at the young love at the table is strong, but I push it away instead. That would lead to me becoming more sentimental and maudlin than I am already, to saying the wrong things, and that is not the way to impress Sophie. No more wine for me.

'So, really,' Sophie is saying, 'we only go up to the Lakes for Christmas. And a couple of weeks in the summer, so I think my parents will probably sell the property.'

I see Paul nod thoughtfully, take a drink of his wine, and then I watch as a frown forms. Sophie is telling us about her parents' house in the Lake District, and her last sentence makes him narrow his eyes and shift forward in his seat in a way that rings alarm bells. I've seen that look on his face before. I've been listening absent-mindedly, but now I snap to attention.

'So, your parents,' Paul says slowly, 'they have a house up in the Lake District that's just . . . empty?'

120

Sophie takes a careful sip of her lemonade and I shoot Paul a warning look.

'Well,' she says, 'they go up there some weekends, and they rent it out from January to May, when they know it's not needed, so it's not entirely empty.'

Paul shakes his head slightly and looks across at me. He lifts his glass in a mock salute. 'A holiday home. Second property. It's all right for some, eh?'

Sophie lets out a small, embarrassed laugh and something changes in the atmosphere. Paul is about to ask another question, but Felix cuts in.

'Dad,' he says quickly, 'how's the darts team going?' He catches my eye, and his look says everything.

'Tell them about Denise,' I say, following Felix's lead. 'Your dad's teaching this woman to play darts. He's doing something really lovely—'

'No one wants to hear about me teaching Denise,' Paul says as he reaches across the table for the wine bottle. 'What we all want to hear about is this holiday home. I hope I'm not being too forward here, love, but how much do your parents make from renting out that house? Approximately?'

'Dad!' Felix exclaims. 'You can't ask that!' His hand goes over Sophie's, and I watch as he gives it a quick squeeze, an apology for his dad's rudeness.

'Paul, really!' I turn to Sophie. 'Sorry, Sophie. Ignore him, he's just—'

'You don't need to apologise for me!' Paul interrupts, and I see now that he's a bit drunk. His cheeks are flushed and his eyes slightly glassy.

'Paul, maybe you should—'

'I'm asking, Sophie, because we're about to enter the world

of renting out a property.' He raises his glass to her. 'We're going to be landlords! How about that!'

I grit my teeth. 'Paul. We're not doing—'

'What?' Felix looks from Paul to me and back again. 'You're renting out Gran's house?'

Paul nods, and takes a large gulp of his wine. 'That's why we're having all the work done.'

'We're not,' I tell Felix. 'We're not going to rent out anything.'

'We bloody are!' Paul says.

'But I thought Gran would never move.' Felix is frowning, understandably surprised at this new information. 'Mum?'

'Your gran isn't going anywhere. We're not renting out the house.' I smile at Sophie, trying to convey that everything is fine. I lean in, lower my voice. 'Your dad's just had a bit too much to drink.'

Paul lets out a loud laugh. I obviously didn't lower my voice enough, and I instantly regret my choice of words.

'Too much to drink? Is that what your mum just said? I'm sober!'

Felix squeezes Sophie's hand again. She looks at him and then gives me an awkward smile.

'Dessert!' I announce in a voice louder than I intended. 'Who wants cheesecake?'

Felix and Sophie start to make noises, but Paul cuts across them, not reading the room, not noticing the way I'm glaring at him, the way Felix is behaving, the way Sophie is gripping Felix's hand.

'No one wants cheesecake yet,' he says, 'and stop telling them to ignore me. Me and Sophie are talking property, something you don't understand, Lou.'

'Sophie doesn't want to hear about—'

'Let me tell her!' He leans towards Sophie, who moves back in response. My hands curl into fists. 'Felix's gran doesn't want to move. She's clinging to that house like her life depends on it. It's because of what happened. The accident. It was years ago, but—'

'Paul, please, you're—'

'I'm not telling any family secrets!' Paul says, and I can see it's the wine talking. He's not just a little drunk, he's further along than that, and I move the wine bottle away from him. 'I'm just explaining the situation. So, Sophie. Felix's gran lives in this gold mine. Massive house. Lots of land, just off the A road leading into the city. Perfect location for commuters, families. Tony says we'll get over a couple of grand a month! But she won't move out. She's in her eighties, should be in a care home, because she can't look after herself and she's got everyone running around after her. And if we rented out that house, the money we'd get would pay for her care, as well as bringing in an income. Everyone is happy, but she won't do it.' He leans in again. 'Was it like that for your parents? This second home in the Lakes. Was it a relative? Did someone die? Was it an inheritance? Is that how it—'

'DAD!'

Paul looks up suddenly at Felix, and the wine haze lifts from his eyes for a moment. He glances around at us all, his face registering shock at our expressions, and for a second I think the evening might be salvageable, that he will see he needs to stop talking about the house and my mother, and asking Sophie, who we're all trying to impress, awkward questions.

'Sorry.' He looks at Sophie. 'Didn't mean to make you . . .' He shakes his head. 'Sorry, Felix. I know it's not polite dinner time conversation. But Sophie here is practically family now, and—'

'I think it's time we all . . .' I begin, but Paul talks over me and it's apparent that he isn't finished, that this line of drunken thought isn't going to go away. My stomach recoils. I hate what he's doing. I hate the way he's making me feel, and I shoot him a look. Try to shout at him telepathically, to will him to just *stop talking.*

'I'll get her to move out.' He gives a nod and smiles at Sophie. 'One way or another.'

'Paul, can you just—'

'She's coming out of that house. She's coming out. Even if I have to drag her out of there myself!' He gives a laugh as if he expects us all to join in, and when no one does, he stops abruptly.

The silence in the room is heavy.

I look at his flushed face, his lips tinted red from the wine. I look at Sophie, who has her eyes down. Felix's hand is tightly on hers, the two of them so close together. I try to think what to say to get back to where we were before, when the conversation was easy, but no words come. Paul drains his glass, and the silence stretches out.

'Cheesecake?' Felix says after a moment, and the way he looks at me, the silent message he conveys, makes my eyes suddenly heavy. With horror, I realise I might cry.

'I'll go get it,' I say quickly, and picking up a few dishes, I leave for the safety of the kitchen.

Dumping the plates on the countertop, I put my hands to my burning face. I'm hot with embarrassment. I want to go to Sophie and tell her we're not really like this. Explain that we don't talk about houses and money all the time. Tell her that we don't constantly argue about Felix's gran moving out and talk over each other; that we usually listen to each other and agree on things. But then I realise with a shock that it would be a lie.

The Lou and Paul who met and fell in love all those years ago have been replaced by us, and I curl my hands into fists so my nails bite at my palms. We are exactly like the people we've been at this table tonight.

This is who we are now.

EIGHTEEN

The next morning, I drive to my mother's as early as I can. I don't want to be in the house, the dishwasher still full of the plates and glasses from the previous evening, the table still adorned with the fancy tablecloth and place settings. After Felix and Sophie had left, I cleared the table while Paul talked about how much he'd drunk. How the alcohol would interfere with what time he could drive the next day and how it had given him chest pains and he felt awful. I knew it was him making excuses for what he'd said, a roundabout way of some kind of apology, but I couldn't forgive him. I couldn't even talk to him about it. I kept remembering the way Felix and Sophie had looked at him, the way he'd made me feel, interrupting me, talking over me, not listening to anything I had to say. I was hiding in the kitchen, close to tears. I was embarrassed for him. Embarrassed for *us*.

I drive through the dark streets, the wet roads shimmering in the early-morning sunrise. I grip the steering wheel at the

mingle of emotions that wash around in my head. The humil-
iation is strong, and it's not only because of Sophie and Felix.
I was embarrassed that Paul got drunk, but it's something
else that makes me want to run. It was the admission of it all.
The meal was like looking into a mirror, and I keep seeing the
reflection and want to smash it. I want to slam my fist into
something hard, because I don't like it. I don't like who we are
or who I am, and seeing myself through my son's eyes made
me realise that.

I let myself in, and for the first time in a long time, I lean
against the closed door and breathe out a long sigh. It feels
weird, to be grateful to be here, to be looking forward to spending time in this house. For ages now, I've had a sense of dread
whenever I have to visit, but lately, I've wanted to be here.

'That you?' my mother shouts down. 'You're early, aren't
you?'

'I am,' I say, taking off my coat. 'Couldn't sleep.'

As I help her with her morning routine, she tells me about
her dreams.

'But here's the thing,' she says as we sort her laundry, 'I'm
not sure it was a dream.'

I stop. Frozen, with her cardigan in my hands.

'What, Mum? What did you say?'

Rick's words flash back to me, her sleepwalking . . .

'The noises,' she goes on, oblivious to my panic. 'The banging I kept hearing. In my dream it was a trapped animal. I got
up to let it out, to open the door, and that's when I realised I
wasn't dreaming.'

'Mum,' I choose my words carefully, 'when you realised you
weren't dreaming, were you . . . I mean, were you still in bed
when you woke up, or . . .'

127

She starts to laugh. 'Course I was still in bed! Where did you think I'd be?'

She tells me how the banging was outside, not in her dream, and how it scared her until it stopped. I notice how fast my heart is beating, how I'm shaking slightly, and I sit on the edge of the bed.

I make us an early lunch of eggs and soldiers. The conversation about her dreams and how they mixed with the reality of the sounds in the night is never far from my thoughts. Probably an animal outside, we concluded – a cat at the recycling, a fox looking for food – but I can't shake it from my thoughts. I know I should do something, but what? What on earth can I do about my mother's dreams?

'Not done this in a while,' she says as she dips a slice of toast into her egg. 'Not since you were living here.'

I smile. She's right. Normally I watch as she eats, eager to leave, to get back to my own house. For what? What am I running back to? Paul is always working, Felix is never home, and more often than not, I end up eating alone in front of the television.

'We'll do it more often,' I tell her. 'It's nice. Me and you here together.'

Her hand reaches across the table. Cool, dry, smooth skin. Fragile fingers squeezing mine. I give her a gentle squeeze back in return, looking at our hands together, an older and younger version. My hands and what they'll become.

'It is,' she says. 'It's nice that you're here when you don't have to be.'

I nod, pushing down the guilt of how I've come to view these visits as something to get through. Done with a sense of duty and loyalty and nothing else.

'Anyway, here,' she says as I'm clearing up the plates, and holds out a twenty-pound note.

'What's that for?'

'The pub,' she says, putting it down on the table. 'I was talking to Oscar and he told me he's taking you to the pub tonight, after your Spanish lesson. That's for you to buy him a drink. Buy him several. He's my knight in shining armour, what with everything he's doing here.'

I go over and pick up the twenty-pound note. 'Mum,' I begin, 'we're going to the pub to talk over the cost of fitting the cameras and the alarm. We didn't include the price of that in our arrangement. I'm not sure my Spanish lessons cover it all.'

'I'll tell him to give me the bill,' she says with a nod, 'so you can stop worrying about that.'

'I didn't mean that. I meant we'll sort it together. Your pension is for your food, the heating bill. I don't want you getting into debt over this. I don't want *you* worrying. I'll see how much it's going to be, and then we'll have a chat. I've printed out some flyers and Rick says there might be . . .'

She shakes her head and bats me off. 'I said I'll pay.' She raises her hands when I go to protest again, and I pick up our plates thinking what I'll say to Oscar later. I'll ask him to give me the bill first. Once I know how much it's going to be, I can make some sort of plan. I can't have her worrying about money on top of everything else. I don't want her worrying about anything.

The day unfolds in one rushed event after another. The time I had with my mother earlier is like a long-forgotten memory by the time I'm back there and getting ready for Oscar's Spanish lesson. Paul texted me about his heartburn from all the wine and how he was knocking back the Gaviscon, and I sent a thumbs-up emoji in return. Unable to reply properly. It's not good, this underlying feeling I have. But I know from experience that it'll fade. It's sharp now because it was just last night, but in a couple of weeks it won't be so cutting, and it'll be pushed down along with everything else.

I called Felix to see how the land lay, to try and smooth things over, but it went to voicemail and I left a long, rambling message about him bringing Sophie again. How next time we'd meet at a restaurant, where Paul would drive and stay off the booze. I check my phone before Oscar arrives, but there's still no reply.

The lesson is difficult, and I'm not sure if it's because I'm still bothered about Felix or because I can't really relax with Oscar. After about three quarters of an hour of repeating verbs, I start to look through his homework, but he puts his hand over it, stopping me from reading.

'I don't know about you,' he says, 'but my brain might have had enough for one week. Shall we go to the pub?'

The Wilmot is designed so that even when it's busy it looks just the right amount of full. Tables are positioned in booths, with plants and lights separating them. The walls are full of art, photographs of the pub as it was a hundred years ago, right up to the present day. There are framed newspaper clippings, tasteful landscape paintings and reconditioned decor from old mills that give the place a hipster feel without it being pretentious.

'I'll get the drinks,' I begin, but Oscar puts his hands up.

'Please,' he says, 'this was my idea, so I'm buying. You take that table,' he points towards the open fireplace, 'before someone else pinches it. What you drinking?'

I leave him at the bar and commandeer the table, taking off

my jacket and suddenly very aware of what I look like. Getting ready for the evening was a bit of a nightmare. I decided to dress in my usual uniform of jeans and jumper, albeit a little flashier than normal. I've gone for a black jumper dotted with silver sparkles and tight black jeans, thinking it would be right, but it suddenly feels all wrong. The idea that people will think we're on a date flashes into my mind, and I flush. An older woman with such a good-looking younger guy. A giggle escapes me, and I surprise myself. I run a hand through my hair and a wonderful sense of mischievous enjoyment fills me. I look around the pub. No one is paying attention, but for a moment I want them to. I want them to see me, and see myself through their eyes, be that person instead of the woman being belittled by her husband at the dinner table.

Oscar brings our drinks over. He looks at me and a smile spreads across his face. 'What?'

'Oh, nothing.' I shake my head. 'I was just ...' I raise my hand to the other people in the pub and then shake my head again. 'Nothing. I was just people-watching.'

He narrows his eyes and looks at me for a moment. I can tell he's deciding if he should press it, ask me what I was really thinking, but he slides my wine towards me instead.

'Hope it's chilled enough,' he says. 'White wine is awful if it's anything but freezing.'

I take a sip. It's delicious.

We drink for a moment in silence, the crackling of the fire and the muted conversations of others filling the air around us.

'So,' he says after a while, 'how did you get into teaching Spanish?'

The question is so unexpected I falter. I'm ready to talk about figures and costs. After my flirtation with the idea of us being on a date, in the silence I've been reminding myself that this is a business meeting, nothing more, so to hear such a conversational opening throws me.

'Oh, I . . .' I look at him. It's been so long since I've been asked. I take a moment to remind myself. 'When I was young, I was obsessed with travel. Would take book after book about trips abroad out of the library and my dad booked a package holiday to Spain. Nothing too fancy, but it was the first time I'd been on a plane, first time we'd gone somewhere foreign, and after all my reading about it, the whole experience blew me away.' I take another sip of wine. Everything feels off between us. Awkward and stilted. 'How did you get into gardening?' I ask.

'Took a course at college, really liked plants.'

We look at each other for a second, and then for some un-known reason we both burst out laughing.

'Do you come here often?' He shakes his head and I nod in agreement. 'Sorry,' he says as we stop laughing, 'I was trying to be . . . I dunno! Polite.'

'You're always polite,' I reassure him, and it's like something has broken between us, the tight pull of tension has shattered. I take another drink and feel myself relax. Maybe this is what Helen was talking about. I've been waiting for Oscar to reveal himself as an idiot, but he clearly isn't, so maybe a nice chat will do the job instead. Make him become a normal, ordinary bloke and nothing more. 'I was thinking you were about to tell me the cost of fitting the cameras,' I say. 'I was bracing myself for—'

'About that,' he interrupts. 'No charge.'

'No charge? No. You can't, I mean . . .'

'It was just a couple more hours here and there. I did it around the other jobs, in between coats of paint on the window

132

frames. Don't worry about it. I'll tell you what, though, you can get the next round in.'

'My mother will get the next round in,' I tell him. 'She gave me twenty pounds this morning for me to buy you a drink. Called you her knight in shining armour.'

He beams. 'Did she? How lovely of her. We've become friends, she's been telling me about her programmes, about the one where they make money from selling junk they find in charity shops.'

'Did she tell you about the teapot?'

'The fifty-quid one? What a find!'

We both laugh, and it's so good to be talking about my mother like this, without all the underlying assumptions and hidden motivations. For someone to just be nice about her.

'She *is* lovely,' I tell him, and go to get us another drink.

When I return, we talk about his love of gardening. He tells me of projects he's worked on, and time passes quickly.

'Another wine?'

'I can't,' I tell him. 'I may have had too much already, and if I want to drive . . .'

'We'll get you a taxi,' Oscar says. 'We'll share one, because they've got Theakston's Old Peculier on draught here and I'm not about to leave that at two pints. Have another glass and then we'll call it a night, and in the meantime, you can tell me about this true-crime obsession of yours.'

'I wouldn't call it an obsession.'

'I would. Rick told me what you two talk about. Body parts in freezers? Cooking them up for dinner?'

'You're thinking of a film,' I tell him, 'unless you're talking about that woman, who did try to feed her husband to their kids?'

Oscar lets out a laugh, nearly choking on his beer.

The rest of the night goes in a blur. I tell him the most grue-some true-crime stories I can think of, and he tells me about his trip to South America. About how long it's taken him to plan, the places he's going to visit, the route he's taking. We get lost in travel stories and dreams, and when we hear the shout for last orders, I can hardly believe it.

I drain my glass and look around the pub. Somewhere be-tween the first glass of wine and now, we've had several, and I realise as I stand up that I'm drunk.

We make our way outside to the car park. The night is still. Calm.

'Taxi,' Oscar says, and takes out his phone. The rain has stopped. I wrap my coat around me. It's an open sky, the stars shine down, and a full moon makes everything glow. I take a deep breath and smile, feeling something I haven't felt in a long while.

'Don't,' I say, and put my hand on his arm, 'not just yet.'

I don't say that I can't bear the thought of Oscar calling Dilenby Taxis and Paul turning up to spoil it all.

'You want to walk a bit?' he asks, putting away his phone. 'My flat is about fifteen minutes away. We could get a taxi from there.'

We start walking, my boots loud on the pavement, the night so still around us. But as I ask him about his upcoming trip again, ask him to tell me what he's most looking forward to, I stumble suddenly and almost fall. Oscar catches me. I start to laugh, giggling at myself and at how drunk I am.

'I've got you,' he says, and puts his hand on the small of my back to steady me. It's nice.

'I'm so glad we did tonight.' I stare up at him, his face so beautiful in the moonlight. So close. 'You're just a normal person.'

He gives a confused laugh. 'I am?'

I nod. 'You are. You see, I've had this ridiculous crush on you, and my friend Helen said I needed to get to know you and you'd become normal and I'd stop fancying you.' I giggle drunkenly, expecting him to join in, but his face is serious, and I stop. His eyes are locked on mine.

'And have you?' He looks at me intently. 'Have you stopped fancying me?'

His hand is still on the small of my back. I feel a slight pressure there. He's bringing me towards him, and I don't protest.

There's a moment, a half-second, where I comprehend what's about to happen. When I feel the change. A ripple of disbelief and excitement surges through me, and before I can talk myself out of it, I press myself into him.

'I really hope not,' he whispers, 'because I fancy you too, Louise,' and he leans in close to kiss me.

NINETEEN

Time slows. My every sense is overwhelmed with him, the smell of him, the taste of him, the feel of him.

I pull back, finally. I can't get my breath; my lips feel swollen.

His eyes are black pools. He goes to pull me towards him again, and I put my hands on his chest, stopping him. Shake my head.

'We shouldn't have done that.'

'Shouldn't we?'

I stare up at him, his face half in shadow. My heart is pounding, and I don't trust myself. I feel dizzy, intoxicated, but it's not the wine, it's him. There's a sound further along the street, a movement of something, litter being scraped against gravel. It's probably the wind, but I cling to him and then my thoughts rush in on themselves.

'Is someone there?' I whisper. 'Back at the pub? Did they see us?'

Loud voices come from the pub car park, just a little way

down the street, and I push him away. Put some space between us, suddenly aware of exactly what I'm doing and who I am.

A married woman snogging a much younger man in public.

'Oh God,' I moan.

'Walk with me,' he says calmly as a group of people appear, walking in our direction. I stare at the shadowy figures. Were they there the whole time? While I was kissing Oscar? There's something about one of them, their posture. Something I vaguely recognise about the way they walk. A voice that sounds familiar.

We begin walking again, Oscar's hand on the small of my back once more, reassuring and firm.

'I think I know one of them. I think ... Oh God, do you think they saw us? I think I might know ...'

'What?' Oscar looks behind us, but the street is now empty. The group of people have turned off towards the smattering of takeaway shops down a side street.

'Listen,' he says as we walk, 'you've had quite a bit to drink and we just got ...' He lets out a laugh. 'It was just some blokes. A group of fellas who were all drunk themselves. They were paying no attention to us at all.'

I stare up at him, his breath coming out like steam as he talks, my heels clicking loudly in the silent streets. It all feels so surreal, so intense.

'You're sure?'

We stop walking and he brings me in closer. 'I'm sure.'

My stomach somersaults. I still have the taste of him on my lips.

'Just along here,' he says, and we start walking again. 'We'll be at my flat in five minutes and I'll make us both a strong coffee. Sober you up, call you a taxi and get you safely home.'

I take his hand, and in silence we continue to his front door, up a flight of stairs and then through another door and into his flat.

He switches on a couple of lamps, and we stand in his lounge, staring at each other for a moment. My heart thumps in my ears. Under the artificial light, everything seems different, and the intensity is magnified. As if every movement I make, every slight action or word, is vital.

'Please, sit,' he says. 'I won't be long.'

He goes into the kitchen. I can hear cupboards opening, cups tinkling. Then he darts back into the lounge and scoops up a jumper and a pair of socks that have been left on the sofa.

'Sorry, sorry,' he says as he takes them away. 'I wasn't expecting company.'

I perch on the edge of the sofa and take in the room. Trying to ignore my heart, which is making my whole body vibrate with its thumping, trying not to think about what the hell I'm doing sitting in Oscar's flat. Trying to act like I haven't had too much wine, that it isn't daring me to do what I shouldn't. I fuss with my hair, change position several times, put on more lipstick.

A large, expensive flat-screen TV dominates the room. It's attached to the wall, a gaming control on the seat beside me. Bookshelves line the walls, and I get up to see what he reads. Gardening books mostly, and an awful lot of biographies. House plants are on every available surface, and it gives the room a light feeling.

'Here.' He holds out a mug. 'I put two sugars in. Thought we needed it.'

I take it off him and go back to the sofa, trying to pretend I'm in control, but I take a sip of the coffee and it burns my mouth. I start to cough, and he takes the mug from me, puts it on the table.

'I'm not used to this,' I say. 'Not used to . . .'

I look up and see how close he is.

He lifts his hand and lightly strokes a finger along my cheek. I don't know if it's that, or because I can no longer ignore how close he is standing, or the memory of the taste of him, but something shatters within me, and in that instant, before I can catch the pieces and try to put them back together, I step towards him and kiss him hard.

My hands aren't my own. I watch as they go to his chest, tug at his T-shirt.

What am I doing?

I push it up, suddenly desperate to see him. To see what's been hiding under the material, what I've been daydreaming about, wondering about.

I'll just do this and then I'll go, I tell myself, but I know it's a lie.

He takes my lead and yanks his T-shirt over his head, dropping it on the floor, and his chest is exactly as I imagined it would be. Taut and hard from all that gardening, skin fresh, dewy almost. I trace my finger over it, dragging my nail along his skin.

He closes his eyes at my touch, lets out a moan, and I feel a surge of power. Of something I'd completely forgotten about.

This. How could I have forgotten about this?

The intensity of it is thrilling. When he opens his eyes, they're dark, black almost, and I very nearly step back. I very nearly pay attention to the voice in my head that asks me what the hell I'm playing at. I very nearly tell him it's all been a terrible misunderstanding and go home to my empty, dark house.

To my empty, dark marriage. To pretending that everything is fine. That *I'm fine.*

But then he does something that makes me stop, that makes me lose myself completely. He reaches out and places his hand gently on the sensitive place where my jaw meets my neck. I lean into his hand, tilting my head. His touch is unfamiliar. Exciting.

His eyes are intense and his face is so beautiful, and I think that if I was younger, if I was still in that place where I was innocent to certain parts of life, this would be the point where I'd fall in love with him. Where I gave everything over to the sensation he's creating in me, to the glorious pull of him. I see myself through his eyes in that moment, and it's intoxicating.

I am about to do the unimaginable, the unthinkable, the exquisite forbidden. I hear a gasp, and realise it's me. I lean into him, letting him kiss me, and my mind stops. Everything stops.

For a blissful moment, the chatter, the noise, the worry, the cares, the heavy weight of my life is lifted. Gone. And it is wonderful.

TWENTY

I met Paul when I was twenty years old, got pregnant at twenty-one, and in all that time, I've never once been unfaithful. I believed those days of lust-filled passion were over for me. They were over even before I met Paul. They were over as soon as the accident happened.

I overheard my dad's friend at the funeral. He was outside smoking with another of Dad's colleagues, and he said something like 'She'll either go off the rails completely or never leave the house.'

I left the house, but I didn't go off the rails. I stayed on the rails so much I had tracks running down my insides. Paul was part of that.

After the accident, I didn't go back to university. I couldn't. My tutors said to take a year off, take some time to get my head around what had happened and come back when I felt ready, but how could I? When it happened, I hadn't seen my father or brother in four months. *Four months*. I'd left them after the Christmas holidays. I was in Spain. Completing my year abroad before finishing my degree.

I wasn't due back for the summer for another eight weeks. Mum had arranged a four-night break for us all at a holiday park. She'd signed us up for some kind of activity, sailing or something, and had all the evening meals booked, and I was dreading it. Wondering why we still had to take family holidays together when Mark and I were grown up.

I had a summer job lined up teaching Spanish at a camp for kids. Mark was just finishing his first year at Liverpool and was going to spend the summer in Newquay, surfing and working at a surf shop. He was only home for the weekend to see his mates and help Dad with the garden.

He couldn't be dead.

They couldn't both be dead.

They couldn't die in a car accident on a Saturday afternoon. We had plans. Holiday plans. Summer plans. We were only just starting out.

I made that journey home knowing I'd never see them again, and it was unbelievable. Literally unbelievable. Mum met me at the airport alone, and it wasn't right. None of it was right. Where were they?

I got off that plane as someone else. Was I still a sister? Was I still my father's daughter? Part of a family?

It didn't feel like it. It felt like I'd been left behind. Abandoned. It felt like falling and falling and never hitting the ground.

I was spending days in bed, alternating between crying and sleeping, not sure of who or what I was. Paul visited because he was a friend of Mark's. He and some other friends had started raising money for the air ambulance in Mark's memory. He came to sit with us, tell my mother about how much they'd made, how it was going, how close to the target they were.

'You should come,' he said to me one afternoon. 'We're holding a fun day at the golf club this Saturday, got a few stalls and a bouncy castle for the kids. You might enjoy it. We could do with a few more marshals.'

I looked at my mum and realised this was contrived. It was another of her attempts to save me. Something to take me out of the house, get me interacting with other people. I was about to say no when she leaned over and answered for me.

'She'd love to. It'll do her good. Be with people her own age, get some fresh air.'

And that was the start of it. Afterwards, Paul asked if I wanted to help with the summer fair in the village, and I nodded. It had been good to do something for Mark and my dad. To make up for not being there for them. And so I began to help with the fund-raising, and by the time we reached our goal, Paul and I were together.

When I think back, I can't entirely remember how it happened. Those days all bleed into each other, and it seems that I woke up and was Paul's girlfriend without ever having agreed to it.

My mother was nice to him back then, before I got pregnant and announced I was going to marry him. I think she thought he was going to be the stepping stone to me getting my life back, not the bank on the other side where I stayed. She'd invite him in to eat with us. Encourage me to go down the pub with him, and when she brought up the subject of me finishing my degree and going back to Spain, it was too late. I was already pregnant.

*

It's half two in the morning and I shut the door quietly behind me. For the first time, I'm grateful that Felix isn't here, that Paul works late and will go straight to the spare room, his eye mask on and ear plugs in. The house is empty, but I creep upstairs anyway. My heart is thumping loudly in my ears, my legs shaking, and a surreal feeling is all around me like a heavy fog I can't shake off.

It's like I'm watching myself from afar. As if it isn't me who's walking into my bedroom and kicking off my boots, throwing my clothes in the laundry basket and running my hands over my face. As if it isn't me with the words *I've done it now* repeating over and over in my head.

But I have. I've done it. I did it. I kissed Oscar.

I went back to his flat and we had sex. I've had sex with Oscar.

It was a one-time thing, the voice says, *not to be repeated, not to be done again.*

But as I shower, scalding water running down my back, my skin still thrumming from his touch, I can't stop replaying it in my head.

Sex. Sex with Oscar. I haven't had sex like that in years. If ever.

When I was first with Paul, did we . . .? I push the thoughts away. Comparing Oscar and Paul is cruel, mean, and yet my mind won't stop.

I love Paul.

I repeat the words over and over to myself, and each time, a wave of something hits me, something so hard and crushing that it almost feels as if I've been physically hit. I do love Paul; I know I do. I think about the man he was when I met him, how we were together. It's a different kind of love I have

144

for him now, but he's the father of my son, he's the man I've spent the last twenty-odd years with, all the mundane, tedious parts of life that go to make up a marriage. All the hard parts.

But as I let the warm water run over me, I can only bring up a collection of memories of us housed in normality. Days filled with repetition, along with a huge sense of duty and loyalty. I can't muster up the last time we had fun, the last time we laughed properly, the last time we were together that wasn't without a nest of difficult emotions.

Is that love?

If he were to find out about last night, about what I did . . . I swallow at the thought, shame and regret running through me.

I go into the bedroom and stare at myself in the mirror. I drop the towel. I haven't looked at myself naked in years, and as I turn from side to side, I see myself not through Paul's eyes, but Oscar's. I don't see the unfit, unexercised body of someone who's let themselves go over the years; I see it as Oscar did when he traced kisses along my stomach. When his fingers trailed lightly over my back, when his legs were tangled with mine. I flush at myself in the mirror.

I love Paul, I insist to myself, and something pushes back at the words.

Do you?

I put my hands to my face and climb into bed, hide under the duvet, where I hope the inner voices will stay silent. But it's no use. Behind my eyes an array of images scroll as if on a screen. Felix. My mother. Helen. My students. The people in the village. Paul. What would they all say if they found out what I had done?

I feel their judgement, hear the gossip, and I squeeze my eyes tight.

It's too much. It's all too much. The giddy, free feeling I had with Oscar, when we kissed under the moonlight and I felt like anything was possible, has been replaced with reality. I'm a middle-aged married woman with debts, a mortgage, loans, and a son who doesn't need the scandal. I've behaved dreadfully.

I groan as I think of Felix and Sophie, at their reaction to me with someone as young as Oscar, and curl up into a ball.

I wake at nine. Thank goodness it's Saturday morning and I don't have any lessons planned. My eyes are hot and stinging. I had a fitful few hours' sleep, waking at five and then falling back to sleep at six. And in that time, I made a firm decision.

I'm going to stop all contact with Oscar.

When I left him, it was still with the headiness of my desire. I laughed, kissed him and made some non-committal joke about our next lesson, but I didn't make it clear that what had happened was a one-off. I swore him to secrecy, begged him not to breathe a word of it to anyone, and even though I'm seventy per cent sure he won't say anything, the other thirty per cent of doubt swirls in my stomach like food poisoning, making me feel nauseous and unwell. I pick up my phone, ready to text him a panicked message asking him to forget everything. Me. Our lessons. I'll think of some other way to pay. Hell, I'll even get an evening job in the village, anything to wipe away what I did.

And then I see it.

A message from Oscar.

I loved last night. I don't regret a second of it and I
want to see you again. Let's talk at the next lesson x

It fills me with a happiness I'm not entitled to. I run my
thumb over it, and then, like a schoolgirl, hold the phone to
my chest, hugging it close.

I squeeze my eyes against the voice that reminds me of
the horrors I thought about in the early morning, the fear
of Paul or Felix discovering what I did, and I look at the
message again. How can I reply and say I *do* regret it? But
do I? I don't want to think about answering that question,
because the truth of it is, I don't regret my time with Oscar,
I only regret that I might get caught. I go to reply and then
stop. How to word it? The last thing I want to do is come
across as dismissive, because this is not something to be
dismissed. This has the potential to explode, and I need to
keep a lid on it.

It can't happen again, I type, then press send before I can
think too much about it. Immediately three dots appear to
show he's writing something, and I hold my breath.

Can't it?

I stare at the words. He wants to do it again?

A bubble of something rushes up into my chest. His desire
blindsides me. I didn't even consider that he'd want to meet
me again. Do what we did again. I assumed it was a one-time
thing, a drunken encounter that we'd both agree was best
never talked about. But now . . .

The three dots appear again, and my mind scrambles to
what's going on. An affair. If I see Oscar again, if we have
sex again, it will jump from a one-night stand into an affair.

Am I really going to risk everything to sleep with him again?

His message comes through, and I stare at it for a long time.

I can keep a secret if you can x

TWENTY-ONE

I've managed to avoid Paul, nipping out as soon as I was awake, knowing that he would rise about eleven and make his way into the taxi office for the afternoon. I saw to my mother and then went to the big Tesco and did a huge shop. Got in all his favourites. The beer he likes, the sugary break-fast cereal, the peanuts and crisps, even the chewing gum he keeps in his car.

As I'm chopping onions for the lasagne I'm going to make him, my phone notifies me of another message from Oscar.

Are you ghosting me?

A GIF of a cartoon ghost bobbing up and down is alongside it, and I can't help but smile. It's his third text. I've not replied to any of them. I tried to, but it was impossible. My first at-tempt was more of an essay than a text, so I deleted it all.

I look at the ingredients out on the worktop, all the things I need to make Paul's favourite meal, and my guilt hangs like a haze over them. I briefly wonder if I'm making it obvious that I've been unfaithful, then brush the idea off. I needed to do something, and cooking him a lasagne was it. I pick up my phone.

I'm not ghosting you, I reply to Oscar. I'm just trying to get my head around last night.

I press send before I start to overthink it and stare at the screen, watching for the dots to appear so I know he's replying, but there's nothing. I'm just about to put the phone back down when a message comes through.

I understand.

I deflate a little. What the hell is wrong with me? The guy has just said he understands, that he gets something of what I'm going through, and I feel . . . disappointed? As I pick up the knife again, giving a low groan of anger at myself, my phone buzzes on the countertop.

I wish we'd met at a different time.

Oh God. So do I.

A brief fantasy of meeting Oscar as a single woman with no responsibility shows itself before I push it away. My heart is beating fast. I go to type something in reply, but my mind is a blank. How to put in a text everything I'm feeling and thinking? Impossible.

We'll talk on Monday is all I manage, and press send.

I wait, staring at the screen, hoping I've not put him off, and hoping I *have* put him off at the same time. My stomach knots itself and then the three dots appear. I stop breathing.

Already counting down the hours x

I take a deep breath and try to focus on the meal I'm making, but God, it's hard. Hard when a beautiful man is giving me more attention than I've had in ages. I pick up my phone and then put it back down. I remind myself that I'm doing this for Paul. He'll come home from his shift later to-night and find his favourite meal and his favourite beer waiting for him. It doesn't matter if he doesn't eat it, I just need him to know I made it for him. That I did this for him. It seemed important this morning, when I first woke up and my guilt was heavy, but now it feels ... well, to be honest, it feels a bit futile. I swallow and go back to chopping.

My phone hums again against the worktop. Another notification. I pick it up quickly, eager to see what he's sent, but it's not from Oscar. It's from Handy Gary.

For me and you on Wednesday, it reads, and he's sent a picture of a fan in the back office where we hold our lessons. My mood swings to dread. I send back a thumbs-up emoji. I find the best thing to do with Gary is to acknowledge his texts but not respond fully if possible.

I'm just about to put my phone down when it rings, the word MUM lighting up in large letters.

'Mum, is everything—'

'Everything's fine, it's all fine, but that alarm. It keeps beeping. Going off. Telling me someone is at the door when there isn't. I get up and check, look through the window, but no one is there.'

'Hang on.'

I flick to the app and pull up the images on the camera. The porch and driveway are empty.

'Mum, no one is there. Are you sure you—'

'I know what I heard. It beeped, saying someone was there, and I heard them. I heard voices, but when I went, they'd gone. Perhaps I was too slow, perhaps I've missed someone ...'

'No, Mum, the camera would've picked them up. I would have a notification here if that was the case. They've literally just been fitted. I can't think of anything that would be wrong with them so soon.'

We talk for a few more minutes and I reassure her, tell her I'll check everything when I visit later. I end the call and go to send Oscar a message, to ask him what could be wrong with the alarm and camera, then stop myself quickly as I bring up our last conversation.

If I ask him about it now, he'll think it's some awful attempt at me arranging a meet-up. A surge of adrenaline suddenly whooshes through me. It would be so easy. Paul always works late at the weekends, it's his busiest time, and I could send him a quick message about the cameras and how they're playing up and how I've got Oscar out. No lies. We could meet up, check the cameras and then I could follow him back to his flat and . . . I stop. My heart is racing.

My phone buzzes in my hand and I jump, almost dropping it. I look quickly, expecting a message from Oscar, as if he can somehow read my mind, but it's Instagram. A new comment under my latest post.

I click on it and go to the page. Another post about my ten per cent off was scheduled this morning; perhaps it's a prospective student, someone who needs lessons.

But when I get to the comment, it makes no sense.

I read it twice and then click on the user who made it. They've no posts. No followers.

I look at the comment again: **Breaking news: you shouldn't have done that.**

Done what?

Made an offer on my Spanish lessons?

I delete it and navigate back to Oscar, wondering how I can word a text to him about the cameras. I pick up the knife and start chopping again, mentally cursing myself for how awkward I've made everything.

Felix arrives as I'm just taking the lasagne out of the oven.

'Perfect timing!' I tell him as I hug him. It's the first time I've seen him in the flesh since the disastrous dinner, and it feels like a different lifetime. 'This is a nice surprise,' I say. 'I'm just grabbing a slice of this before I go to your gran's. Want some?'

He shakes his head, and I wait a moment before a grin spreads over his face.

'Go on then, but just a small piece. Not much, I'm taking Sophie out later.'

'Anywhere nice?'

'Momolina.'

I stare at him, waiting for him to elaborate, and he laughs.

'It's a fancy restaurant. Thought you might have heard of it.'

I smile, shake my head and take our plates over to the table.

'Tell me how everything is,' I say as we sit down. 'Tell me what's going on with you.' I'm ready to lose myself in hearing about his job, his workmates, the fancy restaurant I know nothing about. It's been ages since I last had a meal alone with my son, and I realise it's been far too long.

He pauses for a moment.

'You mean, what's been going on since the dinner from hell where Dad quizzed Sophie and made everything really awkward?'

I put down my fork. 'I'm sorry that happened. I'm sorry that I—'

153

'It wasn't you; it was Dad. He was drunk.'

'We'd all had wine . . .'

'But we don't all get like that. He was really embarrassing, Mum.'

'He's under a lot of pressure.'

'He's always under pressure.'

'Your dad, he—'

'Mum.' Felix stops me and puts his hand over mine. 'You don't need to defend him all the time. I came over to talk about him. That's why I'm here.'

'Because of the meal?' I busy myself with cutting up the food on my plate. 'Felix, you're overreacting, he only—'

'Not just the meal,' he interrupts. 'All that talk about renting out Gran's house, how he wants to move her. I know he's been talking about it for a while, but at the meal he seemed certain about it, and I know why.'

I glance up at him.

'Look at this.' He fishes out an envelope from his pocket and puts it on the table between us. 'It's from when I was packing. I must have picked it up by mistake. It's addressed to Mr Whitstable and I just thought it was mine, but it isn't. It's Dad's.'

Putting down my fork, I pick up the envelope. I know before I open it that it's from the bank. I can see the unmistakable blue logo.

'The taxi rank,' Felix says in a flat voice. 'Did he tell you he's behind on the mortgage for it?'

'Mortgage?' I shake my head as I pull out the letter. 'There is no mortgage. Your dad owns that property. The building is probably worth more than the business now, but it was your grandfather's, he bought it, and when he retired, your dad bought it off him for ...' I stop as I see red words at the top of the letter.

Behind on payments. At risk of losing the property.

Dated the beginning of this month, addressed to Paul. This is madness. Paul owns the property, he doesn't have a mortgage.

I look up at Felix.

'He hasn't told you, has he? He's losing it, Mum. He's ten grand behind. That's what all that talk was the other night. That's why he was grilling Sophie about her parents' holiday home.'

The figures swirl in front of my eyes. We owe money. It's one of the only things we talk about. It's all we talk about. We're not good with money, never have been. We're the type of family that lives in the red, always in the overdraft, but this?

I stare at the letter and will myself to concentrate, but the words slide on the page. The taxi rank was the one thing that kept me from really stressing, knowing that if it came down to it, we could sell the business. Sell the property, a central building in Dilenby. That was our only saving grace.

'It's a letter demanding payment,' Felix says in an angry whisper.

I look up at him. His face is constricted as he speaks. We don't own the building at all.

We own nothing. We owe money on it instead.

'None of this makes sense.' I turn the letter over, trying to find more information: when the mortgage was taken out, how much it was for. 'I'm sure that—' I begin, but Felix stops me.

'Sure that what, Mum? That Dad hasn't borrowed thousands against the taxi rank and is now about to go bankrupt?

He's been lying to you. Lying to me. Lying to everyone about what he's been up to. What else has he been lying about?'

TWENTY-TWO

'Your dad is not going bankrupt.'

'Do you even know what that means?' Felix goes on, not listening to me. 'This is serious, Mum, it means that everything will go to pay the bank. It means that this house could go, maybe even Gran's house if that's viewed as an asset.'

He stabs his finger on the letter, and I look back down at it, trying to read it at the same time as Felix talks.

'You could lose your home, Mum,' he goes on, 'you could lose everything, and then what? He can't keep secrets like this from you. From us, I mean . . .'

'Just hang on a minute.' My voice slices through the air. 'You're getting carried away. Calm down, we are not losing the house. Your dad is not going bankrupt, and even if the taxi rank does have to close, it's a limited company.'

'Limited?' Felix asks, his breath coming out in a rush, and I nod.

'So you can stop worrying. We are not going to be homeless.

The taxi business is separate, this house and your gran's house have nothing to do with it.' I look at him a moment, his face etched with concern. 'Did you ask your dad about any of this before coming to me?'

He gives a laugh. 'Ask Dad?' He shakes his head. 'The last time I talked to Dad about money, he gave me a two-hour lecture on the clothes I buy.' He makes a face. 'You know what he's like if you even mention it. All his hackles go up, so no, I thought it best to come to you. Let you ask him about it.'

I stare at him, unsure what to say. He's absolutely right. Money has become such a touchy subject that we skirt around it, never actually talking about it directly. But to witness Felix's concern is saddening. He shouldn't be worrying about his parents' financial situation.

I plaster a bright smile on my face.

'Thinking about it,' I begin, 'your dad did mention something about this.'

Felix raises an eyebrow.

'You know me, love, I'm useless when it comes to all this kind of stuff. I just leave it to him, but I'm sure he has everything under control.'

He looks at me. 'When has Dad had anything under control?' he mutters under his breath.

I fold the letter and stuff it in my pocket. 'I'll ask him about it later, make sure it's all OK, but he does this, shuffles money about so he always gets the best deal on interest rates and stuff.' My heart beats frantically in contradiction of my words. 'Don't worry, it'll be fine.'

He stares at me.

'It will!' I smile and go back to my lasagne, though it tastes like cotton wool in my mouth.

After a moment, Felix picks up his fork too and starts to eat.

'I just . . . well, I wanted to make sure you knew. I panicked, thought that you might lose everything if . . .'

'It's OK.' I reach out to him. 'Thank you for worrying about us, but you don't need to.'

'And you'll talk to Dad? Ask him about it? Find out what . . .'

'Promise! I wouldn't say so otherwise, would I?'

I go to talk about something else, but see that he's still staring at me, his face full of concern. 'I'll sort this,' I tell him. 'So you can stop worrying. You'll always be my baby boy and I'll always be the parent, so let me worry about this letter and you can just forget about it, OK? I'll not let you down, everything is fine, sweetheart.'

By the time he leaves, Felix is calmer. After he's gone, I take out the letter and examine it. It's everything he said. Mortgage, missed payments, threatening legal action, bankruptcy.

Bankruptcy.

I think about Felix's words. *He's been lying to you.*

There must be an explanation. I know business has been bad, but if it were *that* bad, he'd have told me. Wouldn't he? It looks like the loan was taken out a year ago. What has he been spending all the money on?

I call Paul, but it goes to voicemail. I start to leave a message, then stop, unsure what to say. Instead, I ring the taxi office.

'Sheila,' I say when the phone is answered, 'it's Lou. I need to get hold of Paul. Do you know where he is? He said he was in the office. Could you find him?'

There's a moment's silence, then, 'He's taken an airport run. Want me to get him on the radio if he's not picking up?'

159

'No, no, it's fine,' I tell her. He won't be able to talk properly in front of clients anyway. 'I'll catch him later.'

I grab my laptop, bring up the bank website and log in to our account. I can see our joint account and our savings account – which is a complete joke as there is exactly forty pounds in there – but I can't access Dilenby Taxis. Paul is the only one who sees those bank details.

I go to the joint account and bring up the transactions. I do this regularly, but then I do something I never do and scroll back through the history.

Bloody hell, it makes for terrifying reading. All those debits and hardly any credits. My hands start to sweat, my fingers slipping on the keyboard.

A new phone for Felix, kitchen gadgets for my mother to make her life easier, the work that needed doing on my car, a new iPad for Paul so he could watch TV between jobs when he was at the office. I look at the recent loan we took out, the influx of cash that paid for my MOT, for the boiler that needed to be repaired, and how the money was gobbled up, and now the repayments will increase as the interest rate rises ... I snap my laptop shut as nausea takes hold.

It feels like I can't breathe. Like something is tight around my chest, squeezing me from all sides. I go to the window to get some fresh air. It feels like I'm being dragged down and down, and I can't see an end to it.

I need to get out, to do something instead of sitting in the kitchen thinking about all the debt. I'll go to my mother's early, have a look at the cameras. See if I can fix them, or at least work out why they're telling her people are outside her door when there's no one there.

I hastily clean the kitchen, shoving the plates into the

dishwasher, and leave a note for Paul telling him about the lasagne and the beer in the fridge. Then I look at what I've written, and suddenly a bolt of anger comes out of nowhere.

I know the debt isn't all Paul's fault; I know I spend above our means, but I hate the conversation I just had with Felix, seeing his anxiety. I hate that we're in this position. I hate that I feel so trapped by it all. And in that moment, that split second, I want to blame him for all of it.

Why didn't he tell me? Why didn't he discuss it with me before mortgaging the Dilenby Taxis building? But I know exactly why he didn't want to talk about how bad it was, why he works all hours and I hardly ever see him.

It's because he can't let go.

Can't admit the business is over. Because if he did, what would that mean? What would that say about him? The choices he's made and the choices he has left? What would that mean for both of us?

I get to my mother's in a bit of a state. My jaw is tightly clenched and I'm shaking slightly. I'm going over and over ways I could possibly get us out of debt, but I can't think of anything. There's nothing.

My phone buzzes as I get out of the car, and I pick it up, hoping it's Paul, hoping we'll talk and he'll tell me that everything is under control, that there's a perfectly good reason why he took out that mortgage. But it's not Paul. It's Instagram again. This time I've been tagged in a post. It's from the same account that made a comment on my Spanish lessons post earlier, but this time I read the username properly and freeze.

@Dilenbyscandal4848

Something drops in my stomach as my heart beats rapidly.

I bring up the post. It isn't a picture, it's a text post. Bold

161

letters on a colourful background. I read it twice before it dawns on me what it's all about.

The earlier comment had nothing to do with my Spanish lessons. It wasn't talking about my teaching offer at all.

I look up quickly, stare around me as though the person who posted it might be close by, then read the words again.

I know a dirty secret! It's about someone local, someone pretending to be prim and proper. This is now a game of 'I know something you don't know', but when will I tell?

I'm the only person tagged in the post, and I quickly go to settings to untag myself before screenshotting the image. Then I go to my conversation with Oscar. The dancing GIF of a ghost that seemed amusing just a short while ago.

Someone knows.

TWENTY-THREE

Oscar texts back almost immediately. It's a well-known scam, he tells me. You get an email, or are tagged on a social media post saying they know something about you, and in your panic you contact them, and that's when a demand for money is made.

Google it, he has messaged. Loads of people have reported it. Then block the account and forget about it.

I walk into my mother's, say hello and make my way into the kitchen. As the kettle boils, I do a quick search on my phone. Oscar is right. It's known as 'sextortion' – when someone threatens to publish sexual information about someone else in an effort to get money. The post I was tagged in is a phishing post, tagging random people to hopefully get a bite from someone who is doing something they shouldn't. I block and report the account and try to forget about it, but it's useless.

I make it through the rest of the afternoon being the most self-critical I've ever been. I hate not only Paul, but Instagram, the internet, the fact that sextortion is even a thing. But mostly I hate myself.

By the time Monday's lesson comes around, I have a plan in place.

'Hello, you,' Oscar says as he walks through the back door, and I almost cave immediately. What I haven't prepared for is how the memories of our night together leap in my mind as soon as we lock eyes. How my skin tingles at the thought of his touch, how I instantly remember the smell of him, the feel of his body beneath mine. I flush, and he smiles, a slow, lazy smile that makes me melt.

'I need you to look at the cameras,' I say firmly, and he raises an eyebrow. For a second, I feel bad at being so prickly, but I need him to know how it is between us now. 'My mum thinks they're playing up. Can you check them over, please? We had to switch them off yesterday as they keep detecting movement when no one is there.'

I sit with Mum while he checks, watching a game show with her in the lounge. My body is rigid, taut, and I'm perched on the edge of the seat until he comes back in.

'They're all fine,' he says. 'Nothing wrong with them. What did you say they were doing?'

'That beep.' My mother waves her hands. 'They beeped to let me know someone was outside the door, but when I checked through the window, no one was there. I could hear them, though. Voices. There was someone, but they must've been hiding when I got there. Playing knock-and-run.'

When I look at Oscar's face, a tight pull goes around my chest. He has that look. The one that is sympathetic and pitying and says that my mother is imagining things again, and as he catches my eye, his pity extends to me, and everything he doesn't need to say is obvious. I close my eyes and take a deep breath.

'How about,' I begin, 'we turn off the sound. Can we do that?' I look at Oscar, and he gives a nod. 'That way, Mum, I'll get the notification on my app if anyone is outside the house, but you won't hear anything. We don't want it frightening you with every bird or cat that passes by.'

'Was that it?' she asks, and her face is intense. I can see the fear behind her eyes. 'Was it a cat or something?'

I look to Oscar, and he catches on to what I'm doing. 'Most probably,' he says, and goes over to my mother, puts his hand on hers. 'It's my fault. I should have warned you about that. If an animal gets in the way of the sensor, it can make it beep.'

Mum breathes out a huge sigh of relief, and I see how much this has been worrying her. More than she let on to me.

'Oh, thank goodness,' she says, and smiles up at me. 'I thought I was losing a marble or two for a minute.'

'Not you, Viv.' Oscar smiles at her. 'This one was my fault.'

She laughs, suddenly relaxed, and in that moment, I love him. I love him for his kindness in the lie he's telling her, for going along with my story and making her feel better.

'I've checked the cameras over,' he says quietly as we go into the kitchen for our lesson. 'I think it was just . . .'

I give a small nod to stop him from continuing.

'I need to speak to her GP about her medication,' I tell him. 'It's been on my to-do list for a while. It's making her hear stuff. Making her fearful and paranoid, and I can't bear it.'

'Hey.' He comes over and wraps his arms around me, and for a moment I let myself relax into him, breathing in the scent of him and closing my eyes.

It would be so easy.

I snap myself awake, pushing myself off him, and he tilts his head at me. I give him a look and then point to the table.

'Shall we get started?'

He looks at me quizzically for a second, and then goes to shut the kitchen door.

'No,' I tell him, 'I'd like it kept open, please.'

'But . . .' he glances into the lounge, where my mother has the game show on full blast, 'I might find it hard to concentrate, and I think, given what happened . . .'

'Nothing happened.' My words come out in a rush. 'It was a one-time thing and I'd had far too much wine. I think it's best if we draw a line under it.' I'm trying to keep my voice low, my words hushed, even though my mother wouldn't be able to hear me over the sound of the television.

I sit down and point to the chair opposite.

'I thought,' I say carefully, 'that given what happened on Friday, it'd be best if we had some rules.'

'Rules?'

I nod. 'Lessons with the door open from now on. Sitting opposite each other and . . .' I look up. He's smiling at me, and I flush. These rules sounded a lot better when I came up with them in my head.

'I can't,' I whisper across the table at him. 'I'm married and it can't happen again.' I look at my papers.

'Let's get to it then, shall we?'

I look up. There's a brisk tone to his voice, and he nods.

'I can do professional,' he says quietly. 'I can be a model student.' He holds up his hands. 'I won't flirt, I'll keep my hands to myself. Let's not make any hasty decisions over one night. You're a great teacher, and I need to learn this stuff. OK?'

And it's there again, a childish voice in my head saying, *Not OK! Flirt with me. Tell me you can't keep your hands off me. Tell me . . .*

'OK,' I hear myself say, and I swallow, my throat tight and constricting. 'And you won't tell . . .?'

He mimes locking his lips and throwing away a key, and I smile at the playground gesture.

'Promise,' he says, and that slow smile, the one whose effect he's completely unaware of, spreads across his face. 'You're safe with me, Louise,' he says quietly. 'I wouldn't do anything to hurt you.'

I stare at him. Our eyes lock, and it's an effort to drag them to the papers we should be studying.

'Let's start on this worksheet,' I say.

We begin the lesson, but it soon becomes apparent that it won't work sitting opposite each other.

'Hey,' he says as he changes seats, 'we're OK here. Everything is fine.'

But as he sits beside me, his thigh touches mine and a jolt of electricity runs through me. I look at him, but he's staring at the paper.

I begin to go through the exercise, not even listening to my voice, unable to concentrate on the sounds I'm making. All my focus, every ounce of attention, is on his proximity. The smell of him, the energy between us. I get halfway through a sentence and lose myself, forget what I'm saying or where I'm up to. My words trail off and I look up to see him staring at me, our faces incredibly close. I stop talking, the breath caught in my throat.

I can hear the canned laughter from my mother's game show. I know the door is wide open, that she could be up from her chair and come pottering in at any moment, catch us inches apart, but I lean the tiniest bit forward and our mouths meet. The touch is like a dam bursting. Memories from our night together flood into my mind and I lean into them, into him. Let my hands travel up his chest and his hands move on my thighs. There's another cheer from the television and I pull away, panting and short of breath.

'Oh God. What are we doing? I'm not sure I can ... I mean ...' I look up at him. 'I've never, ever done anything like this before.'

'I haven't slept with any married women either, if that's what you mean,' he says. 'You are my first.'

I get up and shut the door, then lean on it trying to catch my breath, as if I've just run a marathon. His eyes are on me, I can feel them, his stare making my skin tingle, making me come alive like I haven't been in years. I can feel the temptation, the closeness of him, the way I know for certain that if I give into it, if I were to kiss him again, I would feel good. All the worry, panic and anxiety would float away and there would only be him. It's like a drug. A drug that's impossible to resist.

'Look ...' he begins. 'I leave in three months.'

'Three months?' I say, and look back to him, our eyes locking.

'Things like this, like us, they don't happen very often, Louise. We have something here. There is something between us. I know you feel it.' He takes a deep breath, and I notice the way he's holding his hands clenched tightly together, his fingers wrapping around themselves in a nervous knot. The realisation that this is hitting him as hard as it's hitting me is like a push. It's like a shove towards him and everything we're about to do. 'Shouldn't we enjoy it while we can?' he asks in a quiet voice.

I stare at him, his words echoing around my head. The urge to go to him is like a magnetic pull.

'It's not like this can ever be anything serious,' I say, more to myself than him. 'I mean, the age gap for a start ...'

'We're both adults. And we can stop at any time.'

'I can't have my husband or my son or my mother or anyone else finding out.' My words are coming out in a rush. As if I'm not really in control of them.

'Of course.'

'We meet at your flat, where I can make up an excuse as to why I'm there. Extra lessons, for example.'

'Makes sense.'

'No affectionate displays in public, and it ends when you start your trip, if not before.'

'At any time.'

I stare at him. My body is vibrating with excitement. Now that it's real, something we've discussed, it's terrifying but thrilling. He moves towards me as if he's going to kiss me, but I shake my head. 'Thursday,' I tell him, my voice almost a whisper. 'Our next lesson.'

As he collects his things and leaves, an irresistible smile playing on his face, I'm shaking slightly, already unsure about what I've just done. An affair. I've started an affair.

TWENTY-FOUR

When I walk into Gary's shop the following Wednesday, I'm more than prepared.

I see him coming and put my hands on his upper arms, keeping him at a distance as he leans in for a greeting that I ensure is nothing more than air kisses.

He grins at me, as if I'm playing some kind of secret game, and my insides recoil, although I keep a smile firmly plastered on my face.

The letter Felix brought round has been in my handbag since Saturday. I haven't had a chance to discuss it with Paul yet, unable to muster the courage to confront him about it. I can feel it in there, heavy, like a rock. It bumps against my hip as I pull back from Gary. I need this job. There have been no enquiries since I put my flyers out, no messages asking for details on my social media posts, only an email from someone asking if I had space next summer. Next summer! I need the money now.

'See what I've done for you!' Gary says as he takes me through to the back of the shop. Trudy is flipping lazily through a magazine and looks up as I pass. She gives a slight shake of her head at Gary's enthusiastic patter and goes back to the magazine.

He leads me into the room and I see there are two large fans going full blast. Brilliant. Now, not only will I be in a private, confined space with Gary, but I'll also be cold.

'I hope this is enough,' he says as we go to the table. 'If you're not comfortable in here, we could always go up to my flat? Try there?'

'This is perfect!' I shake my head at his suggestion. 'The fans are brilliant. Thank you.'

I get out my papers as Gary sits at the table, his fingers drumming on the surface.

'You're still teaching Oscar at your mother's?'

I falter a little at his name, feel my cheeks flush and keep my head down.

'Yep.' I put the folder on the table. 'Shall we—'

'So not in his flat? You don't go to anyone's flat?'

I frown. 'I teach my students in a variety of places,' I say carefully, 'and this is perfect for us.'

He looks around the back room and gives a nod.

'It's very thoughtful of you to get the fans. Thank you,' I say, and hope I've shown enough gratitude, because if Gary insists we go upstairs, I'm not sure what I'll do.

As I get my laptop out, my phone buzzes. I ignore it. I'm laying out the lesson plan when it buzzes again. My eyes flick to my handbag and Gary leans in.

'You want to see what that is?'

I shake my head.

'Could be important,' he says, and I shake my head again.

'It's fine,' I say, and start to read out the lesson plan, but my mind is on my phone. On the notifications I've had and what they might say.

Since we made the rules for our affair, Oscar has been texting me, and it's rapidly turned into something that's fun and sexy. Something alien to me. I get a thrill of pleasure every time there's a notification sound on my phone. Paul and I have only ever messaged with necessities. What do you want for dinner? Can you collect Felix later? Are you able to pick up some milk? And so now, to have texts that are charming, flattering and sexy is a delight.

How about we do a lesson covering body parts? was Oscar's last message. Or instructions for movement?

The innuendos are ridiculous. Silly. Stupid things that make me blush with embarrassment and smirk like a kid, but they're also incredibly endearing. They make me feel excited and attractive. Having limited experience of any of this, I'm not sure how I'd react if he sent me serious messages, the ones you read about in books, sexting-type messages – like asking what I find hot, or describing what he's going to do to me next time we meet. But wordplay is safe. It's just suggestive enough and makes me feels like I'm not too much out of my depth.

We were messaging well into the night, and now I'm wondering if Thursday is too far away. Twenty-four hours feels like such a long time.

'So, the letter,' I say quickly, as I take it out of the folder. I smooth it out on the table between us, and any excitement I felt is gone in an instant. 'I did my best, but to be honest,

Gary, it didn't read like it was written by someone who ...'
I falter. I haven't thought about how to say this. How to
tell him that I know he's been writing these letters to himself. That I know his Spanish girlfriend is a figment of his
imagination.

'I need to show you something,' he says, and gets up. 'Be
back in a moment, don't move.' He leaves through the door to
the upper flat before I can say anything.

I look around the room at the boxes of stock, the table that
keeps us close together, the whirring fans. I think how I'll
probably tell him that it was my fault. That I didn't recognise
the words and some of the phrases in the letter. That it must be
the region of Spain she's from and that I'm not familiar with
that dialect. But then a surge of anger rises up in me.

Why should I lie and make excuses and go along with
Handy Gary and his pathetic made-up girlfriend?

Because I need the money.

I grit my teeth. I won't be the first woman who's had to
put up with something uncomfortable because she needs the
pay cheque at the end, and I won't be the last. But whereas
thoughts like that used to get me through, now I find myself
wondering what kind of stupid woman puts up with that. Is
it really worth it?

I look over at my bag on the chair opposite. I can almost
see the letter from the bank inside demanding my attention. I
think about the horrid conversation I have to have with Paul,
the talk that I'm avoiding, that I want to hide away from, and
the hatred and resentment I felt towards him at the weekend
surges back. Why do I have to be the one to take charge and
confront him? Seek him out and initiate this awful discussion?
Why is it always up to me? I feel like a grumpy teenager being

forced to do some menial task that they know is beneath them. I want to sulk, to shout, 'It's not fair!' Instead, I pull the lesson plan and worksheet towards me and make myself concentrate. Behaving like a stroppy schoolgirl won't get me very far.

I hear Gary's footsteps on the stairs, making his way back down to me with whatever nonsense he's been making up, and I can't seem to push the anger down like I usually do. A sullen voice whispers in my ear, reminding me how much I hate every aspect of this.

'Here.' He bursts back into the room holding something out. He hands it to me. A box. Pink velvet.

'I bought it for her,' he says, 'a while ago, but she has since told me she hates silver and so I wondered if you wanted it. I'll only throw it away otherwise. I have no one else to give it to.'

Inside the box is a heavy silver chain with a heart locket.

'Open it,' he urges.

I pick up the heart. It's large, and as I open it, I see that it's been engraved.

Mi Amor.

I stare at the words. This is too much. It's all too much.

'You can tell people it's from your secret lover.' Gary gives me a playful push. 'Get that husband of yours all jealous.'

He starts to laugh, and I shut the box quickly and hand it back to him.

'No,' I tell him, and suddenly the room feels too small. It feels tiny. 'I can't do this any more.'

'Lou?'

'I can't be in here. With you.'

I start to pack up my papers quickly. The tight, constricting feeling I had the other day is back. It's squeezing around my chest, making it difficult to breathe, and the anger, the sense of revulsion, is rising like a tidal wave.

I think of him buying that locket, of getting it engraved, knowing all the while that there is no Spanish girlfriend and this is all a sham. The lessons, the letter and now the necklace. I stuff the pages into the folder. I can't get out of here fast enough.

'Lou, please!' Gary protests. 'You can't leave now! The lesson has only just started! We need to go through days of the week and—'

'I can't do it,' I say again. 'I can't be here. I can't teach you any more, Gary.'

He stares at me a moment.

'You can't teach me any more?'

Now that I've said the words aloud, they sound right. They sound like something I should've said a long time ago. They ease the tightness around my chest, and I nod.

'I'm afraid not. I was going to tell you later, but it's better that I do it now. Before we begin. I have other students and can't—'

'Other students? But I've been with you for months.'

'I'm sorry,' I say as I pick up my bag, 'but that's how it is. I can't continue teaching you and . . .' I glance at the pink velvet box on the table, 'you won't be seeing me again.'

Trudy looks surprised as I leave, Gary trailing behind, his face a mass of confusion. She gives a smirk and I almost expect her to start clapping; for the few customers in the shop and the people on the street outside to join in. Applaud me for doing this at last.

I walk quickly to my car, my heart beating fast, but aside from the voice screaming at me that I shouldn't be doing this, that I really need the money, there's a light feeling. I want to run and jump and cheer. I ignore Gary's voice behind me and open the car door, throwing in my bag and laptop.

'Lou, please.' He grabs the door, holding it tight so I can't shut it. I try to pull it out of his grasp, but he keeps a firm grip. 'Can't we discuss this? If it's your hormones, your sudden change of—'

'It's you, Gary,' I tell him, and before I can stop myself, words rush out of me. 'You're inappropriate. The letter, the way you try to be so close all the time, the way you insist on kissing me hello, and now the necklace.' I shake my head. 'It's too much and I've had enough. I've had enough of it all. I think it's best that we don't continue the lessons.'

'But Lou . . . you can't mean . . .'

I get into the car and try to close the door, but he's still holding on to it.

'Goodbye, Gary,' I say and stare at the door, then at him, waiting for him to move.

Slowly he steps away, and as soon as he's clear, I yank on the door and slam it shut.

As I start the engine, I can see his mouth moving, his hands gesticulating, but I can't make out what he's saying. Then, as I back up before turning out into the road, I catch his final words.

'. . . not finished yet.'

I watch him in my rear-view mirror as he gets smaller and smaller. He continues to stare after me, but instead of his usual smile and wave, his hands are on his hips and he's glaring at me.

Not finished yet.

Yes, we are, Gary. We are completely and utterly finished, and I never want to see you again.

TWENTY-FIVE

Later that afternoon, I'm at my pensioners' group.

Usually I really enjoy teaching them and getting lost in the conversations about who is doing what, but my mind is elsewhere. It's filled with relief at ending the lessons with Gary, and it's on my phone. On the notifications. My mind is on Oscar.

It's stupid, I know I'm being stupid and silly and behaving worse than a schoolgirl, but my God, it's ridiculously exciting. When my phone buzzes and I know he's sent me a message, the dopamine rush is real.

I stare at the last one he sent and can't stop myself from smiling.

What do I have to do to get an A in class?

So corny. So cringe and cheesy and absolutely wonderful. He must be getting these gags off the internet, but I lap them up.

I send a GIF back of an eye-roll and marvel at myself. Last week I wasn't even sure what a GIF was.

Do you have a map of Spain? I'm getting so very lost
In my thoughts of you.

I smile and type out a quick reply.

I'M TEACHING! Stop sending texts!

But I can't stop thinking about our extracurricular
activities.

A giggle escapes me, and that's when I realise the room has gone quiet.

I look up to a mass of expectant faces. I set them the task of having a conversation with three topic prompts, and wasn't watching progress. I quickly switch my phone to silent and put it down.

'Sorry, sorry,' I say, 'just having a few problems with . . .' I shake my head. I was going to say 'my mother'. She's been my reason for lack of focus for so long, the words came to me without even thinking, and now I surprise myself with delight at the real reason I'm distracted.

'It's love!' Marie says, a wide beam on her face that shows off her perfect false teeth. 'I'd know that look anywhere. What's that husband of yours been up to?'

The class laughs and I feel the heat intensify in my cheeks.

'Oh, nothing. Right, shall we . . .'

'She's blushing!' Derek declares. He's my best student, has a second home in Palma and skin like leather. 'Look at her! She's blushing like mad!' He's usually charming and sweet, but at that moment, I really dislike him.

'OK, everyone,' I say, trying to regain control, 'let's hear what you've been talking about. Who'd like to go first? Lisa?'

Lisa smiles at me, usually quiet in class but now ready to talk.

'Whatever that husband of yours is messaging you about,

keep doing it,' she says, and there's agreement all round. 'You look the best I've ever seen you!'

Everyone bursts into laughter, and I shout over them and then start to laugh with them. After a moment, I get the lesson back on track and listen to how the weather is and when the bus to the city is leaving, but my mind is half on what they're saying and half on Lisa's words. *The best I've ever seen you.*

And I feel it too. I feel the best I have in ages. I have more energy, more clarity, more everything. I want to study my reflection. See if there's a change myself. I have taken to wearing my hair down, spending a few more minutes on it in the morning rather than just scooping it up and out of the way in my usual ponytail. And I've been wearing jewellery again. Not sure why or when I stopped, but now I'm putting on my hoop earrings and layered necklaces and even a dash of eyeshadow and mascara.

But I know that's not what Lisa is talking about. She's talking about why it's been easier for me getting up these past few mornings. Why I find things amusing and charming. Why I'm no longer just getting through the days but enjoying them.

The lesson ends and I look back at my phone. Three more messages from Oscar before he realised I wasn't replying and signed off with You're teaching me so much more than Spanish, Mrs Whitstable.

I feel the heat in my cheeks again, the delicious whoosh of excitement through my chest.

As I reach my car, there's another notification and I pull out my phone quickly. A voicemail message. I smile, a wonderful anticipation building as I wonder what Oscar was calling about, and then, as I hear Paul's voice, it's like a slap. Like I've been caught out.

'Hello, love, sorry to bother you when you're at work. I

figured you'd have your phone off and I could leave a message. Anyway, I've been chatting with Tony and we've had an idea. How about making your mum's house into separate flats instead of renting it out as an Airbnb or to just one family? That way, the money it'll bring in will . . .'

I don't listen to any more. I end the message and call his mobile. It rings out, as usual, and then kicks in to voicemail.

'Paul. I can't believe you're ringing me to talk about this. Discussing it with Tony. I don't know how many times I have to tell you, but my mother isn't going anywhere. That's *her* house. Not mine, not Felix's and certainly not yours!'

I end the call and immediately go to the taxi rank, but they can't get hold of him either. In any case, this isn't a conversation to have when he's driving. But then when do we have time for conversations? I've yet to confront him about the letter from the bank. Every time I think of calling him, of leaving a message about it or texting, I tell myself I'll do it later, but I've still got my head in the sand. I know we'll need a good hour to go through everything, and at the moment it feels impossible. With him working nights and his darts, and me teaching and my mother, we pass each other as we're either coming or going.

I stare at my phone in the car park. Wondering if he's still giving Denise darts lessons. How can he be so sympathetic to her father, a stranger, but not to his own mother-in-law?

'Money,' I whisper to myself.

If we went ahead with his plan, it would solve our financial issues, but my mum would be in a care home. And as Dilenby doesn't have any of those, she'd be in a care home on the other side of Manchester. A good hour away. A place where she knows no one. I picture her in my mind, sitting in an armchair that isn't hers, watching a television with a group of strangers in a large living room. Or, even worse, shut up in a room on her own. Me making the two-hour round trip to see her, and only able to spend short amounts of time with her here and there. Why can Paul not see how horrendous this is? Why is he pushing it so much?

I pick up my phone and call him again. When it hits voice-mail, I take a deep breath and leave another message.

'We need to talk. Urgently. Can you make time before the weekend? Or at the weekend. What about Sunday? Cancel your darts thing and I'll do a roast. It's important.'

I hang up with a feeling of relief. I'll cook a joint, do all the trimmings, and then, when we've eaten, I'll show him the letter and we'll go through it all. That gives me time to look through the accounts, to work out how much we have coming in, how much we can start to pay back, and what our budget is.

My stomach clenches at the thought, and I feel a little sick. Even though I know we've been living beyond our means for far too long and it can't go on, I still don't want to do anything about it. The familiar feeling of dread and refusal floods over me, and my head fills with the well-worn excuses I've used over the years: how I won't be able to get all the information I need, how I don't have time to go through our finances. I sigh and navigate to my banking app, putting in a request to have the past twelve months' statements emailed to me. Something tangible that I can't ignore, that I can highlight and put in front of Paul along with the letter from the bank. Props to guide me through.

My phone goes again, and I jump. A text from Oscar.

Don't suppose you have time for extracurricular
lessons today?

I stare at the message. I know what it means and suddenly

181

I find my fingers working.

I have time right now.

I see the words on the screen and press send.

Three dots. I hold my breath, waiting for his reply.

See you in five at my flat.

TWENTY-SIX

'It's fine, Mum, there's no one there.' I show her the camera app on my phone. The scene of her empty doorway and drive. 'No one,' I repeat, and she stares at the screen.

It's six o'clock on Sunday morning and I'm at her house, coat thrown over my pyjamas. She called at five, insisting that some-one had been out in her driveway for most of the night. That she hadn't got a wink of sleep and had waited until it was a decent hour to call me. I thought about asking her since when five a.m. was a decent hour, but didn't. Instead, I drove over to reassure her, sipping strong coffee out of my travel mug on the way.

'Shall I make us some breakfast?' I suggest.

'I couldn't eat a thing. Not after the night I've had.'

I go to the kitchen and switch the kettle on. Put a couple of slices of bread in the toaster and take hold of the counter as I try to organise my thoughts.

This is not getting better. I had a look at her medication, a brief chat with her GP, who reviewed it all and was adamant that her meds are not the cause of her confusion. He advised a blood test to check for kidney and thyroid function and a visit for some cognitive assessments.

'Assessments?' I asked him. 'What are you assessing her for?' Though I already knew the answer.

He told me that the tests wouldn't necessarily diagnose anything, but they would be a way to see if further investigations were needed.

Further investigations.

I grip the counter.

'Have you told Paul what the doctor said?' Oscar asked me earlier that week. We were in his flat, in bed. There can be no doubt now that we're having an affair. I've had sex with him four times. That can no longer be described as an accident, can it? I'm in the strange and exciting land of being a mistress, and although I hate to admit it, the thrill of it all is wonderful. I know it sounds clichéd, but when I'm with him, I switch off who I am and become someone else. Someone I never thought I'd get a chance to be.

It was while I was being this other person that reality gate-crashed and my mother called asking me to check the camera app. She was certain she'd seen a shadow pass the lounge window. I sat up in Oscar's bed, his black duvet pulled against my naked chest, and looked at the empty driveway, assuring her no one was there.

'The cameras are fine,' he explained after I'd finished the call, 'and if the doctor thinks that ...' he kissed the back of my bare shoulder, 'maybe you should ...'

'It's fine.'

I shut the conversation down. Dressed quickly, not wanting the two parts of my life to collide. 'I'll sort it. It's fine.'

184

But it isn't fine.

I haven't told Paul; I haven't told anyone. I told the doctor to wait, to give it another month or so. That my mother was under a lot of stress; work was being done on the house and that could be the source of the disorientation. I said I'd monitor her and check back in a month, and book the blood tests in the meantime.

And now here I am. Just gone six in her kitchen, making tea and toast I don't want, refusing to believe that this could be what everyone else is telling me it is.

'Here,' I say as I hand her some heavily buttered toast, 'try to eat something, and then let's get you back to bed. I'll stay here while you sleep. I'll be right here.'

She looks up at me, and her face relaxes.

'You'll stay here?'

I nod.

'What will you do? Watch telly?'

'I've some work to get on with,' I tell her. 'Don't worry, I'll be in the kitchen, working at the table, and I'll be as quiet as anything. If anyone comes by, I'll be here.'

She smiles at me, and I put my hand to her white hair. Soft as feathers.

'That's nice,' she says, and takes a bite of toast. 'I'll relax knowing you're downstairs. Get some rest.'

'That's probably all you need,' I say, and as the words leave my mouth, I clutch at them. 'Of course that's it. You're over-tired. You just need a few nights' decent sleep and you'll be fine.'

I spend the next couple of hours going over the bank statements I printed out. Paul has cancelled his darts lesson and taken the day off work. Lunch is at one, and by then I need to be clear on what I have to say to him and how I say it. What I need to suggest.

I highlight a payment we made for a meal delivery service that we later cancelled, and rub at the back of my neck. I'm swinging between being furious at myself and furious with Paul. All these things we spent money on in an effort to make life easier. Meal delivery, gadgets and gym memberships and subscriptions to various television platforms that we never watch. It's all here in black and white. As is how much I've actually earned over the past year, and although it's more than I first thought, what is becoming apparent is that it's nowhere near enough. Paul's drop in income combined with my irregular wage is barely enough to cover our basics.

Taking off my glasses, I sit for a moment and look out of the window. My eyes rest on Rick's bungalow and I wonder what he's up to. What he does on a Sunday morning with no problems and no one else to think about. My mind wanders to the other me in Spain. It's like saying hello to an old friend, and something I've not done in a while.

I imagine her looking out over the sparkling blue sea with a coffee in her hand. Money in her bank account from the work she does over at the property business, a flat all to herself, no one demanding things, no one making her work out budgets or asking her to cook a roast and discuss shutting down a family business. She can have sex with whoever she likes. Take a different lover every day of the week if she wants to. This unfamiliar landscape I'm navigating, with its dips and thrills, is her home. She looks back at me, her face outlined in the reflection of the window, then fades away. She was never real; she was someone I was growing into before my father and brother died, and she died along with them.

186

I look at myself. Lou Whitstable. Stuck in my mother's kitchen, going over bank statements and trying to find a way out of the mess.

'And now what?' I whisper to the empty kitchen. 'What happens now?'

TWENTY-SEVEN

Later that day, I fill two plates with roast beef and all the trimmings: roast potatoes, cauliflower cheese, carrots and peas, Yorkshire pudding. I debated whether wine was a good idea, but I need it. I take a large gulp of Merlot, then carry the food to the table and call out for Paul. He was only just up when I returned from my mother's, and has spent the past hour and a half getting himself together.

When he enters the kitchen, his face is ashen.

'This looks nice,' he says in a quiet voice. 'It's not often we do this.'

I let out a nervous laugh as I put the plates down.

'But I'm glad you made me cancel my plans today.' He pulls out a chair and sits in it heavily. 'This talk is long overdue.'

I glance up at him, and his eyes are filled with something ominous. My heart speeds up at that look, almost bursting out of my chest. Over the years, I've learned to read Paul's expression, and know when he's disappointed about something.

When he tells me how much the car is going to cost after the scratch I gave it, when he tells me that he doesn't like the meal I've cooked or can't make something due to darts practice. The look on his face now is the one that braces me for bad news, and I freeze.

He knows.

He knows exactly what I did. What I'm doing. He knows it all.

'I'll just get the wine,' I say, and go back into the kitchen. I'm shaking and breathing hard. I try to think logically. How could he know anything? Maybe Felix told him about the letter from the bank after all. Maybe his expression is because of the mortgage. I flounder with possibilities in my head, ready to tell him anything he needs to hear if he should ask about Oscar.

I'm teaching him at his flat now, we were disturbing my mother too much.

I'm doing more lessons with him like you said, trying to get more money together.

The words rattle around in my brain as I top up my glass and take the bottle back into the dining room.

When I walk in, Paul looks up and gives me a sad smile. That smile is terrifying. I hear a strangled laugh escape me. 'Don't look like that!' I try to make a joke of it. 'It's not so bad having Sunday lunch together, is it?'

He stares at me as I sit opposite him, the gravy slightly congealing on our plates.

'Sorry, sorry.' He picks up his knife and fork. Puts them down again. 'This is lovely, really lovely, and so nice of you to ...' He waves at the food. 'I've been awful lately. Avoiding you.'

'Avoiding me?'

He rubs a hand over his face.

'I shouldn't have. I should have come straight to you once I found out. Talked to you. Done this.'

My heart is beating so hard I can feel it in my head. I wonder how he isn't distracted by the sound.

'Is this Felix?' I ask, my voice small. 'Did he tell you about the letter?'

A cloud crosses his face. 'What letter?'

I shake my head. My mouth has gone dry, and I can't find the words. I think about the bank statements waiting in my handbag and almost get up and fetch them as a way to steer the conversation.

'I shouldn't have been skirting around this,' he goes on. 'Honesty is always the best policy and all that, and I think it's time we were honest with each other.'

'Honest . . .'

I trail off, my voice strained. The excuses I practised moments ago are gone; my mind is blank. If Paul were to ask me about my affair with Oscar now, I'd be lost as to how to answer. I have nothing in my defence. My guilt rises like a tidal wave, and an urge to confess it all bubbles up inside of me.

His hands curl into fists on the table. 'There's something I need to tell you about.'

I try to swallow, but my throat is tight, strangling me. I brace myself.

'I've got to have some tests.'

I stare at him.

'What?'

'Don't panic,' he says, and he moves his hands, leans forward and grips mine. 'It's just tests.'

'Tests for what?'

'That heartburn I've been having.'

'You're having tests for heartburn?'

He nods. His complexion is grey, his eyes red-rimmed.

'It's not just heartburn,' he says slowly. 'There've been other symptoms. Palpitations. Dizziness. I didn't tell you because I didn't want you to worry, but the doctor . . . well, he did some tests, and among other things I've got high blood pressure, and he thinks it might be . . . well, they need to investigate further. He suggested I see a cardiologist.'

I stare at him, my hands in his, his face sombre and my heart thumping in my chest.

'A cardiologist?' I repeat, and he nods slowly. 'Your heart? The doctor thinks there's something wrong with your heart?'

'I knew you'd take it badly,' he says. 'This is why I put off telling you. But don't worry. It's just a few tests, and we'll get through it. We have each other and we'll get through it together.'

TWENTY-EIGHT

My head is spinning. I'm sitting in my mother's driveway, staring into space, trying to organise my thoughts. After our conversation yesterday, Paul and I tried to eat the meal I'd cooked, but it was useless. He went back to bed; said he was tired and wanted to get a few hours' rest before starting his shift. Said he felt a bit better about it all after talking it through with me. But I couldn't sit staring at the walls while he slept. I needed to be out.

I took a walk around the village, trying to work out everything in my head, but I still couldn't get my thoughts straight. They swirled around – the money, Paul's heart, Oscar – not a single one making any sense, and when I went to bed last night, I slept fitfully. I got up at six, and now, sitting outside Mum's house, my mind is still flitting about, trying to find a way out, like a bluebottle banging against a closed window.

Paul told me he's got a series of tests with a specialist coming up. Investigative tests. Intrusive tests. Tests that might confirm the doctor's suspicions about his heart and tests that I need to take him to and collect him from, being there for him like the wife he deserves . . .

I put my hands to my face, the weak morning light just breaking through the clouds. I think of what I was doing with Oscar while Paul was working through this alone. The worry, the stress. It suddenly all makes sense, why he was so drunk at the meal with Sophie and Felix. Why I haven't seen him at all the past few weeks.

He's been dealing with what the doctor told him while I was starting an affair.

His parting words from last night are still fresh in my mind. He told me how glad he was that I was there, that he had me, that he could lean on me in times like this, and when I started crying, he thought it was because of what he was telling me, but really it was because of what I'd done. What I am doing. I despised myself at that moment, and I still do.

My phone vibrates with a notification on my lap, and I jump. I'm twitchy, on the verge of tears. My eyes feel as if there's sandpaper behind the lids, and the back of my neck is tight. Oscar texted again last night with another pun on our extracurricular lessons, something about a field trip, and I deleted it immediately, disgusted with myself. And now I'm filled with guilt and shame, but even now, even after Paul said what he did, there's still an excited anticipation when my phone vibrates with a notification. An involuntary giddy sensation at the sound, an automatic response that I have no control over.

I snatch up the phone and stare at the screen.

It's a text. From Felix.

How did the meal go? Did Dad explain it all?

I stare at the words, forgetting for a moment that I told him my plans to discuss the letter with Paul. That he wasn't to worry, as we were going to talk it through and there would be a perfectly reasonable explanation as to what his dad was doing. In the end, of course, I didn't mention the letter. I couldn't even think about it once Paul told me about the tests.

All great, I text back quickly. *Just as I thought. Moving money around for the best deals. Everything is fine. Don't worry x*

All lies. But what else can I tell him? We decided to keep Paul's tests secret from Felix until we know something concrete.

'No point in worrying the lad if it turns out to be nothing more than indigestion,' Paul said with a half-laugh, and I agreed, but now I'm suddenly desperate to tell him. To share it with someone.

I go back to my phone and see that another text has come through.

OK, so you're ignoring my idea about a field trip. Bad idea. I'll make it up to you after the lesson tonight x

A rush of adrenaline surges through me and I'm furious with my body's betrayal. I go to text back and then stop. What will I say? That I feel the same, that I can't wait to see him later, but everything has changed now? That Paul might be seriously ill and the thought of him finding out what I've done is unthinkable?

My finger hovers over the keypad. I navigate to recent conversations instead and go to Helen. Her name calls out to me like a lighthouse in a storm.

Can you meet for a coffee today?

I stare at my words, willing her to reply.

I know you have your calls in Manchester, but can
you meet up?

I wait, and then add, Please.

I look at my three messages, highlighted in blue. The des-
peration is clear in my words. Three dots appear.

Is everything OK with your mum?

She's fine, I type back. Just really need to talk to you.

Sounds urgent!

It is.

A laughing emoji face appears.

Want to come here now? I have a couple of hours
before I need to leave.

I almost weep at the suggestion.

'So this is a first,' she says as she opens the door. 'You never
normally ...' She stops when she sees my face. 'What's
happened?'

Helen's house is always lovely, but this morning it's like a
haven. The comforting smell of coffee fills her large open-plan
kitchen, and anticipating my arrival, she's set out a plate of
croissants with jam and butter. I let the tears fall.

'Hey, hey.' She ushers me in and guides me to the dining
table. I hear footsteps on the upper floor and wipe my face
hastily. Moments later, Simon comes in. Tactfully, he doesn't
mention my tear-stained face. I nibble at a croissant while they
say their goodbyes, and once he's left, I stop trying to pretend.

'The boys are out,' Helen says, 'so tell me everything. I can
delay my morning meetings. What is it?'

I tell her about Oscar, about getting drunk and sleeping with
him. About doing it again. About Paul, his upcoming tests,
and lastly about the letter from the bank.

By the time I'm finished, I feel lighter, and my stomach is a ball of energy, tight and contracted.

Helen is silent. I look up at her. She's staring at me with wide eyes.

'You think I'm awful,' I whisper. 'You think I'm the worst person who ever lived.'

Her face snaps back into our conversation. 'Don't be ridiculous,' she says quickly. 'I think nothing like that, I'm just . . . taking it all in. The last time we spoke, you were meeting him to discuss the price of fitting the cameras at your mother's, and now . . .'

'I know! I know! I don't know how it's all happened so quickly. We were just talking about stuff, we got on so well, and he was telling me about his trip to South America and I was telling him about my time in Spain, and I drank too much wine and then when we were outside, and the thought of calling Paul to come and pick me up . . .' As I say Paul's name, my face crumples and I drop my head.

Helen comes round the table to me, her arm going around my shoulders. She makes comforting noises and lets me cry.

'OK,' she says as I wipe my face. 'It's not the end of the world.'

I stare at her, and she smiles at me.

'You're not the first person to be unfaithful.'

'I feel like the worst woman in the world.'

Helen gives a soft laugh. 'You're hardly that. You had a fling. It was a mistake. But it's all fixable.'

'Is it?'

She nods slowly. 'You can make it right. Tell Oscar. Finish it before Paul finds out.' She reaches across and puts her hand on mine. 'I'm so sorry to hear he's not well.'

We sit for a moment in silence. 'But Lou,' she says, 'if the issues with Paul's health weren't there, would we still be having this conversation? I mean, would you still want to . . .'

My head snaps up, and she raises her hand.

'I'm only asking because you and Paul . . .' she makes a sympathetic face, 'the way things are between you, sleeping in separate bedrooms, you just seem—'

'Paul could be seriously ill!' I shake my head. 'Sorry, I didn't mean to . . . It's just . . . if anything happened, if he found out what I'd done. Now. When he's going through this . . .'

'You think Oscar will keep it to himself?' Helen asks. 'Because it is fixable, but if you don't want Paul to find out . . .'

'He can never find out. Could you imagine if his heart . . . I mean, if he heard that I'd been unfaithful, and the shock . . .'

'So you just need to make sure Oscar keeps quiet for the next few months before he leaves.'

I nod.

'And you need to speak to Paul about the letter from the bank. It's not going to go away. Even with the tests at the hospital, you need to have that talk.'

I cover my face with my hands.

'I know, I know, it's just . . .'

'Hard.' Helen nods. 'But pretending your debt isn't there isn't going to make it disappear, I'm afraid.'

We talk for a long time. Practical talk. Logical talk. That's Helen's best feature. Her ability to stay completely calm in any crisis and offer the best advice. I leave with a plan of sorts. A way to give us some breathing space with the money stuff and a determination to end things with Oscar. I feel sick. I hate the thought of doing either. I want to go back to when everything was boring and normal and I was talking to Helen about nothing more than my mother's falls. I dig in my handbag for my phone. Is it bad manners to dump someone via text? I don't think I can do it in person. If I were to go to Oscar's for our lesson this evening, I'm not sure I'd be able to say the words I need to.

I have a notification. Instagram. I've been tagged again. Frowning, I open the app and see a post of a wagging finger with text underneath.

You've been very stupid, haven't you? Things are getting ugly. Time to reveal what I know.

TWENTY-NINE

I stare at the image of the finger mid-wag. Just a finger. Not even an offensive gesture, but it has the same impact as if someone were screaming the vilest curse inches from my face. My throat constricts, my stomach clenches and my eyes, hot and swollen from crying, can't look away from the image.

I go to the account again. This is only the third post. This isn't a scam or a well-known phishing exercise hoping to catch someone like me who has something to hide. This is personal. It has to be, doesn't it? I'm the only one who's been tagged and it doesn't feel random. It's talking about me. I untag myself and then give a loud groan as I see that the post has comments. The last time I looked at this account, it had zero followers, but now it has forty.

Spill the tea! I read. Tell us what you know!

I look at who wrote it, and see that it's someone who lives in the village, and my breathing gets shallow because I know how these things work. It only needs to attract one person's attention and soon everyone in Dilenby will know about it.

I go to Google. Frantically doing the same searches I did last week, hoping that a long list of results will appear telling me that yes, after they've tagged you in a post about a 'dirty secret', they then send you a finger-wagging post threatening to tell, but of course, nothing comes up. I get the same results as I did last time. An email, a message, a tag in a post, but not this. Not a continued threat, and certainly not from someone with a username of my village.

I look up at Helen's house. Could I go back in and show her? Ask her what to do about this? Get some more of her practical advice?

My face flushes. She already thinks I'm a terrible person; do I really want to add to that? I feel a moment of guilt over dropping all this at her door, but I've no idea what else to do.

I'm about to get out of the car, but stop as her front door opens. I'm parked a little way along the street, and I watch as she gets into her VW on the drive. She's put on her blazer and she's ready for work. Ready for a day of normality and meetings before returning home to her perfect husband and sons.

You'll never believe what Lou has gone and done, I hear her saying to Simon that evening, and even though I know she probably won't tell him, because she's my oldest and dearest friend, there's still a sliver of suspicion that my drama will become a private conversation between them at some point. That's the temptation with gossip, isn't it? That's why we use words like 'juicy' before it. It's a dish that everyone wants a bite of.

I imagine their intimate looks to one another, their *thank goodness we're nothing like that* expressions, and I instinctively duck my head so she won't see me. I want the next time we meet to be back in our usual dynamic.

I look back at my phone, my heart hammering against my chest. I block the account again. Report it again. But even as I'm doing it, I know it's useless. They were able to unblock themselves last time, the account didn't get banned or removed, and I go hot as I think what the next post might be.

Then a thought hits me that leaves me cold.

What if Paul is tagged in the next post? He doesn't have an Instagram account, but Dilenby Taxis does. Felix does.

A light sheen of sweat blossoms on my upper lip. My hands are shaking as I take a screen shot.

NOT A SCAM, I type, and send it to Oscar.

It's nine in the morning and the rush-hour traffic has begun. I inch my car along towards my mother's as my mind races and my heart beats at an ungodly speed. A message arrives. I open it when I'm stopped at the traffic lights.

Don't worry about it. Meet at mine for lunch? x

My hollow laugh fills the car. He has no idea. Of course he's telling me not to worry, what exactly has he got to lose? He's off to South America in a matter of weeks, if someone does know, if they do announce it on Instagram, tag my husband, my son, my students, what will the repercussions be for him? A slap on the back from his friends? A nod and a chuckle?

I shake my head at my stupidity. I will lose everything. I'll forever be known as the woman who had an affair with one of her students. My business will be ruined. Felix probably won't talk to me. If he thought Paul was embarrassing at the meal, how will he react about this?

By the time I get to my mother's, my overthinking and playing out every worst possible scenario is in overdrive. I've mentally given Paul a fatal heart attack and imagined myself in a terrible job as a night shift worker in some shop where no one will ever see me. Wiping my hand across my face, I get out of the car, then stop as Rick's black Land Rover makes its way along the drive. He slows, and I raise my hand, put my head down and start to walk quickly to my mother's front door, but he calls to me.

'Lou? You got a minute?'

I pause. All I want to do is go inside, sort Mum out and get her comfortable, then look at the Instagram account again. See if I can find out who's behind it. I try to arrange my expression into one of calm as he gets out of his car and comes over. The day is dark and cold, with a bitter wind, and I wrap my thin jacket around me.

'I know you must be run off your feet,' he says. He looks towards the house. 'But I was locking up last night and I saw a light.'

'A light?'

He nods. 'Confused me at first. I couldn't work it out, but it was distracting, shining in through my curtains.' He leans in and lowers his voice. 'It was your mother. Vivienne.'

'What?'

'I know it sounds like nothing, but I thought I should tell you. What with everything else.' He gives me a meaningful look. 'Like I said, it was shining straight into my house. At first I thought it was a car, but then, when it became apparent that it wasn't, I walked over here to see what was going on, and that's when I saw her.'

As he's been speaking, my stomach, which I didn't think could get any tighter, has constricted even further. It feels like there's a brick in there, dragging at my gut and making the muscles strain like a tight coil. I put my hand there, make a mental note to get some painkillers.

'She had a torch,' Rick says. 'I asked her what she was doing, but she didn't answer. I think she was looking for something.'

I stare at him.

'Shining it out of her bedroom window, down onto the ground. I asked her what she'd lost, if I could help, but she still didn't say anything. I gave up and went home, but when I went to the toilet in the early hours, I saw it again.'

'Right.' I look to the house, imagining my mother shining a torch out of her bedroom window in the dead of night, like Morse code straight into Rick's house alerting him to her paranoia. 'Sorry,' I shake my head, 'she's been getting herself worked up. Thinking people are there when . . .'

'The cameras, though, I thought . . .'

'We turned the alarm off. She kept thinking she was getting notifications. Hearing the alarm and voices when no one was there.'

We stare at each other, the drone of the traffic on the distant main road a low, depressing hum.

'Well, I'd better make tracks,' he says after a moment. 'You know what the traffic into Manchester is like at this time of the morning.'

'Rick?' I stop him before he gets to his car. 'I'm sorry she disturbed you. I hope it didn't keep you up.'

'Not at all.' He gives me his bright smile and I let myself into my mother's feeling ten times worse.

It takes me a full two hours to get it out of her that she has a torch hidden in her bedside drawer.

'Rick saw you,' I tell her. 'You know he did, so why deny it?'

'Rick's an old busybody. He needs to mind his own business.'

'Well, I'm glad he didn't. You should be sleeping, not shining a light out of your bedroom window like a bloody lighthouse. It woke him up. Why on earth were you—'

'Because someone was there.'

'No one was there.' I take out my phone. 'I would've been alerted. I would know. The camera is set up to record and notify me, and look,' I show her the screen, 'nothing. Not one notification.'

I leave just before lunch. Drive to Oscar's with my head humming. My mind has been flitting between so many different crises that I can't concentrate. I just know I have to put out fires. I have to stop them before anyone gets burnt.

'Kids messing about,' Oscar says as he looks at the Instagram account. 'You're getting worked up over nothing. It's probably some old student you pissed off wanting to get back at you for failing their A level or some shit. I've reported the account, so that should be the end of it.'

I stare at him. It's clear from the way his flat is that he thought I was coming over for sex. It's clean. A smell of air freshener heavy in the air, clogging the back of my throat. His bedroom door is open, Oscar standing in the doorway ready to take me to the bed and undress me.

And why wouldn't he? In the brief time we've been together, isn't this the routine we've got into? I let out a humourless laugh.

'Reporting the account won't do anything. Don't you think I've already done that? And have you seen the comments?' I go to the sofa, sit on the edge, making it clear that nothing will be happening in his bedroom this lunchtime. 'There's two, and I know the woman who wrote the second one. She works at the post office. I see her when I pay my mother's gas and electric.'

'So?'

'So!' I shake my head. 'So if she works it out, if she knows what I did, she'll ...' I take a deep breath as I imagine her relaying the gossip to the whole village. 'You don't understand. Paul ... he ...' I rub my eyes, 'he's having tests.'

'Tests?'

'His heart. He told me yesterday. And my mother still thinks someone is outside her house at night. She woke Rick up shining a torch from her bedroom window.' I stand up and then sit again. 'What I mean is, this ...' I wave between me and him, 'I can't do it any more. I can't run the risk of Paul finding out. Of Felix finding out. I can't trust that this is just some angry student.'

'Louise ...' He comes over to me, puts his hands on my cheeks and kisses me. A long, slow kiss that makes me dissolve inside, and all my thoughts about ending this suddenly seem ludicrous. This is the only good thing in my life right now. *This.*

'No.' I push him away. 'I can't do it. We can't. Paul ...' I trail off. 'I'll have to stop the lessons. I can't trust myself to—'

'Louise, you're overreacting. Just take a moment.'

'I'm sorry, Oscar,' I tell him, and go to the door. 'I'm so sorry for it all.'

I make my way to my car on shaky legs. I feel claustrophobic, like I need air even though I'm out in the open. I feel like I've just done something awful, something terrible. It's like I'm cutting open my insides and sticking pins into my organs. I think I've made a mistake. I think of Oscar, of saying goodbye to him and everything it entailed. Of never seeing ...

I stop as I get to my car. There's something under the

windscreen wiper. A folded piece of A4 paper. I snatch it out and gaze at it. It's not a flyer as I first thought. It's a message. A message for me.

THIRTY

*YOU NEED TO STOP BEING SUCH A WHORE. LEAVE
AND TAKE THAT BITCH OF A MOTHER WITH YOU.
OR I MAKE THE POST.*

I stare at the words. They don't make sense. I let out a high laugh of disbelief. This can't be for me. It isn't for me. Who would write this? And then I read the words again and my heart speeds up. Of course it's for me.

It was on my car. Someone made this and wanted me to find it.

I look quickly down the street. I see an older lady waiting at a bus stop, a middle-aged man walking a Border Terrier. Neither is paying any attention to me. Swinging my head round, I scan in the other direction. An old man on a mobility scooter. Empty pavements. Cars roll past as if everything is normal.

I turn around, the paper in my hand. Nothing. No one. Vehicles parked along the street. Cars with the dull light reflected off the windscreens, making it impossible to see into any of them. I suddenly get the real sense that someone is watching me again. The back of my neck prickles with the awareness of being stared at, and I search for them, for the person who left this note for me to find and is now watching me.

'Oh God,' I whisper as a slither of fear races up my spine. I almost drop my car keys as I spin around and retrace my steps, breaking into a light run as I make my way back to Oscar's flat.

'I've got to call the police,' I tell him. 'This is more than a post on social media, this is someone here. Following me. Watching me. Knowing that I'm in here. With you.'

Oscar is staring at the paper. He opened the door with a lazy smile, thinking I'd changed my mind, but when I shoved the paper at him, his smile vanished. Words tumble out of my mouth in time with my racing heart and mind.

'I mean,' I go to his window, peer out from behind the curtain, 'who would do this? Follow me here? Make a note like that with letters cut from a magazine and put it on my car window, like a blackmail letter from some eighties film?' I spin around. There's a scratch at the side of my mind, a memory trying to claw at me, but I can't think clearly. 'Oh my God, is that what this is? Is it blackmail?'

'Calm down.' Oscar rubs the back of his neck. 'It's not blackmail. There's no demand.'

'They're demanding for me to leave. Leave where? And take my mother? What does that even mean? My mother has done nothing to nobody.'

I wait. Staring at Oscar as he slowly puts the letter on the couch next to him and sits back.

'Well?'

He gives a non-committal shrug. It makes me furious.

'What does that mean?' I imitate his shrug in an exaggerated way.

'It means I don't know,' he says, shaking his head. 'Who have you pissed off lately?'

I go to tell him no one when I remember Handy Gary. That weird locket. But he wouldn't stoop so low as to do this, would he? And what would the dirty secret be? That I'm menopausal?

'That's who it is,' Oscar says. 'Whoever you're thinking of right now, that's who's behind this account.'

I shake my head. 'It doesn't make sense. He knows no secrets of mine, unless . . .' I pause. 'Gary, the man who owns the off-licence in the village. He knows you, said you did some work for him?'

Oscar looks at me blankly, and then I see something on his face, a memory surfacing. 'Him? He wouldn't say boo to a goose.'

'I cancelled our lessons the other day because . . .' I stop. 'Did you . . . do you see him? Could he know about us, about this?'

Oscar lets out a laugh. 'I'm polite to him. Say hello when I pop in the shop, but he's not a mate. I don't talk about stuff to him, and I haven't spoken about us to anyone.'

'Are you sure?' I ask. 'What about an old girlfriend? Someone you speak to regularly, who might get jealous, who—'

'I've told no one. NO ONE. And believe me, none of my exes would do this. If they were posting on social media out of revenge or jealousy, everyone and their aunt would know. My exes are . . .' he looks away for a moment, 'not the type to be shy about letting their feelings be known.'

I stare at him. Look back to the letter. The mention of my mother. Who would be upset enough to call my mother a bitch? Who would be upset enough with me to do this? And suddenly it's obvious. The only person we've collectively pissed off.

'That charity man.' I look back out of the window, as if he'll suddenly be there, down on the street, staring back up at me with that sarcastic smile. 'The man you called me about. The one who was on his way to fleecing my mother before I got there and stopped him. And that night, when we kissed outside the pub . . .' I take a ragged breath, 'I knew I recognised one of those people. If it was him, if he . . .'

Oscar stands up. 'You think . . .?'

'I think I need to call the police. Tell them about him. About how he might be stalking me because I stopped him from taking all my mother's money.' I bang my fist on the window. 'I knew I should have called them that day. I knew I should've . . .' I trail off when I see Oscar's face. 'What?'

'If you call the police,' he says slowly, 'you know you'll have to tell Paul about us. Tell Felix.'

I blink rapidly. He lifts up the paper.

'It says you're a whore,' he says gently. 'The first thing they'll ask is why. What are you doing that warrants that description?'

I stare at him a moment before putting my head in my hands.

He's right. Of course he's right. I can't call the police without confessing everything. Could I ask the police to keep quiet about my affair? Shame hits me like a wave, the thought of that conversation, talking to an officer about my younger lover and my husband's heart condition and why he must never find out.

'Look,' Oscar says, 'the best thing to do in this situation is nothing.'

I glance up at him.

'Think about it, this letter isn't making any demands. It's not blackmail. It's a scare tactic. Someone is trying to frighten you.'

'It's working.' I'm close to tears, my eyes smarting. 'I'm terrified.'

He comes over to where I'm standing by the window and puts his arms around me. 'Don't be. Whoever is behind this, and those Instagram posts, is a coward. If they meant business, Paul would already know. Felix would already know. The post they're talking about would already be up.'

'So they want something from me,' I say, 'but what? What the hell do they want? For me to leave?'

He looks back to the letter. 'They just want to rattle your cage. Let you know they know about us. But there is no more us, is there?'

My eyes dart to my rear-view mirror an unnecessary number of times on the drive to my mother's, and when I pull up in the driveway, I park so I'm facing the road and sit for a while. Waiting. I'm not sure what for. A car to crawl past the house and park up? A suspicious person lingering outside?

Oscar made me a cup of tea and helped calm me down. Pointing out that whoever was behind this had limited cards left to play. That it was all hot air and if they meant business they would have done their worst already. I listened and tried to believe him. When he offered to come with me to my mother's, I had to argue with him to convince him not to. I don't want whoever it is to see us together. I want to let them know it's over, so can they please, please leave me alone. I think about DM'ing the Instagram account, begging for forgiveness, but stop myself. As if they'd just write back and say, OK, glad you did what I asked. And that would be that.

When I let myself in, my mother glances up in surprise. 'What are you doing here so early? Is everything OK? You look like someone's walked over your grave!'

I am early. I usually have my online students around this time, but I cancelled them, making up an excuse about the flu. There's no way I can teach like this. I'm shaking. Jumpy. Bordering on tears. My thoughts swinging between Handy Gary and whether he's capable of doing something like this, and the charity man and what his motives might be.

'I'm fine,' I tell her, and plaster on a smile. 'But I need to ask you something and I want you to be honest.'

She lets out a confused laugh, and then stops when she sees my expression.

'Lou, you're making me scared. What's going on?'

I take a deep breath and go over to her. Take her hand in mine.

'Remember last month, when that man claiming to be from a charity came over? I had to get rid of him, he was . . .' I stop. My mother is staring at me. Her eyes have turned into wide pools of terror and her hand has tightened its grip.

'Did he do it?' she asks me in a whisper. 'Did he report me?'

'Report you?' I put my other hand on her arm in an effort to calm her down. 'Report you for what?'

'Lou, I'm so sorry. I didn't mean to, I didn't!'

'What are you talking about?'

She shakes her head, her bottom lip trembling. 'Am I in trouble?'

'Trouble? Tell me what you're talking about, Mum. Tell me what happened.'

'He came back,' she says, and closes her eyes. 'After he'd been here the first time, he called in again.'

I knew it. I knew something had happened. I feel rage build up inside me.

'Why didn't you tell me?' It's only after the words have left my mouth that I realise I've shouted them.

'I didn't want to worry you!' She snatches her hand out of mine and turns away a little from me in her chair. 'And I didn't do anything wrong. I didn't even let him in. I told him I was calling the police on him. That it was wrong of him.'

I stare at her, my heart pounding. 'And when was this?'

'A couple of days after he was first here. He wanted to explain. Said he could prove he was from a charity and was sorry he'd upset me. I told him to go away, did exactly as you said, and he . . .' She lets out a little noise, and my insides clench.

'What did he do?'

She shakes her head.

'Mum?'

'He called me a miserable old bitch,' she whispers, 'and said he hoped I was happy that I was leaving those poor children to die.'

'Right,' I say, grabbing my phone, 'I'm calling the police.' I won't be able to tell them about the letter on my windscreen, but I can tell them about this.

'NO!' I look up, and stop. My mother is shaking, her hands clenched tightly. 'I did something. Something that upset him. That's why he keeps coming back. That's why he keeps watching me at night, and why he left that doll on the back doorstep.'

I stare at her.

'Doll? What doll?'

'When I was telling him to go away, he shouted at me and threw a doll. One of those dolls he gives to people after they make a donation, like the key rings, and I got scared. He

213

tried to come in, kept saying he wanted to explain, so I ...'
she shakes her head, 'I pushed him with my stick, gave him
a sharp jab. It knocked him backwards a bit and he started
saying how he was going to press charges against me. How I'd
assaulted him.'

'What?'

'He was filming me on his phone. Filming my stick. Saying
I was using it as a weapon, and it was evidence and I'd go to
jail.' She's shaking all over, her frail body convulsing in terror.
'Please don't get the police involved. He'll tell them what I
did, he'll show them that video he took of me, and they'll
arrest me.'

THIRTY-ONE

'No one is arresting you.' I put my phone down and quickly go
over to her. I've never seen her like this; she's terrified. 'Don't
be ridiculous.'

I put my arm around her, and the sharpness of her bones
under her jumper amplifies how fragile she is. I feel a surge
of anger for Josh. The bully who told her this, who got her so
scared, who threw a creepy doll at her, leaving it on the doorstep to intimidate her. What kind of joke is that to play on
an old lady? Who would do that to such a vulnerable person?

'Hey.' I make her look at me, her eyes large and rheumy. 'You
won't go to jail, OK? You are not going to jail, but we need to
report him. He's playing sick games here, Mum, getting off on
scaring you. He was threatening you in your own home. You
were defending yourself.' I pick up my phone again.

'No, Lou, no! That's just it. It wasn't in my home; he wasn't
inside. He was on the steps. He said it would be GBH. I at-
tacked him and he was outside, so it was unprovoked.'

'Listen to me, Mum.' I try to make my voice gentle, amazed at how much he's got into her head. 'We need to get the police involved in this. He threatened you. He threw a doll at you and left it on your doorstep to frighten you. He's probably round at someone else's house now trying to fleece an old lady out of her pension. We can't—'

'We can.' Her face is etched with anxiety, her voice thin and pleading, and I sit beside her again.

'I'm sorry, it's just got me so angry, seeing you scared like this.'

She looks at me, and I see how tight and still she's holding herself.

'It's OK,' I say. 'I won't call the police.' I see her soften slightly. 'But we need to—'

'I did call the police. You told me to, remember? They found nothing. No one. And since then, it's only got worse. I think,' she swallows, 'that if we ignore him, he'll get bored and leave me alone. He's not been back recently. I think he's stopping.'

I stare at her, my mind racing to catch up.

'And what can they do anyway?' She pulls a tissue from the box on the table beside her and starts to fiddle with it. 'I don't even know his full name, and even if I did, even if they found him, he'd tell them what I did, how I pushed him, and . . .'

She's talking in fits and starts, sobs and gasps of air breaking up her words. It pains me to see her so upset.

'Hey, it's OK.' I make a big show of putting my phone away, zipping up my bag. 'I won't call them.'

She stares at me.

'I won't! I promise—'

The shrill ring of the doorbell makes us both jump.

'Hello? Anyone home?'

I exhale. It's Rick.

He comes into the kitchen as I make us all a cup of coffee, and over the noise of the kettle, I tell him what my mother has just told me.

'She's insisting I don't call the police. He's got her terrified. Convinced her that she'll go to jail for pushing him.'

I shake my head and open the fridge for the milk. Part of me wants to ignore her. To call the police immediately and tell them what this creep has been doing. Another part whispers that if I do that, it's inevitable that everything will unravel. If he is behind the posts on Instagram and the threatening letter, he's been toying with both of us. I could ask the police to warn him off, if that's something they even do, but I'd have to admit that I have no idea who he is. And I'm going entirely off what I've gathered from my true-crime box sets here, but then I guess they would start to investigate everything. I'd have to tell them about my work, my students, and they'd learn about Handy Gary and how I ended our lessons, and they'd discover that I'm teaching Oscar. They'd ask questions about our lessons at his flat, about the time I spent with him, and Paul would find out about our affair, and all this trouble with his heart would . . .

'Did you see him at all?' I ask Rick.

He shakes his head. 'Oscar told me he'd been around that first time, but I had no idea he'd come back.'

I take a deep breath. 'Neither did I. He must have really scared her; she's been keeping this to herself all this time.' I grip the counter as the words leave my mouth, thinking of the late-night calls, the terror in her voice, the paranoia, the sleeplessness and anxiety.

'So that's what the torch out of the window was about?' asks Rick. 'She was looking to see if this man was there?'

'And the doll.'

'The doll?'

'He threw it at her and then left it on the doorstep for her to find, from what I can gather. That must have been the one you saw her with.'

'What an absolutely vile thing to do. Did the cameras catch him?'

I shake my head. 'I had no notification. Maybe it was before they were up. Those bloody cameras. They've added to it all, her panic. She convinced herself she was hearing the sound that tells you someone is there, but it always turned out to be nothing.'

'Nothing? So she was . . .?'

'Oscar checked them over and said they were too sensitive, going off with every cat or dog that passed by. I asked him to turn the sound off.'

'They can be very sensitive,' Rick agrees, and starts to tell me about how he has them at his house and how they go off if a leaf blows past, but I'm not listening. I'm looking at my phone, suddenly realising that in all the time since Oscar fitted the cameras, I've not had one notification. Not from the postman, or my mother opening the door. Nothing.

'Everything OK?'

He's staring at me, and I slip my phone into my back pocket.

'Fine,' I tell him, 'just something I need to look into later.'

I place his cup of coffee on the table in front of him, and look off to the lounge, where my mother is currently watching one of her shows and trying to calm down.

The weight I've been feeling on my chest over the past few weeks pushes down with renewed vigour. I think of her being scared, of searching around the house with a torch from her bedroom, and I feel so helpless. And then it hits me.

'Of course,' I say, turning back to Rick, 'with everything that's now happened with Paul, he'll have to agree.'

He looks at me, confusion on his face.

'Sorry,' I shake my head, 'I'm all over the place today, but I've just realised. For ages I've been telling Paul that the answer is for us to move in here with my mother. Be on hand for her. He always refused, claiming work and . . .' I falter a little. 'But our circumstances have changed recently, and he might need some time off, so . . .' I trail off as I think of Paul in bed recovering from his tests in one room and my mother in another, and me going between the two. Looking after them both.

Rick's mouth has opened in shock. 'But Lou, didn't you say that your husband and mother . . .'

'Hate each other? They do, and it's not ideal,' I tell him as the idea takes hold, 'but it means that when she thinks she can hear that man again, when she gets paranoid and wants to look out of her bedroom window with a torch, I'll be here. It also means Paul and I can make some money from renting out our house, and if Paul has to take time off . . .' I take a breath. 'Let's just say that now, with everything going on, it suddenly all seems doable.'

He stares at me for a long moment, then takes a sip of his coffee.

'That seems a bit . . . Well, I mean, how will you and Paul . . .? And Vivienne? I don't mean to interfere, but won't that be awful for all of you? Before you do anything drastic, maybe just take a moment. You don't seem yourself today. It's clear this guy has frightened you both, and I'm worried that you're acting out of fear and not logic. You have the cameras to alert you if he comes back, and—'

'But that's just it.' I take my phone out of my pocket. 'The cameras aren't alerting me. I told Oscar to switch off the alarm here, the one that my mother would hear, but I should still be getting notifications. And I haven't. Not one.' I turn the phone around to show him.

'But that's good, isn't it?' He takes another sip of his coffee. 'Means that no one is here. And you can clearly see the door, the porch. It's a great picture.'

'But no one? Not even my mother when she's been out to check if someone was there?' I stare at the screen, suddenly realising that I haven't even had a notification when *I'm* the one outside the front door, and I suddenly feel stupid. Like it's something I should have realised a lot sooner. 'Shit,' I mutter.

I navigate to the settings, trying to search for where the controls are, but I'm at a loss. I didn't read the information booklet; I left that to Oscar and let him tell me what I needed to know, and now I curse my laziness.

'I'll bet it's the timer,' Rick says. 'With mine, I can set it to start and end at certain times. It's probably something like that.'

I give a low groan, staring helplessly at the image on the screen. The empty driveway outside the house. I stand up and go to the front door, Rick following. Outside, I look up at the camera and then back at my phone.

I'm not there. Just the same image of the empty driveway.
'What the . . .?'

I wave my arms in front of the camera, then look back at the phone and the image that hasn't changed. It's mid-afternoon; surely the cameras should be on now, no matter what timing we've set them to.

I peer at the screen, and then go back inside to get my glasses.

'Lou?' Rick is standing in the hallway, leaning on his stick, confusion etched on his face. 'Is everything all right?'

'No,' I sigh. 'I'm so stupid. I've been looking at an old image.'

I point to the date in the corner of the screen. It's the date the cameras were fitted.

'An old image?'

I nod and show him the option that I've only just found. A menu that I didn't even know existed asks me if I want to 'connect live stream'.

'I don't think it's ever been activated,' I say slowly.

'Did you forget to do it? Turn it off without realising?' he asks.

I let out a laugh. It sounds hollow, but I try to make it convincing, suddenly seeing how this must look from Rick's perspective. How we're bothering him so much about my mother, getting him up at all hours, and then I have cameras fitted that I don't even know how to work.

'Yeah, I must have done that, now I come to think of it. Oscar must have told me to do it when we had all the trouble with the alarm disturbing my mother, and it must have slipped my mind to turn it back on to live stream.'

I activate the camera, and suddenly the screen changes and I see the date on the bottom of the image. Today's date. A flush of embarrassment works its way up my neck at my stupidity as I take off my glasses and put my phone back in my pocket. If Rick notices, he says nothing.

We go back into the kitchen to finish our drinks. He talks about the charity man, and how the area is getting worse, with petty crime and antisocial teenagers, and then we're back on the safe ground of crime books and shows we've been enjoying, but as Rick starts to tell me about a new podcast he's found,

I can only think of Oscar, and why he didn't tell me about connecting the cameras to my phone properly. Why he told me there was nothing wrong with them, and why he would lie to me.

THIRTY-TWO

'Are you on drugs?' Helen takes a sip of her coffee and looks at me across the table. We're in the Crooked Kettle, our usual meeting place, and I've just told her my plan. The more I think about it, the more I think it's the only solution.

'I mean,' she goes on, 'if you're not on drugs after saying that, you should be. Paul? Your Paul, living with your mother. Living with her? All of you under the same roof? Even if he is ill, or recovering from whatever, and I also need to point out that he hasn't yet had any tests to say he has anything wrong with him, so you're massively jumping the gun here . . .'

'But he can't say no this time,' I tell her, and give a nod. 'There's too many problems it will solve.' I start to count on my fingers. 'The debt. We can rent out our house and get some extra income that way. Me having to run to my mother's all the time. I'll be living with her. Paul can take time off if he needs to, because with renting out the house, we won't need so much income.'

'But you're missing one vital thing,' Helen tells me, and I look up. 'You'll all kill each other. Paul will definitely kill your mother; there's no way he can live with her. Remember the last time they got together, for Felix's graduation?'

I remember the car journey to Leeds; it was a disaster. Just under two hours, but it felt like we were in that car for years. The bickering between Paul and my mother was unbearable. By the time we reached the university, they were no longer speaking. It was so bad, Paul refused to be in the car with her again. He got the train home separately and my mother called him names all the way home, told me how immature and stupid he was.

'And what does Paul think about it?'

'I haven't mentioned it to him yet.'

Helen lets out a laugh. 'Wish I could be a fly on the wall for that conversation! And your mother?'

'Refuses.' I shake my head. 'She told me there was no way, but it's not like we have options. This is the best solution.'

'Best for who?' Helen's question hangs in the air. 'Because this solution will make you into a full-time carer, you know that? While putting more stress on your already stressed-out husband, who is in the process of having tests for his stressed-out heart. And renting out a property isn't a walk in the park either, Lou.'

'But what else can we do?' I take another sip of my coffee and look out onto the high street.

It's Valentine's Day. The card shop has love-heart balloons in the window and the Crooked Kettle has put out red napkins with pink hearts on. I run my thumb over one of them. Paul left me a card on the kitchen countertop. A picture of a kitten with *To my wife* written on the front. Inside he'd signed his name. I did the same for him, a non-descriptive card with my name written inside. No special message, nothing offensive or interesting. The same thing we do every year.

Oscar didn't get me a card. Of course he didn't and I didn't expect him to. It's over. Even when I asked him about the security cameras at my mother's and why my phone wasn't connected to the live stream, he sent back a very professional message.

Sorry! Thought you understood it had to be connected. I didn't check your phone. Just the cameras.

It's true. When I told him about the problem, he gave the cameras the once-over, but he didn't look at the app on my phone. The disconnection was my fault.

I stared at his message for a long time. No kiss. No talk of our extracurricular activities. I longed to send something flirty back, something about me needing to be checked by him, but I stopped myself, and that's another reason to move in with my mother. I'll be so busy with the house move and renting out our home, it'll remove any temptation to message Oscar or mope about.

'Lou?'

I blink and look up at Helen.

'Lost you there for a minute. What were you thinking about?'

I shake my head. 'Nothing.'

'Is it him? Oscar?' she whispers, and I shake my head.

'I can't think about what a mess it all is any longer. Talk to me about something else. Please?'

Helen stares at me a moment. She goes to say something and then stops herself.

'We need a night out,' she declares. 'Screw my diet. This is an emergency. How about this weekend? We could go to the

Chinese restaurant on Shepherd's Way and then,' she flashes a smile, 'hit the bars. Get dressed up. Forget everything for a few hours. Pretend we're different people for the night. What d'ya think?'

'Helen,' I give her a smile, 'you know I've got no money to—'

'Here's the genius part of my idea. This Saturday is bingo night at the Duck and Bucket. We go there first and win, and that takes care of the rest of the night!'

A laugh escapes me. It feels good to laugh; it feels like I've not done it in so long.

'Since when did they start doing bingo at the Duck and Bucket?'

She gets out her phone. 'I'm on their email list and this new landlady is behind it. She's doing all sorts, quiz on a Friday, bingo on Saturday.'

She shows me the email claiming 'huge prizes', and I'm about to say no when a photograph catches my eye. Blonde hair. Up in a high ponytail.

'Who's she?'

Helen glances at the screen. 'That's her. The new landlady. Denise, I think she's called.'

I take the phone out of her hand and peer at the photo. 'Paul knows her. He's teaching her to play darts.' I hand the phone back. 'Her dad's got dementia and Paul's helping out.'

Helen looks at me. 'Paul's helping her out? This new land-lady, with her dad who has dementia?'

'That's all her dad can do. The only thing he remembers. She wants to play so she can reconnect with him.'

Helen's face says everything she doesn't say out loud. I see her mouth move, as if she's going to speak, but she stops herself again. Instead she puts her phone away and talks about the bingo and how much we could win, and I let her ramble on about what we'd wear and where we'd go, knowing that it'll never happen.

After Helen leaves, I sit in the café and stare at my phone. I'm scrolling through the Duck and Bucket's social media, and suddenly there she is. Under an announcement about bingo, the image Helen showed me. She's pretty. Got a nice smile. I imagine her and Paul together. Him with his hand on her wrist, like he used to do when he tried to get me involved in the game. I wonder if she's married. And as I stare at her image, I let the scenario develop in my mind. Testing myself to see how it feels.

Does it hurt? If Paul were to start a relationship with this woman, would it hurt?

I swallow, my throat tight in preparation, and it's suddenly all so sad. So very sad that these thoughts are in my head. That I'm testing myself. My feelings. And that if he were to have an affair, to do the very worst like I've done to him, my overriding reaction would be one of relief.

I could move into my mother's alone.

'But the money,' I whisper to myself. Leaving Paul now and moving in with my mother won't get rid of the debt. And Paul. The tests. His heart. The fact that he might be seriously ill.

I put my phone down, and as I glance out of the window, I see a man come out of the chemist opposite.

Handy Gary.

He looks up, and our eyes meet. My heart jumps into over-drive. This is the first time I've seen him since I ended our lessons. Since the note on my car. I look away quickly, but it's too late. He's seen me. He crosses the road, approaches the café. I think about getting up and leaving, but suddenly he's in front of me.

'Lou,' he says, 'I was hoping to see you. We need to talk.'

He pulls out a chair as if he's about to join me, and I shake my head. 'I'm just leaving,' I tell him.

He puts a hand on my arm. 'Please?'

I look around the busy, crowded café and think about how there is safety in numbers, and he takes my silence as consent and sits down opposite me.

'Oscar called me,' he says. 'He said someone is sending you threats.'

'What?'

'Oscar. That odd-job man you teach at your mother's. He called and said that if I was posting things about you on social media, I needed to stop.'

'Oscar called you? Said that?'

He nods, and it's an effort for me not to show my confusion.

'Is someone posting about you on social media?' he goes on. 'Is that why you ended our lessons? I would never do that to you. Do you think I would do that?'

I stare at him. Do I?

'I can't bear it if you think it was me, if you think . . .'

My heart begins to pound as I remember the stacks of magazines in his back room, the scratch at the back of my mind when I saw the note, each letter carefully cut out from a printed page. My throat goes dry.

'Is it you?' I ask quietly. 'Have you been posting on Instagram and tagging me in those posts? Did you follow me here? Did you send that letter? Have you been—'

He frowns. 'What letter?'

228

'I know about your girlfriend,' I tell him. 'The Spanish girlfriend. Josie.'

'Josie?'

'She's not real,' I say. 'You invented her so you could spend time with me. Making me translate that love letter. And after I stopped our lessons, you lashed out by posting on . . .'

I stop as his face crumples. It's shocking. His bottom lip protrudes as his mouth curls downward, his eyes close, and I watch in horror as he starts to cry.

'Gary?' I expected denial, bravado, not . . . this.

It's over in a moment. He regains control, wipes his face with the back of his hand and looks at me.

'She is real.' He takes out his phone. 'I met her last year. When I went over there on holiday. We did keep in touch. She would call, we would talk.' He shows me the screen: a photograph of him with a slightly younger woman. Dark hair, big earrings. They're both smiling. 'I don't have much luck with women, and then she said she wanted to visit, to come and stay with me, but she didn't have the money, so I sent her . . .' He looks away for a moment. 'It was a trick,' he says as he looks back at me. 'She tricked me for money. When we started our lessons, I thought she was coming to visit. After she did that to me, I couldn't . . . so I kept going. I told my family, my staff that she'd got delayed. That I was still having Spanish lessons and . . .' He shakes his head. 'I wanted everyone to think . . .'

He trails off, looks at the photograph again and then puts the phone away.

'I had no idea,' I say.

'Why would you?' He gives a half-laugh. 'I thought it was love.'

We sit in silence for a moment.

'But I would never post things about you on social media. When Oscar called me, I told him what I'm about to tell you. I would never do that, and whatever is happening, it'll be his fault.'

'What?'

'Oscar,' he says, 'he's ... he's not who he pretends to be. I know him, and he's one of those that acts a certain way. The way you want him to act. He'll say the right things, do the right things to get what he wants. Like Josie used to with me.'

I go to ask him what he means, but he stands and collects his bags.

'*Adios*, Lou,' he tells me. 'I really did enjoy our lessons. Please don't lose everything like I did over a pretty smile.'

I watch as he walks out. His comparison of Oscar and the woman who swindled him replays in my mind.

My eyes still on Gary, I hear the dull buzz of my phone as it vibrates with a notification against the table. I pick it up, thinking that if it's a message from Helen, I'll call her and tell her what just happened, but as I look down, I see it isn't from Helen at all. It's a direct message from Instagram. From the @Dilenbyscandal4848 account.

My fingers shake as I go to my inbox.

I'm watching you. She's not safe in that house. Don't make me post proof and let your son and husband learn the truth.

THIRTY-THREE

Heart pounding, I navigate to the main grid. I go to @Dilenbyscandal4848, but there's nothing. No new post. No tags. But the account has a hundred followers now, and as I scan them, I recognise a few names.

Local businesses, some parents I used to know when Felix was at school, a couple of students. There are more comments under the last post, and one is from a friend of Felix's: *What's this? Gossip in Dilenby? I need to know what it is NOW!*

I feel sick at the thought of them seeing a post about me and Oscar.

Proof. What proof? What proof could they possibly have? A picture of us together? I feel sick. Of course they could have a picture of us. They followed me to Oscar's flat, left that message on my windscreen. It wouldn't be hard for them to take a photo of us together. But he's my student. I'd say we were in a lesson. Unless they had something . . . The sick feeling builds.

My stomach rolling as my mind races through times when we weren't as discreet as we should've been. Oscar reaching for me as we left my mother's, holding my hand and caressing the small of my back before we made it to his flat, kissing me as he opened the door to me. My heart pounds, the dull thud of it behind my eyes.

I frown. Gary's hands were full of shopping when he left the café. He couldn't possibly have been using his mobile phone to send me threatening messages.

It isn't him. Was never him. It's someone else.

I look back down at the text.

She's not safe in that house.

I turn around and scan the café, then look back out of the window at the high street filled with people. The chatter and clinking of cutlery on plates is suddenly too loud, too much. I get up quickly, certain that whoever sent the message is watching me, and almost jog back to the car park, my mind scuttling from one thought to the next. I collide with a woman and apologise, and eventually reach the safety of my car, my mouth dry, my heart pounding.

My hands are sweaty as I put my key in the ignition. Paul will be making his way to my mother's; we've planned to meet there. I told him he needed to see the work that Oscar has done on the house so far, when in reality it's so I can discuss us moving in there. But now I don't know if I can do it. Act as if nothing is wrong. Have the difficult conversation and stand my ground when someone has sent me this.

I go back to my phone.

Who is this? I hit send. They say never to interact with trolls. Block and delete. But I need to know.

I stare at the screen, but there's no reply. I'm not sure the message has even been sent; how do you know with direct messages on Instagram? I think about texting Oscar, but instead find myself searching the street for Gary. I need to find him and ask him what he meant about Oscar. Could it be something to do with one of those exes he mentioned? I look back at the message. If it's the man from the charity, it makes no sense. If he's trying to blackmail me for something, where are his demands?

I smack my fist on the steering wheel in frustration.

What do you want? I type.

My last message is still in the ether. No 'delivered' or 'read' notification. I send the new message and then bring up Oscar's number.

Got another message, I text him. Are you sure you've no ex-girlfriends it could be?

I watch the screen as the small 'delivered' sign appears. I give it a few seconds, and when there's no reply, I set off for my mother's. How I'm going to pretend that everything is fine is beyond me. I've got to meet Paul, have one of the toughest conversations I've ever had with him, and I'm shaking so much, it's all I can do to focus on the road and make sure I get there in one piece.

Paul is waiting in his car when I get to my mother's. He's got a paper spread out over the steering wheel and is turning the pages slowly as he reads. Rather sit in his cold car than go in and see my mother; not a great sign. I take a deep breath and tell myself that for the next couple of hours I need to pretend that the text hasn't happened. Everything is normal. Everything is fine.

That Oscar hasn't happened.

I need to be the wife Paul thinks I am.

'Hey,' I say, and smile. It must come across as thin and fake, as Paul frowns at me as he gets out of his car.

'Everything OK?'

'Fine!' I tell him, and make my way towards my mother's front door. 'Helen just went on a bit.' I rummage in my bag for my keys. 'She was trying to get me to go on a night out with her, even though I told her I can't afford it. She says there's a bingo night at the Duck and Bucket. Denise arranged it. I didn't know she was the landlady there. That's the Denise you're helping, isn't it?' I'm rambling. My words tripping out of my mouth as if I've had a gazillion espressos.

He nods. 'She's letting us practise in the pub. It's where I've been teaching her.'

'How is all that?' I swallow, my throat tight, my heart still racing. I try to take a deep breath, mentally tell myself to slow down, to pretend everything is *normal*. 'You still helping her out?'

'Now and again,' he says, and nods towards the front door. 'Shall we have a look? I need to see the window frames around the back of the house. I've got Tony coming over in half an hour or so. I did want a little bit more time to get her prepared, but seeing as you're late, it's—'

'Tony?'

'Thought he could have a look at the place as well. You got me to cancel him the other day, but I'm here now and Oscar's almost finished with everything, isn't he? So I told Tony to come over.'

'Paul, you need to ring him. Tell him not to come.'

'Don't be daft. Once we've broken it to her, you'll feel much better about it all. The prospect of doing something is always worse than actually doing it.'

'No, it's not that. I'm not telling her anything because she's not moving out. We're moving in.'

'What?'

This is not how I wanted to tell him. Standing in my mother's porch, against the chill of the February weather, speaking in hushed whispers.

'It's how we can work this whole thing out. It's obvious. We move in here, then Mum doesn't have to go anywhere and I can be on hand to look after her, and we rent out our house.'

Paul shakes his head, gives a half-laugh to dismiss me like he always does.

'Tony will take a few pictures on his phone. He's not bringing the photographer with him—'

'Will you shut up about Tony?' I hiss. 'For the umpteenth time, we are not renting out this house.' I turn to him. 'Don't you see? Can't you understand how it makes perfect sense? Especially with the tests. If you have to take time off work because—'

'Whoa, whoa, who said anything about taking time off work?'

'Paul ...' I take a moment, 'you're having tests for a suspected heart condition. Now is the time to think about taking it easy. You need less stress, not—'

'The only stress I have in my life is this house not being rented out because you won't see sense.'

'But if we—'

'There's not a chance in hell I'm moving in there. With her.' He jabs a finger at the door, 'I'd rather move into the taxi office than live with your mother.'

I hold my hands out, warning him to keep his voice down. 'Have you asked her? What did she have to say about it?'

'She said—'

'Oh, I'll bet she did!' he booms. 'I'll bet she had a thing or two to say about allowing me to live in her precious house. She won't even let me through the door most of the time!'

I put my hand to my head, which is starting to throb. Before I can reply, the door opens and my mother looks out at us, her stick lifted at her side.

'Let me guess,' she says. 'Lou suggested you move in here again?'

'Mum!' I move myself between them. My mother half closes the door, as if to stop Paul from stepping inside.

'Don't worry.' He holds up his hands. 'I want that about as much as you do, Viv. It's never going to happen.'

My mother makes a sound.

'We're here to talk about you moving out.'

'Paul!'

'Into a care home. It's time, Viv, that's what we're here to—'

'We are not!' I look at my mother. She's staring at me, and as our eyes meet, I see her confusion.

'Viv,' Paul lowers his voice, and it takes on a softer tone, 'we're concerned over how forgetful you're getting. The stuff that's been going on. The late-night calls, thinking people are watching you . . .'

'PAUL!' I shake my head. 'Mum, no one is moving you out, we're just—'

'Of course we are.' Paul puts his hand on my shoulder. 'I know this is hard, Lou, it's really hard, and I feel for you, Viv, I feel for you both, but it's high time we had this conversation.'

'What conversation?' My mother steps towards me. 'What's he talking about?'

'We're going to rent out this house,' Paul says. 'We've talked about it before, we can—'

'Over my dead body!' She looks at me. 'Lou, did you know about this?'

'Why do you think we've had all the work done?' Paul asks. 'Why do you think we paid Oscar to—'

'*I* paid for it. I paid him this morning. He came round and—'

'Oscar was here?'

They both look at me, and I realise my voice must have been louder than I intended. 'No, Mum,' I shake my head, 'you've got that wrong. Oscar still has the outside wall to finish. I told him to contact me, that I'd pay him.'

'He came this morning,' she repeats, 'said he was finished and collected his tools. I paid him for the work he's done, but he wouldn't take anything for fitting the cameras – he said there was no charge for those.'

'Those bloody cameras!' Paul looks up, and I follow his gaze to the camera above the front door. 'They've been no end of trouble. I knew they were a bad idea, I did say . . .' He narrows his eyes as he reaches up towards it. 'What the . . .' He lets out a laugh. 'No wonder they've been going off every two minutes. Look at this!'

I watch as he fiddles with something behind the camera.

'This'll be why he didn't charge for fitting them; he obviously hadn't a clue what he was doing!'

I stare at what's in Paul's hand. My mouth going dry.

'Every gust of wind would blow this in front of the lens and set the motion detector off. What even is it?'

I take it from him and my heart drops. There's no mistake. The silver chain and ring. The flimsy ribbon. It's the key ring that Josh the charity man tried to give me.

THIRTY-FOUR

My mind tries to scramble around the timeline. When did Oscar fit the cameras? When did Josh make his second call?

'This is exactly what I'm talking about,' says Paul. 'You're vulnerable, Viv. You need to be somewhere safe, where people can't take the mickey. Anyone can take advantage of you here, all alone in this big house. This joker's been telling you he's doing a good job of fitting the cameras when he's clearly been doing sod all. Can't even spot that a bit of rubbish has got caught on them. Getting you to pay for him doing nothing. No wonder he asked you for the cash. Let me—'

'I'll ring him,' I say quickly before Paul can get his phone out. 'Leave it to me. I'll sort Oscar, and for now . . .'

'For now, Tony is due here.'

'NO!' I snap, and Paul looks at me. 'Call Tony and cancel him. For the last time, Paul, my mother is not moving out.'

He goes to argue, but I stop him.

'Just forget the idea of renting this place out. It isn't happening.'

Paul says something about how it's best for everyone, and my mother snaps at him saying he only ever thinks of himself and what would he know, and it's all I can do to get her back inside so they don't start a full-scale shouting match on the doorstep.

'We'll lose it. You know that?' he says, and I look up at him. 'Felix will lose it. The money tied up in this place will all go to pay for carers once it's too late to get her in anywhere. Once she becomes too old and too ill. She'll need round-the-clock care, and if she won't move out . . .'

I put my hands up. 'Please. Stop. Just . . .' I dig into my bag, ready to get out the letter from the bank that I've been carrying around. Ready to tell him that we'll lose the building, the taxi rank, everything, if we don't *do something*. It was the conversation I had planned for today; I meant to talk about the letter, tell him I knew about the loan and then suggest moving into my mother's, but instead . . . I look at the key ring in my hand and feel sick.

I put my hand to my chest. I can't seem to get air in.

'Let me just . . .'

He looks at me for a moment.

'Let me talk to her,' I finish, 'let me think. Just give me . . . I'll come up with something. I'll think of something.' My words sound desperate, but Paul gives me a nod.

'You think on it,' he says, 'but time is running out, Lou.' He walks away, then turns back, calling to me over his shoulder. 'Got that appointment tomorrow afternoon, don't forget.'

'How could I?' I wipe my face and look up at him. 'I'll be waiting for you outside the main hospital door.'

'Great. See you there. I'm working late tonight, so don't wait up.'

I watch him walk away and think how that could be on the gravestone to our marriage. *Don't wait up.*

Leaving my mother to calm down with a hot drink and her favourite show, I go into the kitchen, close the door and study the key ring. I turn it over and over in my hand. It's definitely the same one. I clearly remember the cheap ribbon, the flimsy chain. The way he brought it out as if it were proof of him working for a charity. Paul said it was lodged behind the camera. The ring stuck around the back, the ribbon hanging down over the sensor so every gust of wind, every light breeze would make it move and set off the alarm. No wonder Mum was up in the night with a torch out of the window.

I squeeze my eyes shut. Can I have been this stupid? Has Oscar got something to do with it: the messages, the threats and the charity man?

I go to my phone, take a photograph of the key ring and send it to him.

Found this on the camera. Explain, please.

'Please,' I whisper as I watch the message go, the small 'delivered' sign. Please let there be a good reason why this was on the camera and why you didn't find it.

The rest of the day is a bit of a write-off. I cancel what lessons I have and sit with my mother, the fire blasting out heat, the television on loud and the key ring in my hand, ruminating on what could be going on and why. Every so often, when an idea hits, I get out my phone and google something. Try to find out who makes the key rings and if I can find out the charity man's identity from that somehow. Do a search on fitting security cameras and see if it's possible for Oscar to have missed the key ring.

'Tell me again,' I say to Mum in the afternoon as we open another packet of biscuits, 'what exactly did Oscar do here this morning?'

She gives a shake of her head, a slight shrug. 'He said he was all done, that he'd moved the date for his trip forward and I wouldn't be seeing him again. We chatted a bit about his travels, then I went to get the cash I keep in that box under the bed. He tried to stop me, said he'd get in touch with you, but I paid him anyway. Is it true, Lou? Was he a con man? Was he like that other one? Trying to trick me because I'm here alone?'

Her face twists in on itself, deep lines etched around the corners of her mouth and eyes, and I reach over and wrap my arms around her. 'I liked Oscar,' she says quietly, 'I thought he was one of the good ones.'

'I'm sure there's a reason for it all,' I whisper. 'He was nice. I'm sure he wasn't trying to trick you out of anything.' I lean back, hand her another custard cream. 'And it wasn't just you. I gave him lessons, remember? If he did trick us, he tricked us both.'

My mother nods and we go back to the show. Both of us lost in our own thoughts.

I'm making us an easy dinner of fish finger sandwiches when my phone goes. I rush to pick it up. Oscar. At last.

Meet me at the Gatehouse Inn, 8 p.m., and I'll explain then x

Relief washes over me. I want him to explain so badly. I want him to tell me that it was all real, that we were real. That the words he said, the way we were together, meant something. That all of this is easily explained. I'm desperate to talk to him.

I help my mother upstairs early. Let her watch television in bed with a hot drink. She's jittery, panicked, and keeps asking about Oscar. About the cameras and what happened. I've told her several times that it'll be OK, but my reassurance only works for half an hour before she asks again. I should stay with her. I should sit with her and make sure she's all right. I should take her to my house, stay there with her until I know exactly what's going on. But I do none of that. Instead, I get in my car and drive to the Gatehouse after I've triple-checked all the locks and made sure the camera app is working correctly on my phone.

It's not a place I've been to often. Just on the outskirts of Manchester, its main clientele are people needing food and drink before they hit the city and city prices. It's the kind of place that serves breakfast all day, that has a happy hour from five until seven, and as I walk around trying to find a seat, I realise it's the kind of place that's always busy.

Finding a table towards the back of the pub, behind a partition wall of distorted glass, I order a glass of white wine and a pint of something ale-like for Oscar, and text him telling him where I am.

I look at my messages and a fresh wash of panic sweeps over me. No replies to the messages I sent to the @Dilenbyscandal account. No 'sent' notification. I look at the posts again. Try to see something I may have missed. Try to work out why this man pretending he's from a charity wants me to leave. Why he wants me to stop seeing Oscar and what he could possibly have to do with him.

I take out the key ring again, run my thumb over the ribbon, and wait.

'C'mon, Oscar,' I breathe, and then, as my wine is nearly finished and his pint is going flat, I call him.

It rings out. I imagine him looking at his phone, seeing my number but not answering. It goes to voicemail and I consider leaving a message, but don't. He must be on his way.

I order myself a tonic water and go back to my seat. There's a change in customers now. The families and parties who were here eating when I arrived have left, and people dressed for a night out are coming in. Couples, groups of girls with big blow-dried hair, groups of lads with loud banter. It feels intimidating. Like I don't belong, a middle-aged woman sitting alone staring at her phone. I call Oscar again, and this time I leave a message.

'Where are you? It's almost nine. I have to leave soon.'

I wait until 9.15. Oscar doesn't return my calls, or my text, although I can see that he's read it, and as I stare at the little 'read' notification, it feels like the rug is being pulled from underneath me.

He knows I'm here. He knows I'm waiting for him. He knows what's happened today, and he's not coming.

THIRTY-FIVE

I leave the pub feeling numb. An emptiness fills me as I get in my car. It's half past nine. I have no answers, no explanation. Clearly Oscar doesn't want to explain. He doesn't want to confess to whatever this is.

Despite the voice in my head telling me not to, I call him again, praying that he'll answer, and when it clicks into voicemail once more, I end the call and put the car in gear.

I haven't been to Manchester in so long. Used to be that I was nipping in all the time, to go shopping, to visit museums or walk around, but somewhere between Felix growing up and me getting older, all that stopped. I told myself it was because of the traffic, the bus route and speed cameras that make driving so difficult, but as I navigate the one-way system, avoiding the areas that I know will be busy, I wonder if it's something else.

Why did I stop venturing out here? There's a wonderful energy to the place, a liveliness that I've missed. I've been spending my free time with my mother, both of us behind locked doors, in warm rooms where we're safe, but maybe we should have gone out more.

I pull into the street and slow down as I inch towards Felix's block of flats. I haven't told him I'm coming. I wasn't even sure I was going to come until now. So this is where he lives. This is where he's left home to come to.

He asked me to visit with Paul in a few weeks – that was the vague arrangement we had when we were officially invited to see his flat. But sitting in that pub, stood up by Oscar, knowing my son was only fifteen minutes away, an idea hit, and it suddenly seemed like the obvious thing to drive here.

As I get out of my car, though, I'm not so sure. I consider getting back in, calling him first and making sure he's home, but before I know it, I'm knocking on his door.

Sophie answers. Her hair is thrown up in a ponytail and she's wearing gym gear.

'Oh!'

I laugh at her response. 'I know,' I tell her. 'I'm sorry. I know I'm the last person you expected to be knocking at your door at this time.'

'Mum?' Felix comes up behind her and his face breaks into a wide grin when he sees me. 'What are you doing here?' His expression clouds. 'Is everything all right? Is it Gran? Is—'

'Everything is fine, it's all fine,' I lie. 'Honestly, I was just at a loose end and found myself driving here. I just wanted to say hello. If you're busy, I can—'

'No, no, we're not busy, come on in.'

Sophie stands aside and I walk in. The flat smells of their evening meal, something tomatoey and garlicky. The main thing I notice is the light. The wooden floors are whitewashed, and the walls are all white too, with colourful paintings on, meaning that the whole place feels light and airy. I go through to a lounge that is small and cosy and sit on the edge of a deep blue sofa made of some kind of corduroy material.

I run my hand over it.

'Quirky, isn't it?' Felix sits down beside me. 'We found it in a second-hand furniture shop over by the canal. Got it for a song.'

'I thought it was from Rick's shop for a second,' I say. 'This is like something he'd sell. Something he'd have in his bungalow.'

'Rick?'

'Your gran's neighbour owns that shop in the centre near what used to be the big department store. He's an interior designer.'

Felix and Sophie both look at me blankly.

'Haymoss Interiors? I think that's what it's called.'

'I don't think so,' Sophie says. 'I'd have been in it if it was there. There used to be a shop with house stuff in, but it closed a few months back.'

'Yeah,' Felix says, rubbing his chin. 'It seemed to be closing down for ages. It was really poky, not somewhere you'd—'

I shake my head. 'I'm sure that's where Rick said his shop was, but I must have the wrong place.' I look back at the sofa. 'Anyway, this is lovely.' I smile at them both and then clear my throat.

'I don't know if you can help, but you're better on social media than me, so . . .' I make an effort to sound calm. 'Is there a way of finding the identity of someone behind an Instagram account?'

Felix frowns. 'What do you mean? Like find out their name and address or something?'

'Exactly that,' I say, but I must say it too quickly, as Felix frowns.

'Is everything OK, Mum? Is someone . . .?'

'No, no, not me.' I try to smile. 'One of my students is getting messages, being tagged in posts, that kind of thing.'

'They need to go to the police,' he says in a matter-of-fact tone. 'Even if the account gets shut down, it's easy enough for a troll to open up a new one.' He gives a shrug. 'Though there's no guarantee anything will happen. Police resources and all that. Best if they just ignore them.'

I nod. I don't know what I was hoping for. Felix to suddenly come up with some high-tech way of revealing Instagram accounts?

I start to chat to him about his work, his friends, as Sophie makes us all a drink.

'And Gran,' he says, 'how is she? I mean, do you think she's . . .?'

'I . . .' I don't finish the sentence. I can't. With everything that's going on, I can't suddenly tell Felix that I think she needs to be out of that house for a while but it's not for the reasons he thinks. We sit for a moment in silence.

'I think . . .' Sophie begins, and we both look at her; she's been mainly quiet while Felix and I have been chatting, 'that you have to gently show your mother what she's missing out on by refusing to look at other options.'

I raise my eyebrows.

'My grandad,' she goes on, 'he moved into an assisted-living flat. My gran died years ago and he's always been this big independent character and I don't think any of us were ready to let go of that version of him. Especially not him. But it got to a point where he wasn't doing anything. His world got smaller and smaller until it was just his lounge and television set and none of us realised. Not until he finally moved into his assisted-living accommodation and was doing things again. Making new friends, going to the social get-togethers . . . he even joined the chess club.'

Felix puts his hand over hers. I watch as he gives it a squeeze and I see it again like I did when they came for dinner the other week. His love. My son's love for this girl, and at that moment, I understand why he loves her. Why he left his life with us to start one with her.

'What made him move in the end?' I ask.

'A fall.' She gives me a small smile. 'He fell and slipped a disc or something in his back. Had to have an operation and never really recovered his mobility, so we had to look at moving him.'

'And how is he now?'

'He passed away last year,' she says quietly, and then raises her hand as I go to say something. 'It's fine, fine. He was in the assisted living for five years before, and I'm just so glad that he was happy there. Because he wasn't at home on his own. None of us realised, not even him, but he was lonely. So with your mum,' she says, 'it might be an idea to talk to her about the possibility of it. To find out what she wants. Not in terms of living accommodation, but how she wants to live. What she wants to do with her days now.'

I leave the flat with a strange feeling. Sophie's right. We've been focusing on where Mum wants to live, but we should be asking what she wants to *do*.

Does she want to spend her days watching television, like

she is now? Or does she want to do something different? She used to be a member of a book club, used to go out to lunch and keep-fit classes with other people, but gradually, over the years, all that stopped.

As I drive back to her house, I make a mental note to have that chat. Not about her health, medication, diet, but about activities. About how she lives her life.

When I was leaving, Sophie took our cups to the kitchen and Felix walked with me to the door. It must have been all that talk about her grandad, but before I left, he put his hand on my shoulder and said, 'You know, Mum, if you don't like something, you can always change it.'

I gave a laugh. 'It's not me we're thinking about putting in assisted living. I'm not there yet. It's your gran.'

'I know, I know,' he said. 'I'm talking about Dad. You and him, you always seem to be bickering.' He glanced away, and when he looked back at me, his eyes were so sad. 'You don't need to stay together because of me. That's what I mean.'

'Where's this come from? We're not ... Me and your dad, we're fine!'

He looked at me for a long moment.

'Course you are, I just wanted to say it. What with all the money stuff and ... well, when we talked last, you said that you'd never let me down, that I'd always be your baby boy. I just wanted you to know that you could never let me down, it's impossible, and I'll always be your son, but not your baby boy any more. I'm a grown man. Look,' he opened the door a little wider, 'I've got my own flat, a job and a girlfriend, so don't feel ...'

His words trailed off, and I shook my head, unable to talk. Unable to articulate how proud I was of him, how happy I was for the life he was making, but how much it hurt to let him go.

The traffic is bad leading out of Manchester, and while I'm at a standstill waiting for the lights to change, I think back to Felix's words. I almost told him about my affair. About Paul's tests. About the amount of debt that's binding us together. Told him all the reasons why everything needs to stay as it is. Everything needs to be fine. Everything needs to be normal. Instead, I reassured him that me and his dad had a great marriage, but the words sounded empty and hollow.

I check my phone in its holder. Still nothing from Oscar. No messages. No calls. Is this what it feels like to be dumped? Ghosted? Ignored? And so much worse, because aside from all of that, I have the feeling that something much more sinister is at play here. It's like I have all the pieces of the puzzle but just can't make them fit.

I think about calling him again, not sure what my next move is. I don't have time to play it cool; I need to think about what to do now. The lights go to amber, and as I change gear, my phone starts to ring.

Oscar!

But as I stare at the screen, I see it's an unrecognised number.

'Hello?'

'Is this Lou? Lou Whitstable?'

The voice is a woman's, high and breathy, one I don't recognise.

'My name's Denise, and I'm so sorry to have to tell you this, but it's Paul.'

'Paul?'

'Your husband. I'm so sorry, but he's in the hospital. He's had a heart attack.'

THIRTY-SIX

As I pull over, the woman's voice echoes around my car, high and rambling, her words a jumble. I can hear what she's saying, but it's like she's speaking in another language. I can't process the information.

'You're at the hospital?' I ask.

'St Martin's,' she says in a small voice. 'He's OK, the doctor said they got to him in time. But they've taken him into theatre, he needs new stents or something, he's under now.'

'Under?'

'In the ... operating room. They're operating on him. It's ...'

My mind suddenly catches up and I feel myself shift from shock to action. I need to get there. I need to call Felix. I need to get to Paul. I need ...

'Are you a nurse?'

'No, no.' A hesitation, a sniff. 'I'm ... I was with him when he ...'

At that moment, I don't care who or what she is. She tells

me the hospital again and what ward they're planning to take him to, and I speed off. I need to tell Felix, to ask Helen to see to my mother, and I press my foot hard on the accelerator, making the calls as I drive.

'He's fine.' She's waiting for me outside the ward, and as her words tumble out about Paul, I make the connection of who she is, this woman who called me with the terrible news. It's Denise. The woman Paul is teaching to play darts. 'They're still with him in the operating room, but a doctor, a surgeon, a consultant, I don't know who he was, he did tell me but I've forgotten, anyway, a man came out and told me. Paul's OK.'

Her face is blotchy from crying. Her eyes are red-rimmed and swollen and I can tell that she started the day with a full face of make-up but most of it has been wiped away. Her blonde ponytail swings as she speaks; she's one of those people who talk with their hands and wave them about to punctuate their words, and it makes her whole body move in time.

I let her tell me about Paul's condition. I speak with a nurse, and then the consultant, and then I go back to Denise and we talk over how he is, what exactly happened, how he got to hospital and what the specialist said, and then we look at each other.

'You're the new landlady,' I say, 'the one at the Duck and Bucket. Paul's teaching you to play darts. For your dad.'

'Yes.' She sniffs again. 'He's been so helpful, so wonderful. He's such a lovely man.'

'He is,' I agree. And it's the strangest thing, seeing Paul through her eyes. How much she thinks of him.

I can tell by the way she's talking, the way she's so open about how many times they've met and what they've been

253

doing that they aren't having an affair. Not yet, anyway. She gets a flush at the top of her cheeks as she talks about him, her eyes dancing a little. Even now, even in a drab hospital corridor, she sparkles when she talks of my husband.

Yet I don't feel any jealousy or anger. Sitting there in that corridor under the harsh fluorescent lighting, waiting to hear when we can see him, I just feel tired. Denise seems like a nice person, and although it sounds insane, I can see her and Paul being a good fit. She clearly fancies him in a way I haven't for a long time, and it feels like there's nowhere to hide from this realisation any more. I can't push it under the debt we have. I can't keep it behind his heart condition, and I can't refuse to look at it because of being distracted with my mother. I love Paul, of course I love him, but I'm not *in love* with him. I'm no longer in love with my husband, and it's so sad, so terribly, awfully sad.

When Felix arrives and sees my tear-stained face, he automatically thinks the worst.

'He's fine,' I tell him when he runs up to me. 'He's fine, all good. The operation went well and we're just waiting to see him. He's had two stents fitted and he's going to be fine. They caught it in time.' I look to Denise. 'It's lucky he had Denise with him. She spotted the signs and drove him straight here.'

We go in to see Paul together, the three of us, and even though he's full of drugs, I can see how much it means to him. Denise was going to leave once we knew he was OK, she said it was a family time, but I insisted she stayed. She cares for my husband in a way I no longer do, and she saved his life – because of her, Felix still has a father, for which I am beyond grateful.

As we chat and make plans for the next few days and future

visits, my mind can't catch up with itself. I can't think clearly about how I feel. It's all too much and too soon, but I do know we need to talk. And not a talk I can keep avoiding. We can't go on living like strangers in the same house and pretending we're a normal couple. That's not who we are any more and we need to own up to being the people we've become.

Driving to my mother's in the early hours, I'm exhausted.

In the space of a day, everything has changed. Felix has gone home, and Paul will be on the ward for the next few days under observation, which at least gives me some time to think about it all. To get my head straight and try to come up with some kind of plan of what to do.

'Wow,' says Helen after I tell her everything. 'I mean. Wow. Are you OK?'

'D'you know what?' I take a sip of my tea. 'I am. I really am. But it's all so hard. And so sad.' I feel tears threaten and grit my teeth. 'I feel such a failure. Over everything.' I give a half-laugh and wipe my face. 'But I know I can't go on like this. I need to do something. Felix was just saying tonight that I didn't need to stay with Paul on his account. He knows we're not . . .' I trail off. 'But you did as well, didn't you?'

Helen gives me a sad smile. 'I've known something hasn't been right with you two for . . .' She shrugs. 'But you never know what goes on behind closed doors, do you? And you seemed happy enough. It was only when you met Oscar, when you spoke about him, that I saw it. I saw how you were, and I knew you were in trouble. He'd kind of woken you up.'

I nod in agreement and then start to silently cry. Helen comes over and puts her arm around me.

'It's grief,' she says into my hair, 'the death of your marriage.

You're allowed to grieve and I'm so glad that you're making this decision. It's not been fair to you or to Paul.'

We're sitting in the kitchen, whispering over cups of tea so as not to wake my mother, who is sleeping.

It's a lot. So much.

'It's all over between Oscar and me,' I tell her. 'And he's not answering any of my calls or texts because . . .' my stomach dips as it all comes back to me, 'because I'm not sure exactly what it means, but I found this.' I fish about in my pocket and pull out the key ring. 'It was attached to the back of the camera on the front door so the alarm kept going off when no one was around. Oscar fitted the cameras and I can't work out when this got there.'

Helen takes it off me.

'What even is it? This ribbon? Does it mean something?'

'It's a charity key ring. Meant to signify helping children or something, and I know that because the man who came here a few weeks ago trying to fleece my mother out of her pension, he tried to give me one.'

'And this was on the camera?'

I nod. 'So now I don't know if it was there as a fluke, blown there in the wind, or whether he came back and put it there after Mum refused to let him in. But it's such an odd thing to do. Why would you fit this to a security camera? And for Oscar to not see it, unless . . .'

'Unless Oscar and that slimeball are in it together in some way. Some elaborate plan to rob your mother out of her life savings?'

'I don't know! And now Oscar won't answer me. Won't reply to my texts.' I stare down at my mug. 'I have no idea who the man I've been sleeping with really is.'

THIRTY-SEVEN

The next morning, I wake in my mother's lounge. After Helen left, there seemed little point in going home and then coming back a few hours later, so I took a blanket and curled up on the couch. I could've gone up to my old room, moved the junk off the bed and laid down on the dusty mattress where I used to sleep all those years ago, but even the thought of it was too much.

The last time I slept in that room was just before I moved out, pregnant with Felix, still reeling from my brother and father's deaths and determined to live a safe and small life. I've certainly done that.

I sit up and rub at the back of my neck, which is aching. My head feels like it's filled with cotton wool. I can't single out any thoughts or make sense of anything. For a long time last night I lay staring at the ceiling, thinking about the question Helen asked me before she left.

What are you going to do?

I thought about marriage counselling, and as soon as the idea came to me, I dismissed it. Would that really fix anything? What's the point in going around in circles? But that conversation and everything it entails will have to wait. I need Paul to recover. The specialist said he needs to take it easy for months. No unnecessary stress. No surprises, like his wife having an affair, or horrible texts and posts on social media to stress him out. That's my priority now.

I go to make coffee and think about how I need to call the bank. Tell them that Paul's had a heart attack and won't be working, and I suddenly wonder if we've got critical illness insurance and what that would mean. If we could just get them to give us six months where we didn't need to make the repayments, we could have a bit of a breather.

I'm waiting for the kettle to boil when I hear a bang from upstairs, my mother's room. I take the stairs two at a time.

'Mum? You OK?'

When I get to the landing, I stop. She looks awful. Her hair sticking up, her face pale and her complexion grey.

'What happened? What did you . . .?'

And that's when I see it. The bang I heard was a torch dropping to the floor. I bend to pick it up. It's one of those heavy-duty ones, the ones used by car mechanics.

Her face contorts, and she rubs her hands over it.

'They were here,' she says, and her voice is small and shaky, 'last night. I heard voices.'

'It was Helen. You know she stayed . . .'

'No, it wasn't you and Helen. I'm not stupid. I know what I heard.'

I step towards her, but she bats me away.

'I saw him.'

'Saw who?'

'A man. Out there. He was looking up at my window. Away from the house a little and around the side, hiding in the shadows so the camera wouldn't get him. He's clever, knew where to stand.'

I look towards her bedroom and then to her. 'For goodness' sake, Mum, why didn't you tell me? Wake me up?'

'Paul's just had a heart attack! I didn't want to wake you after what you'd gone through yesterday, and besides,' she bites her lip, 'I wanted to deal with it myself. I thought if it was that man from the charity I could record him, like he recorded me. Get some footage of him outside my house and take it to the police.'

I stare at my mother. She never uses her mobile phone. Has no idea how to use the camera, so this idea is beyond me.

Her face twists again. 'But that stupid phone is broken. I couldn't get it to work, so I . . .'

'Mum?'

'Well, he saw me. Saw what I was trying to do and . . . He started laughing.'

'Laughing?'

'I heard him. Horrible.'

'Mum, I was right downstairs. Why didn't you—'

'He left. I saw him walk away still laughing, and I thought about waking you up, but then I thought, well, what could we do?' She sags suddenly, her shoulders dropping. 'So I've kept watch. Thought that if he came back, I'd wake you up and *you* could film him.'

'You've been watching out for him all night?' I stare at her, and suddenly the way she looks makes sense. 'Oh Mum. Why on earth didn't you just wake me up?'

259

'Don't get mad at me.' She wipes her face. 'I thought I was doing the right thing, and you needed your sleep!'

'So do you. Shall we get you back to bed?'

She shakes her head, tells me she needs to be up, dressed and downstairs. And she doesn't say it, but I know she's thinking she needs to be ready in case he comes back. This man, this person who's terrorising my mother and making her stare out of her bedroom window all night.

Later that morning, my mother falls asleep in her chair. I made her eggs on toast and a cup of tea, and now her eyes are closed and she's dozed off in front of the television. All morning she's been talking about this figure watching her, and I can't work out if she was dreaming or if it was real. I can't work out why she was so silly as not to wake me up. But then that's the stubbornness of my mother all over. Still thinking she can fix things. Protect me. Still being my mother.

My phone rings and makes me jump. I answer it quickly so it doesn't wake her, walking into the kitchen with it.

Felix.

'Shall I meet you at the hospital?' he asks, and I look at the time. The morning has slipped away from me. Already it's lunchtime, and pretty soon it'll be time to visit Paul.

We go through the arrangements and the latest update from the hospital, and after I've ended the call, I go back into the living room and look at my mother's sleeping face. I can't leave her on her own. Not after what happened last night.

Could I ask Helen? I dismiss the idea. She's at an event with Simon's work later, one of their date nights. Anyway, I leaned on her so much last night, I can't ask the same of her again. I feel so helpless. I make myself a drink as I try to think of what to do. With no solution, I call Felix back.

'I don't think I'm going to be able to come,' I tell him, my voice low. I explain about not feeling comfortable leaving Mum, and what she thinks she saw last night.

'Can't you ask Helen again?' He sounds agitated. 'We're on our way to the hospital now, and we've bought Dad some stuff, but ...' he pauses, 'we got you something too. Some flowers.'

'Flowers?'

'It was Sophie's idea. She said you needed cheering up as well, and we wanted to ask you to come over to ours this Sunday, you and Gran. Both of you for Sunday dinner.'

I stare at the phone.

'Mum?'

'I'm here. I just ... That's lovely. Me and your gran, you cooking for us both?'

'Sophie thought it would be nice.'

'It is nice.' I smile into the phone. 'It's lovely, and—' I'm stopped by a loud crash and a scream.

'Mum?'

'It's all right, I think it's your gran. I'll call you back.'

I end the call and run into the lounge to see my mother standing, and the side table lying on the floor.

'Are you OK? What happened? What was that noise?'

'I woke up and thought there was someone standing over me, and I ...' She looks at the cane in her hand, and I go to her and put my arms around her.

'It's OK,' I tell her. 'Shh, I'm here. I'm not leaving.'

'But Paul?' She moves back. 'Aren't you visiting him? Isn't it—'

'I'm not leaving you, Mum, not like this.'

She waves her hand, tries to tell me she's all right. That it was just a bad dream and she'll be fine on her own for an hour or two. We're still arguing about it when there's a tap at the door.

'I heard about Paul.' It's Rick, with a box of biscuits and his friendly face, and before he can stop me, I'm hugging him.

'It's been . . .'

He nods. 'I saw the torch out of the bedroom window again.'

'The worst part of it all,' I tell him as I usher him inside, 'is that I was here. I slept over last night. If she'd just told me, woken me up, I could've dealt with it. Seen if anyone was actually there. As it is, she spent all night keeping watch and is in a right state.'

Mum smiles when she sees him, and it's all I can do not to cry. Her eyes are so watery, her face so confused.

'Are you OK, Vivienne?' He goes to sit beside her and holds her hand.

My mother tells him about the cameras not working, the ribbon that blew in front of the sensor, the man outside watching her. 'And she's missing visiting that stupid husband of hers who went and gave himself a heart attack because of it all.'

Rick looks at me. 'Is that true?'

'It's fine,' I tell them both. 'Felix and Sophie are with him.'

'Let me stay with her,' he suddenly offers. 'We need a catch-up, don't we, Vivienne? We can have a coffee and you can tell me your news.'

I feel tears spring behind my eyes.

'Really?'

He nods, and five minutes later I'm en route to the hospital. It feels surreal. Up to now, I haven't had time to digest it all. But making my way through the midday traffic, where everyone is going about their lives as normal, it feels like the filter has changed. Like I'm in an alternative universe.

As I pull up at the traffic lights, my phone rings and I press answer without looking at the caller, assuming it's Felix returning my missed call.

'I'm just—'

'Louise?'

Oscar.

There's a moment's crackle on the other end of the line.

'Oscar? Is that you?'

'We need to meet,' he says, and his words are rushed. 'Now. It's urgent. Can you come to the Gatehouse?'

'Why didn't you show up last night? You can't just demand that—'

'I wouldn't say it was urgent if it wasn't. Can you come here? I'll wait for you. I'm in a booth at the back.'

I look at the road, the route to the hospital on my left, and the Gatehouse and Oscar on my right.

I hit the indicator.

'I'll be there in ten minutes.'

THIRTY-EIGHT

My hands are shaking on the steering wheel as I turn into the car park at the Gatehouse. It's lunchtime and it's half busy. Families, office workers, the kind of nondescript people you know you'll never see again strolling in and out of the entrance, and I rush past them into the pub, my eyes searching for him. I walk to the back, to where I was sitting alone last night, the booths that are half hidden, and it's then that I see him – his boot, at least, sticking out – and my heart gallops.

I told myself on the drive here that I was just going to listen to what he had to say. I wasn't even going to sit down with him; I phoned Felix and told him I was going to be late but would still catch visiting time. But yet again, my body is betraying me. I have an overwhelming urge to throw myself at him, to feel his arms around me, to drink in the smell of him and for him to comfort me. I grit my teeth and walk towards him.

'I'm here,' is all I say when I get to the table.

'Louise!' He goes to stand. 'Thank God you came.'

'I'm not staying long.' I grip my handbag, my heart hammering in my throat, and find I can't look at him. Can't meet his eyes, because if I do, I'm afraid I won't hold my nerve. 'So explain. Tell me now what you've got to say. And quick.'

'I ...' He takes a deep breath. 'Please just sit for a minute, this is—'

'Difficult?' I cut in. 'I was here, ready to listen last night. Where were you?'

'Blackpool.'

I look at him then, and take in the stubble on his chin, the creased clothing and slightly greasy hair, and the way he's gripping his untouched pint.

'I was trying to fix things,' he goes on, 'repair what I'd broken, but it didn't work.'

'Is this about the cameras?' I go to my pocket and bring out the key ring, slamming it on the table. 'You mean this?'

He looks from the key ring to me, confusion on his face.

'It was on my mother's camera. Making the alarm sound with every slight breeze, the camera that *you fitted* that you should've checked—'

'Josh.'

The word slices through the air.

'Josh? Please tell me you're talking about someone else, and not the—'

'The man who came to your mother's house claiming to be from a charity, asking her for money?' He gives a slow nod, and it's like the room tilts. The lighting goes dim around the edges of my vision as I realise what he's just said. What he's just admitted to.

'You know him?'

He looks at me for a long moment, his eyes heavy and sad.

'I do,' he says eventually, and I grip the table, afraid my legs might give way.

'Oh God,' I mutter, 'I've been so stupid.'

His hand is on mine. 'No. You haven't, not at all. *I've* been stupid. Please, just let me explain. I need to tell you everything, because Viv, your mother . . . she might be . . . well, I think the two of you might be in danger.'

'Danger?'

'Please sit, just let me talk . . .'

A woman bustles past, knocking me slightly as she makes her way towards the entrance, and I'm suddenly aware of the people around us. The dramatic scene I'm creating by standing at the booth arguing. I've become some kind of lunchtime soap opera for the other customers.

I shuffle into the seat opposite him, hidden by the glass partitions, and he rubs a hand over his face.

'Tell me,' I say tightly, my voice thin. 'I need to know exactly how any of this involves my mother and how you know that creep.'

He looks heavenward, before bringing his head back down and staring at his pint.

'It was about this time last year. I was doing OK. I had a bit of money saved and was ready to go on my trip. I was finishing up a job for him, this was before I'd even met Josh, and he tells me about this property investment. Studio apartments over on the other side of Manchester. Eight per cent return. Says if I delay a few months, he can give me my cash back and I'd have this investment working for me when my trip was over. And I suddenly think that I can go from budget trip to a mid-level one. I would be able to afford some nice hotels, and I'd have a bit of cash to come back to. He swears it's foolproof. He took money out of his business to invest in it, that's how much of a sure thing he thought it was, and so I did it. I gave him all my savings to invest and waited to get my money back.'

He rubs a hand over his face. 'But it didn't work out that way. A few months in, nothing has started with the development, and then we're told the company that took our money has gone into administration.' He waves his hands, swiping them through the air. 'Gone. All of it.'

He swallows, and I open my mouth to ask what all this has to do with my mother, or the key ring, but he holds up his hand to stop me.

'He got lawyers to sue for compensation,' he tells me, 'used up what cash he had left on that, but it didn't work. Hasn't worked. That's where I've been, signing documents to let the solicitors do whatever new thing it is that they think might get us some cash back, but speaking with them, it's apparent we're just clutching at straws.'

He runs his hands through his hair and looks at me. 'That's when he had this idea. When it became clear that our money was gone, he rang me up and told me about this plan he has. That *we* become the developers. Get new investors to work with us.'

'I don't understand.' I shake my head. 'All this stuff about property investment, what has it got to do with—'

'He tells me that if he can get this old woman to move out of her house, he'll be saved. But she's stubborn and won't agree, so we just have to persuade her. Once she agrees to sell, everything will fall into place, because he'll get a nice bit of cash that we can use to continue with the development and attract new investors. We can make our money back and more. He says if I do my bit, I'll get everything I lost, and . . .'

My mind is doing somersaults. It's like that old video game where blocks fall, and you have to fit them into place to build a picture. My heart hammers as the picture I'm forming in my mind takes hold.

Took money out of his business to invest . . .

About to lose everything.

Move the old woman out of her house and it'll bring in the cash.

'Paul?' I whisper, hardly believing what I'm saying. 'When you say he, you mean Paul? Paul is behind all this? You're telling me you've conspired with my husband to—'

'Paul?' Oscar shakes his head slowly. 'No, it's Rick. It's Rick who got me involved.'

'Rick?' I give a laugh of disbelief. 'That makes no sense, why would—'

'The land,' Oscar says, leaning in, 'it's the land he's after. If your mother agreed to sell, he would buy her house, demolish it along with his bungalow and use the land for the property development.'

I stare at him and feel something drop in my chest. 'Rick wants to buy my mother's house? Then tear it down along with his bungalow . . .'

He takes a deep breath. 'That land, on the commuter belt, it's perfect for studio apartments. He was going to use his own house as collateral to buy your mother's and begin the development that the investors could then finance.'

I think back to the brochure at his house, the glossy pictures of studio apartments, and how I assumed he was thinking of moving into one, not actually planning to build them.

'If he could convince you and your mother that she needed to sell,' Oscar goes on, 'he was going to offer a cash sale. Tell you anything you needed to hear. That he'd keep the house as it is, that your brother and father's ashes would be untouched. It'd be nice and easy, no need to involve estate agents, and of course you'd trust him because . . .'

'It's Rick,' I finish, and he nods.

'And then once Vivienne was out, he'd tear the place down and start with the development. Making back what he'd lost and more.'

I shake my head. 'So you've been . . . everything has . . .'

'It was simple at first. When Rick told me about it, he said it was a win–win. He knew you were struggling for cash, and this way everyone would benefit. He didn't make it sound too bad. He thought the best way to convince you that she needed to be out was to play on her age. Make out that she was a threat to herself. He told me he was well under way with doing little bits to confuse her. Nipping in through the back door and messing about with her stuff – hiding her library books, or her house keys, taking food she thought she'd bought and then returning it, dropping the catch on the lock so she'd lock herself out, moving her shoes and cane so she was more likely to stumble if she went out. Little things. Stuff to show you she couldn't live alone any longer. He was planting seeds; he told me we just needed to push a bit harder. Take it up a notch. That's when he got Josh, this guy he knows who's a right scumbag, to visit your mother, to show you how vulnerable she is.

'That was the first part. Then I was meant to do a few things on my way to and from Rick's. He wanted me to scare her – not much, just rattle her a bit – but I couldn't do it.' He shakes his head. 'I ended up lurking in the dark, just watching the house.'

I thought of all those times I'd felt shivers up the back of my neck, like I was being watched, and I grit my teeth. Oscar was watching me, and Rick was doing all those things that made me think my mother was . . .

'How could you?' My voice is loud. 'How could you even . . .?'

'I couldn't,' he says simply, holding up his hands, 'I couldn't. That day your husband got me to do those jobs? I'd just been telling Rick that I wasn't prepared to scare an old lady in her own home. He said he'd get Josh back, and we argued, and then on my way out, Paul invited me to work on the house. Call it serendipity. I just thought I could, I dunno, protect you a bit from whatever Rick and Josh were about to do.' He shakes his head again. 'And then you and me happened.'

'Was that also part of the plan?' My voice is hard and brittle. 'Shag the daughter, get her onside and get her to—'

'No, no!' Oscar grabs my hands. 'Never. Me and you were real. *Are* real. From the moment we met, our first lesson, I've been trying to stop Rick. Trying to persuade him to abandon his stupid efforts at scaring Viv. Scaring you.'

'But after that first visit, the one you told me about, Josh went back to my mother's . . .'

'I had no idea. I knew nothing about that until later, when I confronted Rick . . .'

'And that time when she thought someone was outside her house in the night. When we got the police . . .'

'I'm assuming it was Josh,' he says quietly. 'Rick planning something to scare her, make it so she'd want to leave.'

I think back to that night, how Rick had come running over, and remember how he was dressed and looked like he always did, immaculate. Not like a guy who'd just got out of bed.

'He told me he found her sleepwalking. Carrying a doll. Calling him by my father's name.'

270

Oscar shakes his head.

'And when I asked her, she . . .' I bang my fist on the table. 'It was all lies, wasn't it? My mother wasn't wandering outside in her nightdress. He said that to make me think she had . . .'

Oscar holds up his hands. 'I swear I didn't know the extent of it. It's gone too far, that's why I went to Blackpool, to see if there was any way we could get some cash back, something I could tell Rick so he would abandon this stupid plan.'

'You should've told me.' Anger is rising in me as I think back to my mother's confused face, her fear, everything she's been through these past few weeks. 'When we went out for that drink, before we . . .'

'But then we did,' he says quickly, 'and how could I admit what I'd done? What I was involved in? I didn't want to lose you. I thought I could change Rick's mind. Stop it all.'

I stare at him.

'The cameras?'

'Rick was using them as another way to scare Viv. Every time I came back, they'd been tampered with. Something like that bloody key ring to make them go off.'

'And the messages on Instagram?' My mind is racing.

'Josh saw us that night at the pub and Rick used it. When he put that note on your windscreen, that's when I decided that I had to do something, that he'd gone too far . . .'

'All this time,' I close my eyes, 'while we were in bed to-gether, while you listened to me worry about my mother, you just stayed quiet. You saw what this whole thing was doing to us, and you didn't say a word.'

He looks at me, his eyes heavy and dark, full of regret. 'I tried,' he says quietly, 'but I was so scared of telling you. I thought I could make him stop. I'm so ashamed.'

'You should be.' My voice is louder than I intended. 'You've been awful. Horrible.' I stop before angry tears can fall and stand up to leave. 'I need to tell the police, to get them to arrest Rick, to—'

I stop as a cold slice of realisation grips me. 'Oh God. Oh no, I need to go.'

'Louise?'

'He's with her now. Rick. I left them together when I came here. He offered to look after her for me.'

THIRTY-NINE

I run out of the pub, Oscar close behind. My mind is a scramble of thoughts and images. Everything he has just told me, the lies, the scheming, the deceit – and then Rick. Lovely Rick with his true-crime books and box sets and the image of him plotting against my mother. It just doesn't make sense, it doesn't fit.

But as I make the frenzied drive towards Mum's, Oscar ahead of me in his van, I think of how Felix and Sophie said his shop had shut down in Manchester. I think of him telling me that he was working from home, but how all the clients I used to see come and go had dried up. I think about all the times he phoned me, his flat tone as if he was annoyed at being disturbed. The library books that my mother had forgotten she'd read. All the times he'd subtly asked if she would sell. The popping round to tell me how she'd done this or that, way before Oscar was even involved. Was that all lies? Him sowing the seeds for what was to come?

The mock concern on his face when he said he'd found her

sleepwalking, that her torch had been waking him up in the night, when all the time he knew Josh was over there frightening her. The scumbag who was making her so afraid in her own house that she'd be desperate to leave. To move out. Away from everything she loves, the ashes of my father and brother and ... I bang the steering wheel hard, my hand throbbing with the pain. I'm furious.

Oscar's van is already in the driveway when I pull up. The front door is open. I stall the car I'm so anxious to get in there, and it jerks forward as I pull on the handbrake and jump out.

'Enough. You've done enough.'

I can hear him from the hallway, and when I run in, I see him facing Rick, mid argument, and my mother sitting in her chair between them, a frown etched on her face and her hands fiddling with the strap on her cane. I want to scoop her up and take her away from it all. Put her in my car and take her somewhere safe. Away from two men shouting at each other in her living room. My anger rises like a tidal wave. How dare they do this to her? To us?

'Oscar,' Rick is saying, and his voice is smooth, calm, 'you've misunderstood this whole thing. Please sit down, you're scaring Vivienne. Have a cup of tea and relax.'

'Enough,' Oscar repeats through gritted teeth. 'It's over, Rick. I've told Lou. Told her all of it.'

'All of what?' Rick looks over to me, and as his gaze meets mine, I falter. I peer a little closer at him. Is that a kind of cold calculation behind his eyes? Something hard that I haven't noticed before?

'Rick,' it's an effort to keep my voice level, 'I think it's best if you leave. Right now.'

His eyes flick towards Oscar and then back to me, and

suddenly I know that everything Oscar has told me is true. Everything. I see it in the way Rick is evaluating us, the way he's trying to read me, the way he's not moving, not retaliating, and my hand goes to my neckline in shock. How could I have been so naïve?

'Nonsense!' He lets out a laugh. 'Don't you think you're being a little dramatic? I've not caught up properly with Vivienne yet.' He turns to my mother, smiling. 'How about another custard cream, Viv? And you tell these two to go and cool off somewhere so we can finish our chat?'

'Lou? Is everything all right?'

I go to her, my anger rapidly swinging into fear. If Rick had shouted denial, argued, it would be easy, but the way he's not responding scares me. The way he's not budging, not rising to any of it, is unnerving.

'Mum?' I put my hand on her arm. 'Let's go.'

'Go where? What's going on? Oscar burst in here like a man possessed and said that Rick's trying to mess with me. That he isn't who I think he is.'

Her eyes search the room as I help her stand up. There's a heavy tension all around, like when you go into a pub and know a fight is brewing. 'Sixth sense', that's what we used to call it when we were kids, when we could feel a scrap about to start in the playground. 'My sixth sense is going off!' we'd shout as we heckled the brawlers and cheered when the first punch was thrown. I don't want to be here when the first anything is thrown. I don't want to be in this room, and I certainly don't want my mother here.

I look to Oscar, and he picks up on my silent plea.

'Let's get you out of here, Viv,' he says, and takes her other arm.

275

'Now wait a minute.' Rick's voice is loud, and it stops us. 'We were in the middle of a conversation. We were having a nice chat. You can't just uproot her now, she hasn't even finished her tea.'

'It's all over,' Oscar says, 'all of it. I'm helping Viv get out of here, and then me and you are leaving.'

I see them then, on the coffee table beside the plate of biscuits and the framed photographs. The deeds to my mother's house.

'You have got to be kidding me,' I say, and Oscar looks at the table.

'Seriously?' He moves over and picks them up. 'And how exactly was this going to work, Rick? You'd buy the house off Vivienne while she's still living in it? Did you really think—'

'Stop that!' My mother's voice is harsh. 'Rick offered to look after the deeds.' She turns to me, her face full of confusion and worry. 'He knows that man. The man from the charity. He's been telling me that Josh has put in a claim for the land between our houses. He thinks it belongs to him, was his grandfather's or something, and that's why he keeps coming here. He thinks he owns those fields.' She points to the window. 'So Rick's taking the deeds to his solicitor. He's going to get them to draw up a contract stating that we own this land, divided between us where the boundaries are, and then I'll just have to sign—'

She stops at Oscar's laugh.

'How would that even work?' he asks Rick. 'You really are something. Let me guess, you'd get Viv all confused, persuade her to sign the papers agreeing to a sale, and then what?'

Rick steps forward and shoves him hard on the shoulder. 'Stop interfering,' he hisses. 'What was your idea? Run off to

Blackpool to see if the solicitors could do anything? And let me guess, no good news. I'm using my initiative; what are *you* doing?' He looks at me, and the change in his features is noticeable. Gone is the usual serene, calm expression, replaced with a tight, hard anger. 'Shagging her? Getting lost between her thighs and forgetting about all the money we lost? All the money we stand to make here? Is she worth that much?'

I see Oscar's hands curl into fists, and I grip my mother harder.

'Lou?' She turns to me, leaning heavily on her stick.

'It's OK,' I tell her quietly, 'let's just get out of here and into the kitchen, hey?' I start to inch her slowly away. Away from Oscar and Rick, now shouting at each other over the coffee table. We've only taken a few steps before she stops and turns.

'Rick? It's not true, is it? What they're saying about you?'

'Come on, Mum,' I urge her.

But she won't move. She's watching Rick and Oscar with an expression of confusion and fear on her face.

'Rick?'

He doesn't hear her. He's locked in his argument with Oscar, his posture more aggressive than I've ever seen it. His face contorted with anger as he hisses in Oscar's face.

'We almost had her,' he's saying. 'If you weren't such a coward, we'd be done and dusted by now. And what do I tell Josh? Who's going to pay him? He did all the things you were supposed to. Coming here night after night, spending hours standing outside the house.'

'Josh?' My mother looks to me. 'The charity man?'

'And all the times he came back to fiddle with those bloody cameras,' Rick goes on, oblivious of my mother and her questions. 'You made it so much harder than it needed to be. And for what? A bit of skirt? A quick roll around in the sheets? We stand to make real money here, Oscar. A lot of money. Do you know what it took to get those investors on board?'

My mother grips my arm. 'Rick had Josh working for him?' she asks in a whisper. 'He made him come here in the night? Scare me? Fiddle with the cameras?' She looks at me. 'So I'm not losing my marbles? I'm not headed for the loony bin?'

'Mum, let's just go outside. Get in my car and I'll explain it all.'

'But why?' she asks, her face desperate, and I try to move her, but she's solid, her small frame strengthened by anger and a determination to know the truth. She shakes me off, using her stick to push me away slightly. '*Why?*' she shouts, and the room goes quiet.

Rick and Oscar turn to us, Rick blinking, as if he's momentarily forgotten why we're even in the room.

'Why?' He repeats the question back at her. 'Because of *this*,' he glances around him, 'this big, empty, stupid house that you won't leave.' He takes a step towards her. 'If you'd only listened when I asked you if you'd sell. When I told you how I could give you a quick and easy sale. You'd be somewhere safe and warm by now, oblivious to it all; you'd be *happy.*' He hisses the last word into her face. 'I have investors lined up. The money is almost there. I can smell it. If you'd just agree to sell to me, but,' he jabs a finger into her shoulder, 'you won't. You are the only thing standing between me and a fortune. And for what?' He gives a laugh. 'This place is practically falling down. It's a disaster! Why would anyone want to actually live here?'

He swings round to me. 'And *you*,' he sneers, 'are the biggest fool of them all. You have no money. You live in that little sad house with your little sad life. Gormless bitch that you are. All those times we've talked and I've felt like slapping you. Shaking you by the shoulders and telling you how pathetic and stupid you are. Coward. You're just as bad as him.' He waves to Oscar and then picks up the framed picture of my father and brother from the coffee table. 'And all because a few useless ashes are scattered in the garden. You should've made her move out years ago. Made her sell this awful, decrepit excuse of a place as soon as the accident happened instead of making it into some kind of shrine. Forgotten about the people who are no longer alive and don't—'

It happens in slow motion.

My mother lifts her stick and points it at the middle of Rick's chest. He isn't looking; his arms are wide open as he gestures to the house, showing us all what a dump it is.

She pushes.

He looks down and smiles pityingly at her effort to attack him, and then he realises he's lost his balance. He tries to regain it by stepping back, but his stick is over by his chair, and without his usual support, he staggers. He reaches out for something to grab hold of. Something to steady him, but it's too late and he starts to fall.

His face is pure shock as he goes down. He throws the photograph away; it lands at my feet as he grabs the empty air for something, anything to save him. But nothing does. He hits the slate hearth by the fireplace, the fire still on, my mother's deeds lying on the coffee table.

There's a dull thud as his head connects with the hard stone, and then silence.

FORTY

'Is he dead?'

My mother's question cuts through the stillness.

I look at Rick, unmoving on the floor. Dark liquid oozes from the back of his head and slips into the grouting of the slate tiles on the hearth. I'm stuck. I can't move. I'm not even sure I'm breathing. I should check him. Try to feel for a pulse, but I can't move. I'm frozen on the spot, staring at Rick and his glassy eyes gazing out into nothing.

Did I just see that? Did I just see him die?

'Is he dead?'

I look up, see my mother staring down at him, Oscar too. Then he glances up at me, our eyes connecting and agreeing. We both know that Rick's no longer here. We both know it won't take feeling his pulse or checking his breath to find that out.

'It was an accident,' he says slowly. 'Anyone will see it was an accident.'

My heart is beating wildly. I swallow, my mouth dry suddenly.

I'm desperate for a drink of water. Oh God, oh God, oh God, he's dead, Rick is actually lying dead in my mother's lounge.

'What are we going to do now?' She looks at her stick and then drops it, and I grab her hand. I so badly want to reassure her, to tell her what happened had nothing to do with the slight push she gave him, but that would be untrue; it had everything to do with her push, he just fell badly. What are the chances? What are the chances of him falling and hitting his head on the slate like that? She goes to speak again, and I raise my hand slightly to stop her.

'Just be quiet for a moment.' I swallow, the dryness in my mouth getting worse. I can't seem to get my breath. 'Let me think.'

'You going to call them?' she asks. 'The police?'

'I don't think we can do anything else,' says Oscar, and his eyes meet mine. 'Can we?'

A million words rush between us in that second, a million unsaid things. It's too much. I slowly get my phone from my back pocket. It takes three attempts to put in my passcode and I hesitate on the last try.

I look up at him. 'You should go,' I tell him. 'You shouldn't be here when the police arrive.' I turn to my mother, words at last beginning to form rationally in my head, thoughts and logic finally taking over from the shock. 'What happened was a tragic accident,' I tell her. 'You never meant for—'

'Of course I didn't!' She's fiddling with the collar at her neck. 'I didn't want him to fall, I never wanted him to hit his head like that. I was just so angry with him. For weeks, months now, I've been thinking I was losing it, that my mind was going, and all the time it was him, messing with my things. Making me think I had . . .' She covers her face with her hands. 'And what he said about your father and brother ...' She starts to cry.

'Hey, shh.' I put my arms around her. 'What you did was completely understandable. Completely. But ...' I glance down at Rick, the pool of blood beneath his head now large and beginning to seep into the carpet, 'Oscar should go.'

'I'm staying,' he says. 'I'll tell them—'

'You can't tell them anything,' I say, 'not while you're standing over his dead body.' I look at Rick again. 'He fell because of his dodgy hip. We all saw that. He was off balance, and it was bad luck the way he landed. But if the police come, and we tell them that, and then they find out your history with him ...' I shake my head. 'I can only ...'

'You've been reading too many crime novels,' Oscar says. 'I should be here, I should—'

'You should go,' I repeat. 'With you here it turns an accidental death into a suspicious one.'

We're all silent for a moment.

'We'll tell the police exactly what happened,' I say. 'That my mother accidentally knocked into Rick and he fell. He was without his stick, and he fell badly and hit his head.' I look at them both. 'Everything I've just said is true, I'm just leaving out the parts that they don't need to know.'

I bend down and pick up the photograph from the floor. I look into the faces of my father and brother and then hand it to my mother, who grips it tightly.

'If he hadn't picked this up,' she says quietly, 'if his hands had been free ...'

'But they weren't,' I tell her, 'and he did pick it up. He picked it up to tell us that we should've forgotten about them. But we never will.'

'Never.' She hugs the photograph to her chest as she looks at me, and for a mad moment it feels like my father and brother had something to do with it all. Like they were involved in stopping Rick. I let out a laugh of disbelief before snapping back into the room and what we need to do next.

After a few minutes' more arguing, I convince Oscar that he needs to go. Once he has left, I sit my mother in the kitchen, pour her a brandy from the bottle we keep in the cupboard and then ring the police. I tell them there's been an awful accident. A terrible, horrendous freak accident involving our lovely neighbour. An ambulance arrives with the police. No flashing lights, no hurrying to save a life. This life has already gone.

The rest of the day is a flurry of people asking questions, of movement and hushed voices, and throughout it all I sit holding my mother's hand and don't leave her side. Nodding my head and answering as best I can, retelling and repeating the story of how it happened. My heart aches, throbbing with the knowledge that she's silently berating herself. That once all this is over, she will fall down a hole of guilt and remorse. I can already see her replaying it all in her mind; every time I mention his bad hip, or his stick, she winces. Silent tears fall from her eyes, and I wrap my arms around her small frame, kiss her soft white hair, pass her tissues, make her tea, pour more brandy. I ask her what I can do, but I already know the answer.

At the end of the day, after everyone has left, when there's only a stain on the carpet to show that anything ever happened, my mother crumbles. The emotion she's held on to tightly all day is unbound.

'I'm a killer,' she whispers between tears. 'I should go to jail. I'm a murderer and I'll go to my grave knowing I've done that to another human soul.'

We sit together, me telling her over and over that that isn't true, that it was an accident, while she asks the heavens to forgive her and I curse Rick.

In that moment, I hate him more than ever, because this is the worst thing he ever did to her. So much worse than his petty tricks trying to make her believe she was losing her mind. This trick has made her believe she's a killer.

FORTY-ONE

Eventually it's ruled that the cause of Rick's death was accidental, due to traumatic brain injury from the way he fell, but in that time between the accident and the coroner's report, my mother went downhill for a while.

I moved in with her, back into what used to be my old bedroom, and I watched her become withdrawn, quiet, and more impatient and stubborn than usual.

I told the police about Josh and exactly what he'd done to my mother and we found out the police were already aware of him; there had been complaints. Reports. Apparently he had been visiting other houses, taking money from people for a bogus charity, and was later arrested for fraud, and although we never learned if Rick was a part of that, we suspected he was.

'He was so desperate in the end,' Oscar told me the last time I saw him. 'He was resorting to doing the very worst. I couldn't understand why he got someone like Josh involved, but if he was also doing the charity scam with him ...' He shook his head.

'We'll never know the full extent of it all,' I said, looking across at Rick's bungalow, which was in the process of being repossessed by the bank. 'Only that he was ...'

'Unhinged,' Oscar finished. 'He was about to lose everything, and his pride wouldn't let him. He'd rather scare old ladies than admit he was ruined.'

We were standing in the shared driveway, the late-March wind making me shiver. Oscar had called around before, but this was the first time I'd seen him. I'd been avoiding his calls, waiting until everything with Rick was over.

'How is she?' He looked towards the house.

'Slowly getting there,' I told him. 'We're working through it.'

He looked at me then, his eyes locking on mine, that intensity I knew so well returning to them.

'And how are you?' he asked quietly. 'I know you've moved in here. Your husband, is it ...?'

But I didn't answer. That road that Oscar wanted me to walk down with him one last time was closed. I shook my head. Crossed my arms and gave him a look that said everything I couldn't.

'You have my number,' he said, 'if you need me. At any time. I'll be on the other side of the world, but I'll always be there for you, Louise.'

I shook my head again. That part of us was over. After what had happened, what he'd done, how could it be anything else?

'Have a good trip,' I said. 'I hope you get to do everything you want.'

'I won't get that,' he answered as he turned slowly back to his van. 'Everything I want isn't in South America.'

But I pretended I didn't hear him. I raised my hand in a wave and went back inside, my emotions and thoughts like a twisted vine wrapping around themselves. I couldn't think about how I felt about Oscar, about Paul, about everything.

While Paul was in hospital and then recovering at home, I'd realised what I needed to do. We had breathing space at last, due to a critical illness insurance that paid out a large sum of money once I told them of Paul's condition.

I finally had time to stop. To think.

I'd explained to Paul that I needed to be with my mother after what had happened to Rick, and Felix moved back home for a while. I spent the next few weeks making sure Paul was OK, teaching a few students, and sitting with my mother going over what had happened and why it wasn't anyone's fault. It was an accident, a tragic accident. Gradually she began to agree with me. There was no wrongdoing; the way Rick had fallen was out of our hands. It could have gone a million different ways, but it went the way of a fall. A bad fall.

As the truth about Rick came to light, we learned that everything he'd told us, everything we'd believed about him, was a lie. We had every right to be angry. To react the way we did. He was nothing more than a thief and a liar.

'So stupid,' my mother would say quietly. 'Such a stupid thing to have done. Scaring me and . . . Stupid, stupid man . . .' and then she'd stop, look off into the middle distance, shake her head.

I took her to the doctor, deciding that the cognitive tests I'd been putting off for so long finally needed to be done. I couldn't stand to see her so quiet and disconnected, and I needed to know whether it was because of what had happened, or something else.

287

After a series of questions and tests, the doctor looked up and gave a slow smile.

'I don't see anything to make me want to refer you to a specialist or take this line of investigation further,' he said, and my mother gave a nod.

'So I'm not losing it?' she asked him. 'I'm fine up there?' She tapped her head, and the doctor gave a brief laugh.

'Perfectly fine.'

She turned to me, giving me a look, and then stood, getting ready to leave.

'But I do want you to do this, Vivienne,' he added, and handed her a leaflet that he'd fished out of a drawer. 'Once a week, down at the community hall. Let's try that before thinking of medication.'

'Medication?' I stood, walked over from the corner of the room where I'd been sitting. 'I thought you said she was fine, that she ...' I stopped when I saw what the leaflet was for: a community counselling group run by a charity, for people who had been affected by fatal accidents.

'After what you've been through,' he said, 'I recommend you both attend at least one session before we look at any other treatment.'

It took a lot to get her to go to the first meeting. She insisted that she was fine, didn't need any fuss, but when I threatened to hide the TV remote if she didn't come with me, she relented.

We sat in a circle, on hard, uncomfortable chairs. Lukewarm tea in small plastic cups, soft biscuits, and hushed voices. I looked around. There were only six of us, and in the large hall, we seemed lost. A lost little group of people sitting in a circle. I was normally in here taking charge, teaching my pensioner group, and it was strange to be on the other side, waiting for someone else to lead.

The woman who was running the session stood up. 'Hello, everyone. I see we have some new members this week. Don't worry, I won't put you on the spot. How about you just take this week to listen? Maybe tell us about yourselves when you're ready.'

We listened to a man talk about the car he used to drive before he was involved in a road accident, a couple who didn't answer the phone to their depressed son before he took his own life, a woman who was swimming with her friend when she drowned and she couldn't save her.

Everyone in that room was struggling, and by the time we left, something had changed. It wasn't anything dramatic, but there was a definite shift.

'Let's go back next week,' Mum said on the journey home, and so we did.

After two months, my mother spoke up. And as she told the group about Rick's fatal accident, I could see the beginning of something new. For both of us.

Gradually, as the days got lighter, as spring turned into summer, I could look back on that cold February day and see it for what it was. A desperate man, a tragic accident and nothing more.

FORTY-TWO

Six months later

I always used to hate this time of year. Just after Christmas, the sparkle and celebration of December gone but the debris of it all still hanging around to be cleared away. But now, as I drive through Dilenby, I find I don't mind it at all.

The lights that still hang on the shopfronts are quaint, the decorations waiting to be taken down are comforting, and I smile to myself as I park up and make my way into the Crooked Kettle.

'Hello, you.' Helen leans over and kisses me, and I get a waft of her heavy perfume before she sits back down.

'Can't stop long,' I tell her. 'I'm already running late, I—'

'I know, I know,' she laughs, holding up her hands. 'That's why I got you this.' She pushes a takeout coffee towards me.

'You star!' I say as I pick it up. 'I'm going to miss these mornings with you.'

'Don't start . . .'

'I'm not!' I tell her, and wipe my face. 'I refuse to be sentimental today of all days, but here.' I take out a large envelope and place it on the table in front of her. 'And thank you again. I've given Felix a set of keys, along with all the information on who lives in what room, but he's . . .'

'Far too busy . . .'

'In Manchester,' I finish, and laugh. 'And yes, far too busy should there be an emergency, which there won't be, but thank you.'

She opens the envelope and I watch as she takes out the bunch of keys and the list of tenants who now live with my mother.

It was Felix's idea. As my mother gradually became herself again, and Paul went back to work, he told us of a friend of his who was looking for lodgings. He'd just started work in Manchester but couldn't afford to rent in the city.

'If you ever fancied it,' he said as we ate lunch in my mother's kitchen, 'you could rent out a room to him.' We laughed, thinking the idea was silly, but Mum shocked us all by asking to meet him, and that was the start of it.

She announced that things needed to change, and so, using her savings, we redecorated all four bedrooms upstairs, and made the lounge and dining room into bedrooms as well. It didn't take long to find four lodgers. Felix only had to mention it to a few of his friends, and suddenly we had a waiting list. Big house just outside Manchester, perfect for commuting. After a talk with Paul, we decided to sell our house, and Paul cleared the attic space in the taxi office and moved in there so we could use the money from the sale to clear all our debts.

None of it was easy. But all of it was necessary.

'And Liz?' Helen asks. 'When is she . . .?'

'Moved in a few days ago.' I swallow; it still feels surreal. Like it's a dream. 'Just so we could make sure everything was OK.'

'How's your mum feeling about having a carer? I mean, last time . . .'

'Last time a carer came in, it was for a few hours a day and they were a stranger in that house. This time . . .'

'Your mother has a house filled with chatter and people and can pay for a carer to be on hand full-time to help her out between her volunteering.'

I nod. A smile I can't suppress spreads across my face. The volunteering for the counselling group came about naturally. With us both being regulars at the weekly meetings, when a request came through asking for phone volunteers, people who'd lived through the experience and were willing to talk with others, my mother offered, and it's been the biggest and best thing.

Now she spends her days helping out at the charity and seeing to her tenants. Liz will be on hand to cook and clean and do anything else she needs, and I will . . .

I look down at my handbag holding my passport and euros.

'It's time you went,' Helen tells me softly. 'Don't worry. I'll call in later, meet Liz, make sure your mother has my number. Everything will be fine. More than fine. It'll be great.'

We hug and I leave, making the journey to my mother's one last time. Parking my car in her drive alongside several others, leaving it for Felix to collect later, I go inside to where my cases are waiting.

Mum is watching her programme with Liz, the volume up loud.

'Is it time?' she asks, and I nod. We hug. This has been in the planning for so long, it feels bizarre now that it's actually happening.

As I start to talk in a flurry about medication and contact numbers and the conversation I've just had with Helen, the taxi pulls up. It's Paul. Of course it's Paul. Driving me to the airport and saying goodbye.

'You go for it now,' my mother whispers in my ear as I give her a final hug. 'Do what you should've done years ago.'

I nod, unable to say anything, as Paul puts my cases in the taxi. I get in and recheck my passport, my money, and everything else I need for this trip that I've been saving for. My heart is hammering, and I take deep breaths. Paul tells me about Denise, how he's still teaching her darts; about the business, which is picking up, and as we get to the airport, he turns to me.

'Spain,' he says, and I nod. 'You OK?'

I look at the terminal building, the memories of the last time I was here trying to crowd in. I shake them away. This isn't about the past; this is about now, and if I want to be that person, the woman who loves Spain, who wears long floaty dresses with the sunshine on her face, who has saved and planned for the past six months, then I have to start being her now. I have to start living that life instead of just dreaming about it.

'I'm great,' I tell him, and as we hug goodbye and I walk into that airport, people rushing past, the air filled with excitement and expectation, I realise it's true.

I *am* great. I am Louise Whitstable, middle-aged single woman travelling round Spain for the next six months, and I am finally everything I ever wanted to be.

I'm not only great. I am exceptional.

ACKNOWLEDGEMENTS

This book has been in the making for so long, I must thank my long-suffering husband Stephen first. For all my worries and anxieties that he helped calm, the plot holes he helped me work out, and the listening he did as I talked through the story. I would never have finished this book without his help and support. Thank you, my love.

Aidan and Talia, my two cheerleaders and brightest stars, it's impossible to write here how important you two are, and I need to thank you for putting up with me when this book wasn't quite behaving.

I also need to thank Laura Pearson, Nikki Smith and Lauren North for being such great friends who also happen to be brilliant authors, and who were there at my lowest points when wrestling with this story and held my hand at the tricky bits. I thank my lucky stars that I met you lot at Harrogate and am so grateful to have you in my life. And thanks to the many other writers who were there to offer words of kindness and support when I needed to hear them.

Thanks to my agent Stephanie Glencross for her support, and the wonderful Hannah Wann, who was always so brilliant when I tried to tell her that it couldn't be done. Thank you for your encouragement and belief that it would get finished! Thanks to Tanisha Ali, Jane Selley and all the other amazing and talented people at Piatkus and Little, Brown Book Group who work so hard behind the scenes.

Special thanks to Kirsty Brennan, Jill Pilkington, Heather Peake, mum and dad, and all my extended family, because whenever I doubted myself, you never did, and I am so grateful for that. Also, big thanks to Amy Thompson, Grace Olsen and Caroline Higham for always having my back.

Lastly, I need to thank the humble cheese and tomato quiche. Without this lunchtime meal, I would never have known what true friendship looks like and had my eyes open as to what it is not.

And you, dear person reading this who hopefully read the book and enjoyed it, thank you. I always dreamed of writing to you, and to be doing so now is a real honour. I don't take any of this for granted and am so very happy to be writing stories for you to read.